"I'm sorry,

"For what?"

"For kissing you. I know it was inappropriate but I... It was the moment, I guess. Blame it on being out in nature. You know, the whole primal thing." Noah's chuckle took her by surprise. She glanced at him sharply. "You think this is funny?"

"A little."

Sophia narrowed her gaze.

"We're both consenting adults, and as far as I can tell, we both enjoyed it, so let's not waste the energy on beating ourselves up."

Solid advice. Was it really that simple? Relief bubbled up from somewhere deep inside as she smiled up at him. "Okay, then. I guess we'll just deal with it— whatever it is."

"That's the plan."

It wasn't until they reached the parking area that reality crashed back in.

The sound of breaking glass crunched under their boots. Noah's truck sat alone in the turnout, the driver's-side window shattered. Glittering shards carpeted the ground like fallen stars.

Training kicked in. They approached carefully, scanning the area for movement. A brick lay on the driver's seat, heavy and brutal. Black ink stained one side, the message clear and deliberate.

YOU'RE NEXT

Dear Reader,

On every reservation throughout the United States, stories of the missing and murdered fade like footprints in snow. I wrote *Lethal Betrayal* as both a gripping romantic suspense and a window into the reality where Indigenous women and youth vanish while their cases gather dust—victims of a justice system that consistently fails these communities through uneven resource distribution and jurisdictional complications.

As you follow Noah and Sophia through Stone River, I hope you see beyond the mystery to the resilient spirit of those fighting for justice. Every closed case allows a family to heal; every cold one leaves wounds open. My deepest wish is that this story helps amplify the voices calling for change—reminding us that every person deserves to be found, remembered and honored with the full force of justice.

Warmest regards,

Kimberly Van Meter

LETHAL BETRAYAL

KIMBERLY VAN METER

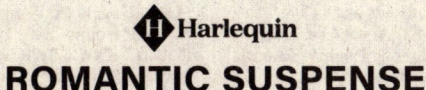

ROMANTIC SUSPENSE

MIX
Paper | Supporting responsible forestry
FSC® C021394
www.fsc.org

Harlequin®
ROMANTIC SUSPENSE™

Recycling programs for this product may not exist in your area.

ISBN-13: 978-1-335-47194-9

Lethal Betrayal

Harlequin Enterprises ULC
22 Adelaide St. West, 41st Floor
Toronto, Ontario M5H 4E3, Canada
www.Harlequin.com

HarperCollins Publishers
Macken House, 39/40 Mayor Street Upper,
Dublin 1, D01 C9W8, Ireland
www.HarperCollins.com

Printed in Lithuania

Kimberly Van Meter wrote her first book at sixteen and finally achieved publication in December 2006. She has written for the Harlequin Superromance, Blaze and Romantic Suspense lines. She and her husband of thirty years have three children, two cats, and always a houseful of friends, family and fun.

Books by Kimberly Van Meter

Harlequin Romantic Suspense

Big Sky Justice

Danger in Big Sky Country
Her K-9 Protector
Cold Case Secrets
Cold Case Kidnapping
Cold Case Reckoning
Sacred Secrets
Lethal Betrayal

The Coltons of Kansas

Colton's Amnesia Target

The Coltons of Owl Creek

Colton's Secret Stalker

The Coltons of Arizona

Colton's Reel Danger

Visit the Author Profile page
at Harlequin.com for more titles.

For the missing and murdered Indigenous women whose voices have been silenced, may this story help us hear your echo and honor your memory with the justice you deserve.

Chapter 1

The frost clung to the earth, brittle and stubborn, refusing to thaw under the fading light of the autumn sun. BIA agent Noah Thunderhawk wasn't sure what had driven him to keep his eyes on the dried-up creek bed as he approached the scene, but the tension in his gut told him enough. This was going to be bad—worse than the usual violence that haunted the edges of life on the Blackfeet Reservation.

People liked to give a lot of airtime to the positives, trying to change the narrative—and that had its place. But the reality on the reservation was that life was often hard, unfair and rife with addiction, violence and poverty the likes of which most people couldn't even fathom.

Being the son of a tribal cop, Noah had seen some things from the time he was young.

In the end, life on the rez had exacted its price on the Thunderhawk family. His father, John, was killed on the job, breaking up a domestic. It could've made Noah bitter and go the opposite direction, but the rule of law was in his blood, and he didn't regret following in his father's footsteps.

But days like this were enough to make anyone wish they'd chosen a career with less death.

The bitter air stung his lungs as he stepped out of the truck. Two tribal officers stood at the perimeter of yellow tape stretched around the site. The younger of the two—Jay

Long, a friend of his sister's—gave Noah a nod, but the stiff posture and the uneasy shifting of feet told the real story.

It'd been a few months since Noah made the lateral move to the specialized Bureau of Indian Affairs task force, and this was his first solo case. He was ready to put boots on the ground but wasn't expecting his first case to send him straight to Stone River.

The small rural Montana town was nestled in the foothills of the reservation—and the place he'd called home for his entire childhood. He knew everyone, and everyone knew him—which was why he'd moved away.

Noah gave a short nod. "What've we got?"

Jay swallowed hard and cleared his throat. "Native girl. Found by a rancher about an hour ago. She's...been dead for a few days, we think. But..." He hesitated, his gaze flicking away from Noah's, unable to hold the weight of the next words. "It's better if you see it yourself."

A heavy knot formed in Noah's stomach. His instincts were finely tuned, sharpened over years of seeing too much death, too many senseless acts of cruelty, but this—there was something different in the way Jay spoke. Something more than just another dead body.

Noah stepped over the yellow tape, moving toward the tarp where the girl's body lay. The setting sun cast long shadows over the ground, the light dimming quickly as the cold crept in. Noah could smell the decay before he reached her—a smell he'd never gotten used to, even after all these years.

The ground was dry, cracked from the hard summer, and he noticed drag marks in the dirt near the body. Someone had tried to hide her here but hadn't cared enough to finish the job. Noah crouched down beside the tarp, pulling it back gently.

She was young—couldn't have been more than sixteen, maybe seventeen. Her face was swollen, bruised, beaten beyond recognition, and the skin around her wrists and arms was torn, raw from what he could only guess had been a violent struggle. But the name scrawled across her arm in black Sharpie sent a shock of ice down his spine.

Travis Longshadow.

For a moment, everything froze. The quiet stillness of the surrounding wilderness swallowed the sound of his breath, the world narrowing to the single name written into the dead girl's skin.

He couldn't pull himself away from the sight. Travis. Fifteen years had passed, and his name was still here, haunting Noah's every step.

He exhaled, standing slowly, feeling the weight of the years pressing down on his shoulders. He hadn't been able to solve Travis's case. He'd sworn to the boy's mother that he'd find the boy's killer, but the case had gone cold, buried under layers of unanswered questions and dead-end leads.

And now, Travis was back in the conversation—but not in any way Noah would've expected.

"Noah?" Jay's voice wavered slightly. "You okay?"

Noah blinked, pulling himself out of the haze of memory. His voice came out rougher than he intended. "Yeah." But his gut twisted, the years of guilt threatening to rise up and choke him. He forced himself to focus on the present, on the task at hand.

"What does it mean?" Jay pressed. "Why would she have his name on her?"

"I don't know," Noah said, though his mind was already spinning, searching for reasons why an unknown girl would have the name of a kid who'd died years ago scrawled on her arm.

And how would he tell the boy's mom, Maggie, the news?

"Unless the reason is hidden in a pocket, we aren't going to find out why just standing around. Let's get to bagging the evidence," Noah said, gesturing to Jay as he donned latex gloves and slipped paper booties over his shoes to prevent cross-contamination. He grabbed his forensic camera and started photographing the scene.

The temperature dropped further as the sun dipped below the horizon, leaving the crime scene cloaked in shadow. Noah moved mechanically through the motions—bagging evidence, marking tracks, interviewing the rancher who'd stumbled onto the body—but his mind kept drifting back to Travis. Fifteen years since the boy had been murdered, and they'd never come close to finding who did it. It had been his first big case as a rookie tribal officer, a brutal introduction to a career that had continued to be full of violence and loss.

He'd seen the kid around town. Travis had been a quiet seventeen-year-old boy with a soft heart, which had always made his friendship with Noah's loudmouth cousin, Michael, a mystery. He supposed opposites attract or something like that, but when Travis had gone missing and was found dead three days later, Noah had taken the case personally. Somehow, that case had gotten under his skin like a bad case of shingles, leaving a mark on his soul.

But with no leads, the case slowly went cold. The mystery of Travis's murder went into a file cabinet until the months turned to years, and Noah left the tribal police to join the BIA.

So, how was it that fifteen years later, a dead girl from out of town was marked with Travis's name?

What was the connection?

A sharp breath cut through the cold air as the sound of tires crunching on gravel pulled Noah's attention back to the present. A sleek black SUV pulled up, and a redheaded woman stepped out, immediately alert and scanning for the person in charge.

He knew she was FBI before she even flashed her badge.

There was a certain way federal agents carried themselves, a mix of authority and detachment that set them apart. And she had it, all right. Tall, confident, with sharp eyes that seemed to miss nothing. She walked toward him with purpose, her hair scraped back in a no-nonsense bun, the weight of the badge in her hand somehow heavier than the one pinned to his own chest.

"Special Agent Sophia Bennett," she said as she approached, her tone clipped and professional. "You must be BIA Agent Noah Thunderhawk."

He wasn't in the mood for feds muscling in on his territory, but professional courtesy dictated a certain level of accommodation. "Correct," he confirmed, folding his arms across his chest. "What brings the FBI out here?"

"The tattoo on the victim's ankle," she replied, nodding toward the body. "It's connected to a trafficking ring we've been tracking. The name on her arm, though… That's new. Travis Longshadow?"

Who called the feds? How'd they know about the details of his case? He shot a look at Jay, who looked like he'd stepped in horse shit, as he mumbled apologetically, "Feds sent out a statewide alert for any cases involving anyone associated with that particular tattoo. I sent the call right after calling the Bureau of Indian Affairs. That's what the chief told me to do."

The kid was just following orders. "You're all right," Noah said, relieving the rookie. He returned his attention to the agent, gaze narrowed. "It's a local cold case," he shared. "Fifteen years old. Never had any leads. I don't know what the connection could be to our new vic. As far as I can tell, she's not from around here, and Travis Longshadow was born and raised right here in Stone River." He gestured. "What's so special about the tattoo?"

"I've been tracking a human trafficking network that tattoos its female victims with that particular tattoo, like a mark of ownership. So far, we've found that tattoo on victims across Montana, Wyoming and Idaho but there's been a disproportionate number of victims identified as Native young women. As soon as I got the call from the tribal office this morning, I booked a flight from Washington and came straight here. I plan to be hands-on with this case."

Federal agencies were supposed to play nice together in theory, but that wasn't always the case in practice. Noah didn't like the idea of partnering up with a fed on his first big case with the task force, but he also knew that his new boss, Isaac Berrigan, wouldn't appreciate him stonewalling the FBI.

"I don't mind working together as long as we both agree this is my case. BIA has jurisdiction as the victim was found on tribal land," Noah said.

"No need to play 'whose dick is bigger,' Agent. I can be a team player. Can you?"

She didn't pull punches. Noah didn't know if he appreciated that quality or not. Too early to tell.

But Sophia had already moved on, clearly believing the matter settled. Her gaze swept the scene again, taking in the full details with a methodical precision that he respected.

"We need to find out who she is and where she came from. We'll start there." Sophia paused before handing Noah a business card, instructing, "Oh, and send me the original case notes on this Travis Longshadow kid. I want to see if anything matches my other cases."

Noah accepted the card with a curt nod, smothering the immediate flare of irritation at her ordering him around. "Will do."

"Excellent." She flashed him an efficient smile. "We're off to a good start."

If you say so.

Sophia walked away to take a call, leaving Noah at the body. Jay sheepishly tried to apologize again, but Noah waved him off. "Don't worry about it. All hands-on deck is a good thing," he said, though the statement caught in his throat. He preferred to do things his way; another person would just get in his way, but he didn't have a choice but to work alongside the federal agent.

There was something bigger here, all right. Bigger than just a cold case. Bigger than just a dead girl with a trafficker's mark. He could feel it in his gut, that little warning tingle that signaled seriously bad shit on the horizon.

His dad used to say, "Listen to your gut, son. It could save your life someday."

The one time his dad had ignored his intuition, he'd taken a bullet to the head, so yeah, Noah made a point to always pay attention when his gut started talking.

By the time the sun had fully disappeared, Noah had finished his part of the work. The tribal officers were wrapping up their end of things, and the scene was growing quieter, more still. Sophia had retreated to her SUV to make calls, no doubt coordinating with whatever federal response was coming next.

But Noah couldn't leave. Not yet. Not with that name burning a hole in his memory.

Travis Longshadow. He had been just a kid—the same age as this girl when they'd found him. Beaten, discarded. Left in a ditch like trash.

The shock of finding Travis's body would always remain in his memory—as would the sound of Maggie's heartrending scream when she learned her only child was dead.

Sometimes life just wasn't fair. Maggie Longshadow had pulled herself out of an abusive relationship. She raised her son alone, pouring all of her hopes and dreams into that boy, only to have him dead at seventeen.

Noah sat in his truck, the engine idling, the cold seeping through the windows. He had thought, maybe foolishly, that he could leave that case in the past. That the guilt for failing to find the killer would fade in time.

But he was wrong.

He picked up his phone and scrolled through the contacts until he found the number he hadn't called in years. He couldn't believe he was making this call, but it had to be done. It rang twice before the familiar voice answered.

"Noah?" she said, her tone incredulous. Amber Laughlin, his ex-fiancée and the best damn investigative journalist he'd ever grudgingly worked with, who specialized in human rights issues facing indigenous people. "Why are you calling me?"

Straight to the point, as always.

"Look, I'm only calling because you were following the case when it first happened, and you're going to find out anyway," Noah said, his voice low, carrying the weight of old wounds. "But we might have a fresh lead on the Travis Longshadow case."

There was a pause on the other end, and Noah could practically hear the gears turning in Amber's mind. "Are you kidding me?" Her voice softened, just slightly. "What's going on?"

"A dead girl was found with Travis's name scribbled in black ink on her skin. I don't know what it means yet," Noah admitted. "But I can tell you, it's big enough to lure the feds in. Whether I like it or not, I've got an FBI agent for a partner on my case."

"Who is it?"

"Sophia Bennett."

Amber's immediate inhale was followed by, "Jesus, Noah, that's not just any agent, that's the national expert in child trafficking and exploitation within the Bureau. Whatever she's tracking... I can guarantee you, it's big. They don't send Bennett for just any case. She's the biggest gun they have. What the hell have you stumbled on?"

Noah didn't know, but he sure as hell planned to find out.

Chapter 2

The small town of Stone River greeted Special Agent Sophia Bennett with the kind of quiet that made her uneasy. Remote towns had a way of concealing secrets, wrapping them up tightly in the routines of ordinary life. Secrets that, once exposed, changed everything. She assessed the situation as her black SUV rolled to a stop in front of Whispering Pines Lodge.

The hotel wasn't much—just three stories, with a faded sign boasting Mountain Views and Authentic Montana Experience. The parking lot was half empty, and the building looked tired, its paint chipped by years of unforgiving winters. Sophia eyed the top floor. It wasn't fancy, but it was the best she'd get out here, and the third floor meant fewer surprises.

Noah Thunderhawk. He hadn't stuck around after they wrapped up at the crime scene, and she couldn't blame him. The case was personal to him. She'd seen it in the hard line of his jaw and how he tried to control the conversation but couldn't hide his frustration.

The question was, could he keep his personal feelings under control or would he let his emotions get in the way of an equitable partnership? Could he handle her being here, or would she have to find a way to work around him?

Sophia cut the engine, grabbing her bag from the passenger seat. *Noah Thunderhawk*, she mused. BIA investigator, clearly competent, clearly a man with deep roots in the community, but not too thrilled about her involvement. That much was obvious.

She'd seen his type before—cops who knew their territory inside and out and resented outsiders coming in. Still, Sophia wasn't here to step on toes. She was here to crack this case wide open and source out the true cancer lurking behind doors held shut with plenty of money.

Trafficking was a cash cow—drugs or people, it didn't matter because both were lucrative commodities. The green flow of greed was an enticing lure for too many people, given that the cost of entry didn't seem too high. The only question was, could Thunderhawk be trusted? Was he immune to the deep pockets feeding resources to key people to ensure their silence?

Trust was something Sophia reserved for those who'd earned it. She didn't hand it out like Halloween candy, especially not to new partners. Professional courtesy, sure. Trust? *Not yet, buddy.* Dirty badges could be anywhere—and Sophia didn't like surprises.

She'd heard of the BIA task force, spearheaded by Isaac Berrigan—they were making headlines with their epic wins, taking down big players like dirty politicians and corrupt officials. But placing bad actors in top positions was how these traffickers kept their operations moving smoothly. Thunderhawk could be clean, or he could be another brick in the wall. She wasn't ruling anything out yet.

He was an imposing man—broad shoulders, keen eyes that seemed to take in everything at once. There was something in the way he carried himself, something she recognized. He was like her—driven but closed off. People like them didn't let others in easily, and they sure as hell didn't trust quickly. If he was anything like her, he wouldn't appreciate the situation they were now forced into—working together.

Sophia pushed open the lodge door, feeling the sudden warmth wash over her from the heated foyer. The old woman behind the counter gave her a friendly but mildly suspicious glance. Small towns. Sophia smiled politely as she checked in, grabbed her key card and headed to the elevator.

Third floor. Always the third floor. Sophia had learned that in her first few years with the FBI. Never choose a ground-level room—too easy to access. The higher you went, the safer you were. Not that safety was ever guaranteed. But after years of tracking some of the most dangerous criminals, she didn't take chances.

The elevator doors slid open with a quiet groan. Sophia stepped onto the third floor, her boots clicking softly against the worn carpet. The room at the end of the hall was hers. Basic. A queen-size bed with a stiff-looking comforter, a small desk in the corner and a single window overlooking the quiet streets of Stone River.

She stood by the door for a moment, listening. It was an old habit she didn't think she'd ever shake. The familiar silence settled around her, and she took a deep breath, surveying the room before she did anything else.

First things first—security check. After a quick closet and bathroom check, she dropped to her knees, checking beneath the bed. Clear. She went to the window, tugging on the locks. Secure. Then she double-checked the door, latching the chain lock and bolting it from the inside. Before she finally moved to her desk, she reached into her pocket and pulled out a small coin, placing it on the door handle—just in case.

Finally satisfied, she pulled her secure and encrypted laptop from her bag and set it on the desk. The machine hummed to life, the screen flickering in dim light. As the room's chill faded away, Sophia made herself focus.

The murder scene earlier had left her unsettled but not for

the reasons most would assume. Noah might have a personal connection to the cold case, but Sophia had been tracking this tattoo for over a year, watching it pop up on young girls who had been found across state lines. At first, no one had connected the dots. It was just another mark, barely noticed in the postmortem reports of each victim.

She'd first come across it on the body of a sixteen-year-old runaway in Idaho. The death had been written off as an overdose, but the tattoo stuck in Sophia's mind. A crude circle with a jagged slash through the middle inked into the girl's ankle. Then, a few months later, another victim appeared—this time in Wyoming. Same age, same tragic end. Same tattoo.

That was when Sophia knew. This wasn't random. It was a marker—a brand, almost like what the Mexican cartels used on their human trafficking victims. At first, the similarities to cartel operations were hard to ignore. But as more bodies turned up, Sophia realized the pattern was unique to the region. This wasn't cartel activity. It was something homegrown, something embedded in the underbelly of the western states.

Her fingers flew across the keyboard as she pulled up her case files, the tattoo image appearing on the screen. She had all the details mapped out—locations, victim profiles, time lines. But none of it explained why a dead girl in Montana had Travis Longshadow's name inked on her arm.

Sophia leaned back in the stiff hotel chair, her mind moving quickly. The dead boy had been murdered fifteen years ago, and yet somehow, his name was connected to a trafficking ring that had surfaced in recent years. It didn't make sense. She didn't like loose ends, and this case had plenty.

She'd asked Thunderhawk for the original case notes on Travis, but he hadn't sent them yet. Probably dragging his feet, wanting to keep his cards close to his chest. *Typical*.

Not one to sit idle, Sophia typed Travis Longshadow murder into her search bar. Small towns like Stone River didn't get much press, but if this case had haunted the reservation for fifteen years, there had to be something—local articles, maybe an investigative piece.

And there it was.

Her eyes locked on a headline from that year: The Forgotten Boy: A Mother's Grief in Stone River.

The article had been written by a journalist named Amber Laughlin, someone Sophia hadn't heard of but whose name she immediately noted. She skimmed the first few lines.

It's been three months since Travis Longshadow was found dead in the outskirts of Stone River, his body beaten and left for the animals to scavage. His mother, Maggie Longshadow, waits for answers that may never come…

Sophia read on, her interest piqued. The writing was sharp and vivid. Amber Laughlin knew how to paint a picture, how to make the reader feel the weight of Maggie's grief, the injustice of a young life cut short. But the further Sophia read, the more her guard went up. Journalists had a knack for mucking up investigations, always poking around in places they shouldn't. They wanted a story, and more often than not, they didn't care about the collateral damage they caused to the official investigation along the way.

Sophia sighed, closing the article. The last thing she needed was a nosy journalist sniffing around the case. However, there was something about Amber's piece that stuck with her. Amber had been close to the case and clearly invested. Sophia made a mental note to contact the journalist and pick her brain. Even annoying gnats—like journalists—served a purpose.

The light outside had dimmed completely when Sophia finished sorting through her notes. The weight of the day pressed down on her, but she wasn't done yet. She'd learned the hard way that staying sharp meant keeping a routine.

Sophia pulled on her yoga pants, cleared a small space on the floor and set a timer on her phone. Thirty minutes of yoga, followed by fifteen minutes of meditation. It wasn't just about fitness. It was about clearing her mind and finding focus amid the chaos.

Her thoughts circled back to the case as she moved through her poses, stretching her muscles and focusing on her breath. There were so many questions—questions that needed answers. How did the girl tie into Travis Longshadow's death? What did the tattoo signify? And how deep did this trafficking network run?

Sophia exhaled into downward dog, feeling the tension release from her shoulders. She tried to push the case out of her mind, but her brain didn't cooperate. The dead girl's image, the brutal crime scene, the inexplicable presence of Travis Longshadow's name—it all flipped through her thoughts. She'd handled some tough cases before, but this one felt different. There was an unsettling undertone that she couldn't quite shake.

Why were the victims disproportionately Native? As a white woman, she knew she'd have an uphill battle getting the locals to talk to her. It didn't matter that she was firmly on their side, seeking justice for the Native victims; the locals would see a white woman with flaming red hair, and immediately their guard would go up. No matter how many cases she'd closed, she couldn't escape the outsider label when it came to places like Stone River.

She'd need a local to smooth the way, someone they trusted. That was where Noah Thunderhawk could come in handy—if he turned out to be worth working with.

Thunderhawk was an enigma. From what little she'd seen at the crime scene, he was controlled but not unaffected. He spoke like a man holding back a storm, someone who'd been forced to live with unsolved cases hanging over his head. He probably had his own list of regrets—everyone in their line of work did.

She eased into a warrior pose, her leg muscles trembling slightly from the effort. Jurisdictional squabbles were a fact of life in her work, but Sophia had gotten good at navigating the egos of local cops and federal agents. Noah seemed like the kind of man who valued control, who wanted to keep the case in his hands.

Tomorrow, she'd get a better read on him. If he showed genuine cooperation, she'd work with him. If he stonewalled her, she'd find her own way in. Sophia Bennett didn't wait for permission, and she sure as hell didn't let obstacles block her path.

By the time the timer went off, signaling the end of her yoga session, Sophia was sweating lightly, but her mind felt clearer. She transitioned into meditation, letting her thoughts drift and not linger. This was her routine, her way of centering herself before the storm of the investigation began.

After fifteen minutes of quiet, controlled breathing, Sophia opened her eyes and exhaled. Tomorrow would bring more digging and more uncomfortable questions. But for now, she needed to shut down her mind, just for a little while.

After a quick rinse, Sophia slipped into bed, her muscles relaxed, but her mind still churning with the day's discoveries. She made one final check of her email, but Thunderhawk still hadn't sent her the case files, and part of her suspected he was hesitating for a reason. Maybe he was vetting her, just as she planned to vet him. After all, just because she was FBI didn't mean she was untouchable.

But Thunderhawk's reluctance wouldn't last. Sophia was

determined to crack this case wide open, and if Noah wanted to stand in her way, he'd soon realize it was a fight he wouldn't win.

She closed her eyes, the mystery of Travis Longshadow's name lingering in her mind. This case might be critical to bringing down the entire trafficking network.

Chapter 3

Noah Thunderhawk stood in the doorway of what used to be his bedroom, now transformed into his mother's beading room. The smell of sage and cedar lingered in the air, mixing with the faint, familiar scent of leather and beads. Grace Thunderhawk had taken up beading after she retired from teaching, turning her son's old room into a workspace for her intricate projects. There was still a small bed to accommodate him when he came to stay, but all other traces of his old bedroom had been packed away.

Glass and bone beads, turquoise stones and thread bobbins lined the shelves where his old sports trophies and books used to sit. He leaned against the doorframe, watching his mother as she bent over the table, her delicate fingers moving with practiced patience, threading beads into patterns that told stories older than Stone River itself.

His old life—the one before the badge, before Travis Longshadow's name had been seared into his memory—seemed like another world. Stone River had always been home, but it had changed while Noah had been away. Or maybe he had changed too much. The burden of years in law enforcement, working through tough cases, had slowly worn away at the version of Noah that had once existed here.

The soft creak of the floorboards announced Lila's arrival. His youngest sister peeked into the room, her dark eyes bright with excitement, as though she was still ten years old instead of in her twenties.

"Big brother's home!" she said with a grin, practically bouncing on her heels. Lila had always been the sunshine in their family.

Despite the exhaustion weighing on Noah after today's discovery, he couldn't help but smile back. "Sorry, not a vacation, though, Lila," he replied, his tone gentle but firm. "Working a case."

Lila's smile faltered for a moment, but her eyes still danced with curiosity. "Yeah, we heard," she said, her expression dimming appropriately. "It's all anyone's talking about in town." She paused, looking around the room to emphasize the small-town nature of their life, where secrets were impossible to keep. "A body found…with Travis's name? That's crazy."

Noah's mouth firmed. Keeping the discovery on the down-low was hard enough—the disquieting detail of Travis's name on the girl's skin was something else entirely. He could almost hear the murmurs spreading like wildfire across Stone River, rumors tinged with sorrow and curiosity.

"What can you tell us?" Lila asked, her voice lowering conspiratorially as she perched on the edge of the armchair in the corner. Her eagerness for details reminded him of how close they'd been growing up. Lila had always seen him as a protector who would be there to watch her back.

"Not much, you know that," Noah returned, his expression softening at his sister's playful persistence.

Lila rolled her eyes but smiled fondly at him. There was no disappointment, just affection. "Fine, be all professional." She rose from the chair and headed to the kitchen, where the smell of coffee hung in the air. Her lightness and energy were the same as always, and Noah was grateful for that. Amid the weight of the case, Lila was a small flicker of normalcy.

Noah turned back to his mother, who had stopped beading and was watching him quietly. Grace wasn't one to pry, but her gaze was thoughtful, filled with unspoken questions.

Noah shifted, wondering if he should reassure her that he was okay.

"What do you make of the Longshadow boy's name on the girl's skin?" Grace asked, turning the needle through a line of turquoise beads. "Pretty shocking to hear his name after so long."

"I think it's a solid reason to reopen Travis's case. How'd you and Lila hear about it?" Noah asked. Trying to keep anything quiet in a small town was next to impossible. The reservation grapevine had a way of spreading news faster than he could keep up.

Grace shrugged. "You know how it is. Someone tells someone else. Word gets around. Can't keep news like that quiet for long. Sad business, though."

He couldn't disagree with that. "Never gets any easier, that's for sure."

His mother had always been well-connected—part-time teacher, community elder and quiet informant. She had a way of hearing things before anyone else did, even if she didn't go looking for gossip.

"Poor Maggie," Grace added, her voice heavy with concern. "I'm sure this newest development, after all these years, must feel like opening an old wound."

Noah sighed, sinking into the chair beside her. "Yeah, I'm sure the tribal police have told her by now. Maybe I should've been the one to do it."

Grace shook her head, her movements slow, deliberate. "That's not your job anymore. Jay Long is a good boy with a kind heart. You need to focus on your part now."

Noah nodded, though the sting of guilt still sat with him.

Maggie Longshadow's grief had been a weight he'd carried for years. The guilt of not solving the case. The feeling of letting her down. But Grace's advice… It spoke to him like it always had. She trusted him to find the truth, to bring justice. Finally, after all these years.

The room settled into a comfortable silence. Noah glanced around, his eyes landing on the shelves lined with Grace's beadwork—a testament to the precision and care she applied to everything she touched. His mom was never in a rush, always taking her time, just like when she had raised him and his siblings.

The quiet didn't last long.

"Mom's talking to someone," Lila said, reappearing in the doorway with a mischievous grin.

Noah's head jerked up at that, his brows furrowing in confusion. "Talking to someone?" The words echoed in his mind, and for a brief moment, he didn't understand. Then, it clicked. Lila wasn't talking about casual conversation. He turned to Grace, eyebrows raised in shock. "As in…dating?"

Grace shot Lila a disapproving look, but the nervous flutter in her hands didn't escape Noah's notice. "Dating at my age? Is that even what it's called anymore?" Grace said, her voice light but her expression uncertain. "I'd say we're talking, enjoying each other's company. Nothing more than that."

Noah blinked, unsure how to process this new information. His mother dating? He hadn't thought about her with anyone since losing their father. Part of him was protective, wanting to step in, but another part knew he had no right to stand in the way of her happiness.

Grace caught his hesitation, her hands busy rearranging beads as if that could hide her discomfort.

Lila, sensing the awkwardness, threw up her hands in mock

defeat. "Good grief, everyone needs to grow up. It's not a big deal. Mom has needs, too."

Grace and Noah visibly cringed, equally uncomfortable with the conversation's direction, but Lila kept pushing. "Honestly, Noah, you should be able to talk about sex like a normal human being. It's natural and completely—"

"Lila, enough," Grace interrupted, standing and smoothing her skirt with quick, nervous hands. "I think I'll call it a night. Biscuits and gravy for breakfast, Noah? I know they're your favorite."

Noah stood, too, pressing a kiss to her forehead. "I'll take a rain check, Mom. I have to be up early to stop by the police station." He smiled. "But I appreciate the offer. I miss your cooking."

Grace smiled, too, patting his cheek gently. "Don't stay up too late."

As Grace disappeared down the hallway, Lila rolled her eyes at him, whispering out of the corner of her mouth just to antagonize him, "His name's Roy, by the way. Met him at her beading class. And he's *white*."

Noah couldn't suppress the grimace that curled his lip. *Roy*. Who the hell was this Roy character? He'd have to add *background check* to his to-do list.

Lila laughed at his expression, disappearing into her room and shutting the door behind her.

Noah sighed, dragging a hand across his face. *Dating*. His mother, dating. It wasn't something he could easily process. The idea of his mom with someone else…made his chest tighten, like he was a twelve-year-old boy again, awkward and uncomfortable.

Shaking the thought from his mind, Noah retreated to the small bed in the corner of the room, lying down with his phone. The room felt smaller than it used to, more foreign, filled with his mother's new life. And yet, this was the same room where he had once dreamed of becoming a cop, of following in his father's footsteps.

The room wasn't his anymore. Just like his mom wasn't the same woman raising five kids alone. She was single, and if she wanted to mingle, well, he'd just have to find a way to be okay with it.

He sighed and pulled out his phone, eager for a distraction. As he scrolled through local news, Amber's intel from earlier about Sophia Bennett popped into his head. Her arrival in Stone River was no small thing, and the way Amber had framed it—the national expert in child trafficking and exploitation coming all the way out here—there had to be a good reason. And Noah wanted to know exactly who he was dealing with.

He typed Sophia Bennett FBI into the search bar and was immediately met with a flood of results. Article after article popped up detailing her cases, accolades and accomplishments. Damn, Amber knew her stuff. Sophia wasn't just another agent sent out to assist in a local case—she was the real deal. This national expert had dismantled some of the most dangerous human trafficking rings in the western states. She'd been on the front lines of high-profile busts, earning commendations for her work.

Impressive, Noah thought grudgingly as he clicked on one article detailing her involvement in breaking a trafficking ring that operated across Montana, Idaho and Wyoming. She wasn't just playing the part of a fed coming to take over; this was her life's work. The intensity of her cases, the sheer number of victims she'd helped, made Noah pause.

He leaned back against the pillow, staring up at the ceiling. What would working with her be like? Their first interaction had been tense, no doubt fueled by the initial friction that came with federal and local authorities being forced to collaborate. But after reading through her list of accomplishments, Noah found himself grudgingly impressed.

Maybe, he thought, having her as a partner wouldn't be the worst thing. She wasn't going to slow him down. With her track record, there was no doubt that she knew how to push cases forward—especially those involving trafficking networks. If anything, she might push the investigation harder and further than he could.

At this point, he couldn't let his ego run the show—not when there was so much at stake.

Deciding to stop overthinking it, Noah pulled up the old Longshadow case notes on his laptop. He'd always kept them with him, even after leaving the tribal police. He'd hoped that the day might come when he'd have reason to reopen the case. Well, that day was here.

First thing tomorrow, he'd send the case files to Sophia. Now, he needed a minute to decompress. Coming home had him questioning which end was up, and he needed to be focused.

Noah rubbed his tired eyes, placing his phone down on the nightstand. He lay back, eyes closed, but the weight of fifteen years pressed down on him harder than ever. Travis Longshadow's face flickered behind his eyelids—ghosts from the past that never quite faded.

The thing about cold cases that no one warned you about was the dangerous element of hope. Acceptance could dull the pain of failure, but hope? It had a way of slicing those old wounds open, raw and bleeding all over again.

The investigation had stalled for so long that accepting defeat had been his uneasy balm. But now, with this new case stirring up everything again, the old wound was bleeding, and this time, Noah wouldn't let it heal until the truth was uncovered.

This time, he wouldn't fail. That was a promise.

Chapter 4

Sophia snapped her laptop shut after five minutes of waiting. Still no sign of Longshadow's investigative file from Thunderhawk. *Strike one.*

She downed the last of her lukewarm coffee and grabbed her keys from the cheap nightstand, already moving. Waiting around for uncooperative law enforcement wasn't her style.

The rental car's engine hummed as she scanned the parking lot—force of habit—before pulling onto the main road. Stone River sprawled before her, autumn leaves blazing against the Montana sky, the kind of beauty that travel magazines tried to capture and always fell short of. The crisp air raised goose bumps on her arms.

Nothing like Houston, where she'd spent her childhood bouncing between foster homes after her parents' car accident. Eight years old and learning the hard way that the world didn't care about broken little girls.

People loved to say that everything happened for a reason, like suffering was God's way of teaching life lessons. Sophia knew better. *Bad things happen because people choose to do them, and others choose to look away.* But she couldn't deny that those years in foster care had shaped her into what she was now—a weapon aimed at the worst kind of predators.

She hunted traffickers. And she was damn good at it.

So, while Stone River might look like heaven with its postcard perfection, Sophia knew better. Paradise made the perfect hiding place for hell.

The tribal police station loomed ahead, a brick building that had weathered decades of Montana winters but wasn't winning any architectural awards any time soon. Sophia spotted Noah's truck in the parking lot as she pulled in. So, he was an early riser. Good. She wasn't in the mood to waste time tracking him down.

The sharp bite of burned coffee hit her nose when she stepped inside. A handful of officers milled about, their conversations dropping to whispers at her entrance. The FBI badge tended to have that effect, especially on reservations. She was used to it.

Noah sat hunched over a desk in the back corner, files spread out before him. As a Stone River alum, local brass probably pulled out all the stops for his comfort while investigating the case. That worked for her; fighting for resources was a pain.

His expression was guarded when he looked up as if he was waiting for her reaction to know the temperature of the room.

"I was going to email those files first thing," he said by way of greeting, though she caught the flicker of guilt.

"Funny how *first thing* means different things for different people." Sophia pulled up a chair, not waiting for an invitation. "I prefer to hit the ground running."

"Duly noted," Noah said, neither apologizing nor making an excuse for his lack of follow-through.

Okay, let's just take the bull by the horns... "Another thing about me, Agent Thunderhawk—I don't sit politely while being disrespected. We're both here to do a job. If you can't find your way to working with me, let's just skip the posturing and make the appropriate phone calls because I need someone who's here to work. I don't have time to dance around egos."

Something flickered behind Noah's expression—respect, maybe?—but it was hard to tell because it was gone in an instant. "Well, then, I guess we better get to work."

Sophia eyed him with suspicion. "That's it?"

"I hear what you're saying, Agent Bennett, loud and clear. I could make excuses as to why I forgot to send the file, but does that matter? I didn't send them. That's on me, and you're right to call me out. It won't happen again. We good?"

His no-bullshit approach to direct conflict was refreshing and unexpected. Relaxing, she nodded. "Yeah, we're good."

"Great." Noah pushed the paperwork her way, moving on. "Travis Longshadow," he said. "Seventeen. Good kid. Smart. Kept to himself mostly. Body was found near Cut Bank River, three days after he went missing." His voice roughened. "Blunt force trauma to the head, but he'd been beaten pretty badly before that. Multiple attackers, based on the bruising patterns."

Sophia opened the file, scanning the crime scene photos, pausing when she read the agent's name on the file. She looked up in question. "You investigated the original case?"

Noah confirmed with a short nod. "It was my first big case as a young tribal officer before I moved onto the Bureau. My younger cousin Michael was good friends with Travis, took his death real hard. Hell, everyone on the rez took Travis's death pretty hard. Like I said, he was a good kid."

Sophia heard the genuine regret in Noah's voice. Every new cop has a case that would eventually leave a mark, and Sophia was looking at Noah's, which made this case personal. That could work for or against them. She'd have to play things by ear and see how it shook out. For now, she'd let it lie.

She returned to the case notes. The boy's body had been posed—arms crossed over his chest, almost peaceful if you could ignore the violence done to him. That detail hadn't been in any news reports she'd found.

"Initial suspects?"

"Lionel Redhorse was the obvious choice. Local bully, had been targeting Travis for months. But his alibi was solid—half the reservation saw him at a party that night." Noah's fingers drummed against the desk. "At the time, John Blackbird and his crew were known for dealing drugs, and there was speculation that Travis might have stumbled onto something. But we could never prove it."

"And the trail went cold?" she surmised.

"Pretty much."

"And who is Logan Crowe?" Sophia asked, noting how the name appeared repeatedly in witness statements, always hovering at the edges of the narrative. "Was he a suspect?"

"We questioned him because he knew Travis and Michael, but that was a dead end, too."

"Is Logan still on the rez?"

"Yeah, he had a rough start, but he straightened out. He started out as a resident at the Clear Skies Residential Program for troubled youth, now he works there. Last I heard, he was doing a good job helping at-risk kids, like he was."

"I'd like to talk to him," Sophia said.

"I'm sure that can be arranged," Noah said.

Sophia didn't trust group homes. She knew all too well what went on behind closed doors when no one was watching. "So, this Clear Skies… Is it a good place?"

"Seems to be," Noah answered. "Clear Skies has a sterling reputation. They take kids no one else wants, give them structure, purpose. The director, Claire Redstone, she's respected. Connected. The program's been running for over twenty years. Never had a single complaint or charge of illegal activity. Claire is known throughout the community for her volunteer work outside of Clear Skies and her willingness to help whenever she can."

"You like her," Sophia surmised.

"I like what I know about her, but it's not like we exchange Christmas cards," Noah clarified.

"I've never entered a group home that didn't have some skeletons in its closet," Sophia said, closing the file. "I know there's a need for places like Clear Skies, but in my experience, group homes can be hotbeds of abuse. I'd like to talk to the director as well as Crowe. I want to see for myself what kind of operation they're running."

Noah paused before sharing, "I read your file. You were part of the takedown of the child pornography ring in Los Angeles operating out of a daycare." He sounded impressed, but added, "That couldn't have been easy on your mental health."

"It wasn't." She didn't elaborate on how she hadn't been able to sleep for months during or after that investigation. The images seared into her brain were nightmare fuel and would be until the day she died. She also didn't like to talk about it. Returning to the current case, she said, "Group homes are a perfect cover. You've got vulnerable kids, high turnover and a steady stream of victims that most people are inclined to ignore because of their pasts. No one asks too many questions when troubled teens run away."

"I get that, but like I said, Clear Skies isn't like most group homes. I've seen it. Claire does good work out there. You'll see when you meet her, she's like the grandma some of these kids never had. I guess you could say Logan Crowe is the best example of her influence. The man today is nothing like the kid he was."

Sophia graced Noah with a short smile. She'd believe it when she saw it. "When can we leave?"

"We can go now, but we need to play this carefully. These people know me, trust me. If we go in too aggressive—"

"They'll shut down faster than a storm cellar in tornado

season." Sophia stood, smoothing her jacket. "Contrary to what you might think, I know how to be subtle. This isn't my first rodeo on a reservation."

"No?" Noah's eyebrow lifted slightly. "And how many of those cases did you close?"

"All of them." Sophia met his gaze steadily. "Every single one." No one could argue with her track record, and she was pleased to see that Noah didn't try. Maybe there was hope for them yet.

"All right then, Agent Bennett. Let's take a drive. Separate cars?" he asked.

Sophia nodded. "Lead the way."

As Sophia followed Noah's truck out of the parking lot, her mind was already cataloging the details she wanted to keep front and center. Group homes were her specialty; she'd seen too many of them turn into fronts for exploitation.

The "perfect" ones were often the worst offenders. After all, a sterling reputation could be bought just like silence could be purchased with the right amount of pressure or money.

She thought about the dead girl's tattoo. That particular mark had shown up on victims across three states, and now it had appeared here, in Stone River, along with Travis Long-shadow's name. The connection nagged at her like a loose tooth.

Noah's truck turned onto a winding road that hugged the base of the mountains. The morning sun caught the autumn leaves, painting them in shades of fire. Beautiful country to hide ugly secrets.

Her phone buzzed—a text from her supervisor back in DC.

Any connection to the Idaho case?

Sophia frowned. Three months ago, they'd found another

girl with the same tattoo outside Boise. She'd been seventeen, Native and had also passed through a group home before disappearing. The similarities were too close to ignore.

"Possibly," she spoke into her phone, using the hands-free text option. "Checking a local group home now. Will update."

She set the phone aside, her attention drawn to the rearview mirror. A dark pickup had followed them since leaving the station, keeping three car lengths back. Could be nothing, small town, limited roads, but Sophia had learned long ago that paranoia was just good sense in disguise.

The truck's license plate was partially obscured by mud. Convenient. She memorized what she could see, making a mental note to run it later.

Her thoughts drifted back to Noah's defense of Clear Skies. He seemed genuine in his belief that Claire Redstone was above board, but that didn't mean much. Good people could be fooled, especially when the deception wore a grandmother's smile and came bearing promises of salvation for troubled youth.

And Logan Crowe… Something about his name kept catching in her mind. She'd seen too many cases where former victims were groomed to become facilitators. Sometimes, it was easier to cope with abuse by joining the abusers than by facing your own trauma.

Or maybe she was just jaded by the job—that happened the longer you stayed in this career.

The road curved sharply, and Noah's brake lights flashed. They were climbing now, the terrain becoming more remote with each mile. Perfect isolation. Far enough from town to muffle screams, close enough to maintain an air of legitimacy.

The dark pickup was still there.

Sophia checked her weapon, a habit born from years of walking into seemingly innocent places only to find darkness lurking behind welcome signs and warm smiles. The weight of her Glock was reassuring against her ribs.

She thought about what Noah had said about Travis being friends with his cousin Michael. Personal connections complicated cases—she'd seen good agents lose objectivity when investigations hit too close to home. She'd have to watch Noah carefully, make sure his judgment wasn't clouded by old loyalties or guilt.

But she couldn't deny that his local knowledge would be invaluable. People here would talk to him in ways they'd never open up to her. She just had to hope his protectiveness of Clear Skies wouldn't blind him to any red flags they might find.

The pickup behind them suddenly turned off onto a side road. Still, she made a mental note of the intersection, just in case.

Noah's truck slowed again, and Sophia caught her first glimpse of Clear Skies through the trees. The facility sat on a ridge overlooking the valley, a cluster of well-maintained buildings that wouldn't look out of place on a small college campus. Everything about it was designed to project safety, stability and hope.

But Sophia knew better than most that hope could be the sharpest weapon when wielded by the right hands. If Clear Skies was hiding something, she'd find out—she always did.

Noah's truck turned into the facility's main drive. A sign welcomed visitors in bright, cheerful letters: Clear Skies Residential Program—Where New Beginnings Take Flight.

Time to find out what kind of wings this place really gave its children.

Chapter 5

Claire Redstone didn't just run Clear Skies—she *was* Clear Skies. Noah had known her since he was a young teen, back when she'd first opened the program. He remembered her gentle persistence with his cousin Michael during his rebellious phase, how she'd had more patience for his attitude than anyone else in his own family.

Even now, watching her bustle down the front steps to greet them, she had that same energy that made troubled kids feel seen. Her silver hair was braided traditionally, and her smile was warm enough to thaw the Montana frost. But there was steel beneath that grandmotherly exterior—you had to be tough to do this work for twenty-plus years.

"Noah Thunderhawk," she called out, her voice carrying the lilt of someone who was raised with their native tongue. "What brings the BIA to my doorstep? And with a pretty guest, no less." Her shrewd eyes flickered to Sophia, assessing but welcoming.

"Just following up on some old business, Auntie." Noah used the respectful term for an older Native woman and kept his tone casual. "This is Special Agent Bennett with the FBI."

"Ma'am." Sophia inclined her head with a polite smile. "Thanks for agreeing to see us on such short notice."

"Well, we're no stranger to having law enforcement as guests around Clear Skies. Sometimes our kids can be a little rowdy," Claire said, her smile never wavering, but something shifted in her posture—subtle, like a deer catching a new scent. "But come, come, any friend of Noah's is welcome here." She gestured toward the main building. "Logan just made coffee, and the cook made fresh banana nut muffins."

Noah caught Sophia's questioning glance. *See?* he wanted to say. *Just a grandmother taking care of lost kids.* As much as he didn't like the reason for stopping by Clear Skies, seeing Claire again felt like getting a warm hug in memory form. She'd always been kind whenever he'd had to deal with her kids on official business, especially when he'd been a nervous new cop, trying to remember all the rules and regulations that came with the job.

Kindness paired with patience was a winning combination when dealing with troubled kids. Sophia would soon see that she was eyeing the wrong person.

The main office smelled of sage and coffee, walls covered with photos of success stories—kids at graduation, college acceptance letters, newspaper clippings about the program's achievements. Logan Crowe's picture hung near Claire's desk: Employee of the Year, 2023. He'd come so far from the angry kid who'd first arrived at Clear Skies.

Claire settled behind her desk, the morning light catching the turquoise at her throat. "Now then," she said, folding her hands. "What can I do for the federal government today?"

The way she said it—like they were all family here, just working things out together—that was Claire's gift. She could make anyone feel like they were on the same side.

But as Noah opened his mouth to explain their presence, he caught a flicker of something in Logan's expression as he set down their coffee cups. Fear? No, that wasn't quite right. More like the look of someone stepping carefully around sleeping rattlers. Some habits died hard.

Whatever it was, Claire immediately caught the discordant vibe and chuckled, saying, "Logan honey, you're acting like a long-tailed cat in a room full of rockers. You remember Officer Thunderhawk, don't you? Well, he's now with the Bureau of Indian Affairs—pretty accomplished, wouldn't you say?"

Logan's expression cleared, and a welcoming smile wreathed his face as he vigorously shook Noah's hand. "Why, I can't believe it, it is you. It's been a long time, how you been?" Then, he answered his own question with a self-deprecating smile, "Obviously, you're doing real good. The BIA? That's pretty damn impressive. Good to see one of our own on the front line, doing good work for the People."

Noah chuckled, shooting a slightly embarrassed look Sophia's way, but her keen gaze seemed to be taking everything in, from details in the room to the temperature of the coffee in her cup. Noah could almost hear the whirring of gears in her head.

"So, what can we do for you today?" Claire asked, returning to business. "I know you didn't stop in just for coffee and muffins."

"No, ma'am, sadly, we're here on official business," he shared.

Sophia took that as her cue to jump in. "I know news travels fast in small places, so you're probably already aware that a body of a young Native girl was found in the area with the name Travis Longshadow written on her skin. As I understand it, Logan was friends with Travis?"

Claire didn't look surprised or horrified by the news, but then a woman in her field saw horrors most people could only imagine. She sobered appropriately, sharing a kind look with Logan. "Travis was a sweet, sweet boy."

"You knew him?" Sophia asked.

"Only peripherally and mostly posthumously," Claire admitted, reaching for Logan's hand to pat it gently. "Logan was beside himself when young Travis was killed."

Logan swallowed as he jerked a nod, confirming Claire's story. "When I was a teen, I landed here at Clear Skies for doing things that could've wrecked my life. I'm not proud, but I was a mess back then." He paused, casting an apologetic look Noah's way before continuing, "You probably remember, but I was running with a crowd known for trouble."

"You don't have to protect my feelings. I know my cousin Michael was part of that group," Noah said, letting Logan know it was okay to be honest. He was fully aware of the path Michael took in life. Unlike Logan, Michael still hadn't found his way and was often in and out of jail, according to his mom.

"Yeah, we were all messed up in the head except Travis. Michael introduced me to Travis, and I thought there couldn't be a more mismatched friendship than theirs because as far as I could tell, Travis was a real good kid. He didn't deserve what happened to him."

"Do you know what happened to him?" Sophia pressed with deceptive calm.

"Just what was said in the papers and that story that was written about him, but what I meant by that was, just that his life was cut short."

"Of course," Sophia murmured. "Please continue."

"Not much else to say, except his death really shook me up. I was only a kid myself. I'd thought of myself as a tough guy until real death was staring me in the face. I hate to say it, but I think if it weren't for Travis dying like he did, I might not be where I am today."

"Oh, I don't know about that," Claire disagreed with a warm smile for Logan. "You're always selling yourself short." To Sophia, she explained, "Logan spent a long time grieving for a boy he'd only known a short time, which showed me that this was a kid with a big heart just looking for the right reason to heal. I love all my kids, but I'd be a liar if there weren't some that just stick to me for reasons I can't explain. Right then, I knew that Logan needed me to help him find his true purpose."

"And that's what she did," Logan said, nodding. "I owe her my life."

"I wish Michael had had a similar awakening after Travis died," Noah said. "He's definitely put our family through it. Especially my aunt. She never gives up hope on him, though."

Claire graced Noah with an indulgent smile. "A good mother never does."

"Do you have children of your own?" Sophia asked, curious.

Claire lifted her chin. "Every child who has walked these halls is a child of mine. I care for them no less than if I'd given birth to them."

"That's very generous of you," Sophia said as her gaze wandered the wall of accomplishments. "It seems your kind heart has helped many kids."

"I like to think so, but I just do what I can and put the rest in Great Spirit's hands."

Sophia's perfunctory smile made Noah wonder where Sophia's personal faith lay. Here in Stone River, a high percentage of residents believed in a fusion of Christianity and their ancestors' belief structure. So, while they might participate in a sweat lodge to purge their souls of negative energy on a Thursday, they'd still show up in church that following Sunday to listen to the pastor talk about Jesus.

Some people didn't quite understand how that fusion worked, but it was all Noah had ever known.

"Was the girl from Stone River?" Logan asked, the crease deepening on his forehead.

"I'm sorry, but we can't talk about an open investigation," Sophia answered before Noah could.

"Right, of course, sorry." Logan flushed with his apology. "Not real used to anything like this happening around here."

"I'd love a tour of the grounds," Sophia said, rising. "If you wouldn't mind, of course."

"We're proud of our facility and happy to show it off," Claire said with a beaming smile. "Logan, go bring the golf cart around. We'll give them the VIP tour."

"You got it," Logan said, disappearing out the door.

"You sure you don't mind?" Noah asked.

"Anything to help," Claire said.

The golf cart hummed quietly as Logan navigated the grounds, Claire narrating from the front passenger seat while Noah and Sophia sat behind them. The facility sprawled across several acres, each building purpose-built and well maintained. No peeling paint or sagging porches here.

"We have separate dorms for boys and girls, of course," Claire explained, gesturing to two identical structures. "The kids share rooms—we find it helps with accountability and teaches them to live cooperatively. Logan, pull over by the garden, honey. I want to show them our latest project."

The cart stopped beside neat rows of vegetables, late-season squash still clinging to browning vines. A teenage girl looked up from her weeding, quickly dropping her eyes when she saw Claire.

"This is Sarah," Claire said warmly. "One of our brightest stars. She's teaching the younger ones about traditional farming practices."

The girl's shoulders hunched slightly at the praise, but she managed to whisper "hello" before returning to her task. Noah noticed how her hands trembled slightly on the trowel.

"Shy," Claire explained with an indulgent smile. "But she's come so far. When she first arrived, she wouldn't speak at all."

"Trauma?" Sophia asked.

Claire's expression dimmed as she simply nodded without elaborating.

Noah hated that so many generations of his people suffered in ways that most people could never understand. Growing up on the rez was both beautiful and tragic. Resources were often stretched so thin it was inevitable that someone, somewhere, would fall through the cracks, which meant help didn't come fast enough sometimes.

They continued past a recreational area where boys played basketball, their shouts carrying across the crisp morning air. Everything looked normal and healthy—exactly what you'd want in a youth facility. But something about the way the kids stopped playing as they passed, their eyes tracking Claire's movement, made the hair on Noah's neck prickle.

You're letting Sophia's suspicion get to you, he thought. Kids always got nervous around authority figures. That was all this was.

"And here's our pride and joy," Claire announced as they approached a newer building. "The learning center. We have computers, tutoring, cultural education—everything our kids need to succeed." Her voice took on that familiar, passionate tone that had always impressed Noah. "You can lock up a troubled kid, punish them, but that just teaches them to be better criminals. Give them purpose, identity, skills—that's how you change lives."

Noah caught Sophia studying Claire's face, looking for... what? Cracks in the facade? She wouldn't find any. Claire Redstone had dedicated her life to these kids. He'd seen it firsthand over the years.

"Logan practically lived in here when he was a resident,"

Claire continued, patting Logan's arm. "Always with his nose in a book. I knew right away he was special."

Logan chuckled at the memory. "Just needed someone to believe in me, that's all."

They passed more kids as they toured—all of them polite. Noah remembered Michael talking about Clear Skies once, saying Claire ran a tight ship. *She's got eyes everywhere*, he'd said. *Nothing happens there without her knowing.*

At the time, Noah had thought that was a good thing. Structure and supervision—wasn't that what troubled kids need?

"Would you like to see inside the learning center?" Claire offered. "We just got a grant for new—"

A sharp cry cut through the air. Everyone turned to see a boy sprawled on the basketball court, clutching his ankle.

Claire's reaction was instant. "Tommy!" She was already moving before the boy's cry faded, her actions smooth and practiced. "Logan, bring the cart around. Officer Thunderhawk, Agent Bennett—I'm so sorry, but would you mind if we…?"

Noah recognized her manner from countless similar incidents—how she'd drop everything when a kid needed help. It was one of the things that had always impressed him about her.

They reached the boy just as he tried to stand, tears cutting down his dusty cheeks. Claire knelt beside him, her movements graceful despite her age, one hand gentle on his shoulder.

"Now, now, let's not make it worse," she soothed, her voice pitched to carry just the right note of maternal concern. "Show Auntie where it hurts."

The other boys hovered nearby, their game forgotten. Noah noticed how they watched Claire's every move, like satellites locked in orbit.

"Just twisted it," Tommy mumbled, clearly embarrassed by the attention.

"Even small hurts need tending," Claire said, checking his ankle with practiced hands. "Logan, help Tommy to the infirmary. Nurse Martinez should be in." She brushed the dirt from her skirt as she stood. "Boys will swear they're fine and then end up having a broken bone," she explained to Sophia with a self-deprecating smile. "Can't always trust what they tell you."

Logan helped the boy into the cart, and Sophia suggested they walk back to their cars so Claire could get the boy to the nurse sooner.

"I'm sorry to cut our tour short. You sure you don't mind walking back to the parking lot?" Claire asked as Logan climbed back into the driver's seat.

"Not at all. It's a beautiful day, and I could stand to stretch my legs a bit," Noah said.

"All right, then, call me if you have any other questions," Claire said, nodding to Logan to start driving.

Noah watched the cart disappear around the corner, then turned to find Sophia already walking toward the parking lot. Fall leaves crunched beneath their feet as they walked in silence.

"I get why you're suspicious of group homes," he said. "Given what you've seen, I'd probably feel the same way. But c'mon, clearly Claire's different. Twenty years I've known her, watched her fight for kids everyone else gave up on, and I've never once seen her give up on a kid in her charge."

"You trust her." It wasn't a question.

"Yeah, I do." Noah thought about all the times he'd brought troubled kids to Clear Skies, how Claire never turned them away, no matter how late the hour. "Look, I'm not saying bad things don't happen in places like this. But Claire Redstone? She's one of the good ones."

Sophia considered this as they reached their vehicles. "Maybe. But in my experience, Agent Thunderhawk, the most dangerous predators are the ones who've earned everyone's trust."

"And in my experience," Noah countered, "sometimes people are exactly who they appear to be." But as he watched Sophia climb into her car, a whisper of doubt tried to surface. He pushed it away. Claire wasn't the monster they were looking for. She couldn't be.

Could she?

Chapter 6

"How about this—we head back to town, and I show you where to get the best coffee in town," Noah offered when they finally reached their cars.

Sophia looked up from her phone, pausing her digital notes. She always tried to jot down her thoughts and feelings immediately after an interview so nothing was lost in the recall. "Excuse me?" she asked, confused.

"I'm taking a wild guess that you're staying at the Whispering Pines, and I can guarantee whatever they're filtering probably tastes more like mud than anything that's supposed to resemble a roasted coffee bean."

Sophia couldn't lie, the coffee was barely drinkable, but it had the caffeine she needed, so she gulped it down. "It could definitely use some improvement," she admitted.

"Okay, then, let me show you where to get a good coffee and where to eat so you don't end up writing a bad Yelp review on all of Stone River."

"Does Stone River have a huge tourist draw?" Sophia couldn't resist the light tease.

"You'd be surprised," Noah quipped. "So, you in?"

She ought to decline. Keeping things professional was the safest way to maintain objectivity, but she also needed to determine if Noah was the right man for this job. She tucked her phone away, studying him. The late morning sun caught the silver threads in his dark hair, and she noticed for the first time how his eyes crinkled at the corners when he smiled. She assessed him further with a critical eye. Good-looking in a raw, traditional sense…sharp jaw, strong cheekbones that would make an ancestral warrior proud and an innate sense of fair play that appealed to her moral compass. "I don't date on the job," she stated bluntly.

"Whoa, slow down, it's just coffee, not a marriage proposal," he said. "Good manners are ingrained in me. Blame my parents, but I can't let a colleague choke down dirt water when I know there's a better option."

"Of course, my bad." Heat climbed into Sophia's cheeks. Of course, he was just being polite. This was Sophia's problem and the reason why she socialized as little as possible. She never seemed to catch the differences between social niceties and flirting. "But I figure, it's best to manage expectations."

"Right. No dating on the job. I have the same rule," he said. "Now, that we have that out of the way…are you interested in the coffee intel or no?"

The thought of choking down that bitter hotel sludge every morning was a daunting prospect. She slowly nodded, accepting his offer. "I'd appreciate the intel. Thank you."

Noah grinned, pushing past the awkwardness with a finesse she envied. "Red Feather makes a decent breakfast, and I don't know about you, but I skipped an opportunity to have my mom's biscuits and gravy for breakfast, and I'm starving."

Biscuits and gravy? "Otherwise known as a Southern heart attack special where I'm from."

"If it is, it's not the worst way to go," Noah said. "I'll be honest, when I'm on the job, sometimes I don't eat as well as I should. I'm actually looking forward to a meal that doesn't come out of a box."

She chuckled. "I can relate. TV dinners and takeout are probably going to kill me someday."

"The hidden pitfall of a career in law enforcement," he commiserated.

"It does feel that way. All right, you convinced me. Lead the way, Agent Thunderhawk."

"One thing, though," Noah said, before climbing into his car. "Please call me Noah."

Sophia hesitated but finally jerked a nod. "And you may call me Sophia."

"Great!" He tapped the hood of his car, pleased. "Follow me, and I'll lead you straight to the best food you've ever had."

"Don't get ahead of yourself, Agent, I grew up in Houston. I know good food," she returned with the slightest tease in her voice.

"Challenge accepted," he returned with a short grin and climbed into his car.

Within twenty minutes, they were parked at the Red Feather Bar and Grill, which sat on the edge of town. The restaurant's weathered wooden exterior was barely visible behind a row of pickup trucks. Classic rock drifted out when Noah held the door, along with the smell of coffee and bacon.

Her stomach growled, reminding her that the aforementioned terrible coffee she'd downed this morning was a poor substitute for sustenance.

Conversations dimmed as they entered, heads turning to track their movement. Sophia felt the weight of dozens of eyes, the silent assessment of outsiders that she'd encountered on reservations before. But then—

"Noah Thunderhawk!" a waitress with silver-streaked hair called out. "Your mama said you were back in town."

"Hey, Martha." Noah's smile was genuine and comfortable. "How's Joey doing at college?"

"Finally getting his master's degree, if you can believe it. Remember when you caught him trying to steal your hubcaps?"

"It was either bold or stupid to try to take the hubcabs from a tribal police squad car," he recalled with a chuckle. "Glad to hear he's doing good."

Sophia watched the exchange with anthropological fascination. This was Noah in his element—connected, remembered, part of a living tapestry of shared history. She'd never stayed in one place long enough to have that. That old ache bloomed in her gut for something she'd never had and likely never would—so she did what she always did: ignored it, pretending it didn't exist.

They settled into a corner booth with a good view of the exits.

"Trust me on the breakfast special," Noah said, not even opening his menu. "Unless you're one of those people who only eats egg whites and dry toast?"

"Did you not hear me when I said I was raised in Texas? I eat meat, and I chase child traffickers for a living," Sophia replied dryly. "I think I can handle whatever passes for a breakfast special in Montana."

Noah's expression sobered slightly at the mention of their work, but Martha returned with a coffeepot before he could respond.

"You must be the FBI agent everyone's talking about," she said, filling their cups. Her tone was friendly but guarded.

"Word travels fast," Sophia noted, wrapping her hands around the steaming mug.

"Small town." Martha shrugged. "Two specials?" she asked Noah.

"Please." He waited until Martha left before turning back to Sophia. "So, what's your real take on Clear Skies?"

Sophia raised an eyebrow. "Trying to get my professional opinion over breakfast, Agent—" she caught herself "—Noah?"

"Just making conversation." But his eyes were sharp, assessing. "Unless you'd rather discuss the weather?"

"I'm not much for small talk." She took a sip of coffee—damn, it was good—choosing her words carefully. "Claire Redstone seems…devoted to her work."

"But?"

"But I reserve judgment until I have all the facts." She studied him over the rim of her mug. "What brought you to the BIA task force? Long way from tribal police."

Something darkened in Noah's expression, and Sophia knew she'd touched a nerve. Good. She wanted to see past the easy charm and find out what really drove him.

"It's not very exciting or unique," he said finally. "You sure you want to hear it?"

"I wouldn't ask if I didn't." If she were being honest, despite her line in the sand about interpersonal mingling, it wasn't entirely professional curiosity that made her ask, but it was in there. "I want to know who I'm working with."

"All right then, well, my father was a tribal officer, and I always just figured I'd follow in his footsteps—which I did—but once I was in the job, I realized there's so much more that needs to be done, and half the time, there just aren't the resources to do enough. I knew if I wanted to really make a difference, I'd have to climb the chain. Don't get me wrong, I'm not saying that good work can't be done as a tribal officer, but for me, I needed more."

"Is your father still on the force or retired?"

"He…was killed on the job," Noah shared.

"Oh, I'm sorry, that's rough," she said, feeling terrible for inadvertently sticking her foot in her mouth. "It's a risk that comes with the job, but I don't think it truly hits home until we're personally affected."

"Yeah, that's definitely true." A beat passed between them before Noah said, "Learning something like that can be a conversation killer, but no matter how it ended for my father, I'll always be proud of his legacy. I try to focus on that—not his death."

"That's very wise of you," she murmured, struck by his quiet strength. "Not many people would look at it the same."

"Again, I blame it on my parents," he said with a slight smile.

"Then, I'd say they raised you right." Something she wouldn't know much about. She took another sip of her coffee, if only to regroup for a minute. "So I have to ask, is it weird to be back on your home turf for this case?"

"A little," he admitted. "It's not like I've avoided home, but my visits to Stone River have been few and far between with everything going on with my job. It's a good place, though. For the most part, good energy."

"The most part?" she queried with a lifted brow.

"Well, no place is perfect," he answered from above his coffee mug. "Evil is everywhere if you know where to look."

"No argument there," she agreed as Martha returned with plates heaped with eggs, bacon and what looked like enough hash browns to feed a small army. The biscuits were golden brown, drowning in peppered sausage gravy. Sophia had to admit, it smelled amazing.

Noah waited until Martha moved out of earshot before speaking. "Three years ago, I was working a missing person's case. Fifteen-year-old girl named Jenny Almond. Her mother swore she wouldn't have run away, but you know how it goes—teenage girl disappears, everyone assumes she just took off." He paused, pushing his hash browns around with his fork. "But something felt off. The girl was an honor student, close to her family. And there had been other disappearances—nothing anyone connected at first. Just kids from different reservations going missing."

Sophia's pulse quickened. This was familiar territory.

"I started digging," Noah continued. "Found a pattern of Native girls vanishing along the I-90 corridor. Local cops weren't talking to each other, tribal police were overwhelmed, and the feds…" He shrugged. "Well, you know how that usually goes."

"Missing indigenous women and girls rarely get the attention they deserve," Sophia said quietly.

"Exactly. But I had this sergeant, Lon Johnson. He listened. Helped me connect the dots to similar cases in other jurisdictions. Turned out there was a trucking company running girls across state lines, using the reservations as hunting grounds."

"The River Rock case," Sophia said, recognition dawning. "That was you?"

Noah nodded. "Took us eight months to build it. Found Jenny's body in South Dakota." His body tensed with the memory. "But we got them. Every last one. After that, when a position came open, Johnson put my name in the ear of Isaac Berrigan for his new BIA task force. At my interview, Berrigan said he needed people who wouldn't give up, who knew the communities, and someone who didn't scare easily. I knew exactly what I was signing up for, and I was all in."

"The River Rock case made headlines," Sophia recalled, impressed. "Changed how trafficking cases on reservations are handled. I followed the case closely at the time. That's pretty impressive."

"Didn't bring Jenny back, though." Noah finally looked up from his plate. "Or the others we didn't find in time."

Sophia recognized the shadow in his eyes—she saw it in

her own mirror often enough. "You never forget the ones you couldn't save," she commiserated. "Sometimes the weight of that failure is heavy enough to crush your soul. They say cops in our line of work age ten times faster than any other department."

"Yeah, I heard that statistic somewhere, too." He shrugged. "Every job out there takes a toll on the mind or body in one way or another. Sometimes both. But I know I'm doing what I'm meant to do, and that's good enough for me."

"It's got to be hard, though, coming back home to investigate a case connected to the one you couldn't solve—that can mess with your head," she said.

He cut into his breakfast, chewing slowly as he held her gaze. "Why don't you ask what you really want to know?"

She paused, fork midway to her mouth, taking the challenge. "Okay, can you be objective when it comes to this case? This town?"

"Guess there's only one way to find out," he answered, neither making any promises nor giving her overconfident assurances.

She liked his honesty, even if it was delivered with a subtle smirk bordering on arrogance. Liked it a little too much. Noah had a quality about him that whispered to something deep inside her that she'd buried for so long she barely recognized the feeling. She'd spent her career so hyper focused on chasing the bad guys that it'd always been easier to keep people at arm's length, preferable even, but Noah made her want to challenge her own rigid rules.

"I suppose so." Sophia studied him, really studied him. Not the surface charm or the easy way he had with people, but the steel underneath. She suppressed a shiver that dragged lazy fingers down her vertebrae. This wasn't just another cop going through the motions. This was someone who understood what they were up against. She trusted him even if they had different ways of going about things.

Which was a good, if not surprising, feeling. "You're an interesting guy, Noah Thunderhawk," she admitted as she stuffed a bite of biscuit smothered in gravy in her mouth. Damn, that was good. She let a small groan escape her lips as she chewed, meeting his smug gaze. "Okay, you were right, it's pretty delicious. But if you tell anyone I admitted that this Montana breakfast can compete with Texas, I'll deny it."

His laugh broke the tension, and for a moment, they were just two people sharing breakfast, the weight of dead children temporarily lifted from their shoulders.

But Sophia knew better than most—moments like these never lasted. There was always another case, another victim, another monster wearing a friendly face.

At least now she knew she had the right partner to hunt them down.

Chapter 7

The late afternoon sun cast long shadows through Grace's beading room window, turning the glass and bone beads into tiny prisms of light. The scent of sage and sweetgrass lingered from her morning prayers, mixing with the metallic tang of approaching much-needed rain.

Noah sat at the worn desk, case files spread before him as his thoughts drifted to Sophia. When her red hair caught the sunlight, it was like a fiery halo erupting on her crown. Red was the perfect color for her—it matched her personality. He'd never put much stock in the stereotype about redheads, but Sophia was putting that stereotype through its paces.

Was it terrible that he wanted to know more about the woman behind the badass agent? But Sophia made it very clear there would be no bending the lines etched in steel, and he respected her boundaries. Just another example of the discipline and professionalism that he admired about her.

But it didn't seem to stop the curiosity from burning in his brain.

The distinctive rumble of a familiar engine caught his attention, switching his focus. The deep, throaty purr echoed off the weathered siding of the house, making the windows vibrate slightly. He knew that sound—the purr of Amber's restored '67 Mustang, a car she'd poured more money into than most people spent on their first house.

It was a gas guzzler with no safety features, and everything about it screamed high maintenance, but if cars matched their owner's personalities, it was a perfect fit for Amber Laughlin.

Well, he knew this was going to happen the second he placed the call. There was no way Amber could resist revisiting the story that had launched her career into the stratosphere.

"Is that—?" Lila's excited squeal from the living room confirmed his fears. Before he could move, his sister had already thrown open the front door. "Amber! Oh my God, what are you doing here?"

Noah rubbed his temples, wondering if he could slip out the back door without being noticed. But Lila's voice carried through the house like a megaphone: "Noah's in his old room pretending to work, but really he's just staring off into space. You know how he gets."

There was no way to avoid the reunion that was coming—and it was his own damn fault. He rose and closed the door behind him to join his sister in the living room.

"Look what the cat dragged in," Amber teased as he entered. The sharp click of her boots on the hardwood floor broadcast her confident stride. "C'mere and give me a hug and don't be weird about it." The familiar scent of her jasmine perfume made his nose twitch, reminding him how that particular perfume had always made him sneeze.

Before he could refuse, Amber wrapped him in a tight squeeze that he awkwardly returned.

"Good to see you, Amber," he murmured, releasing her quickly. "I had a feeling you'd come, but I didn't think you'd drop everything and show up so fast."

"When opportunity knocks, I answer. Besides, you and I both know this case is personal. There's no way I could walk away," she said.

"Yeah, I know."

She looked exactly as he remembered—tall, athletic, with dark hair cut in a sharp bob that suited her no-nonsense personality and dark eyes as sharp as a shark, never missing a thing. "It's been a while since I've been back to Stone River, but I hope the chicken fried steak at the Red Feather is still as good as ever."

He chuckled. "Everything seems about the same since we left."

Their shared history sat between them, but neither felt anything but a lingering appreciation for time spent, which was rare in this day and age. Most people he knew had nothing but bad things to say about their exes. He supposed he and Amber were just built different. Neither wanted to get back together, but that didn't mean they couldn't appreciate what once was.

Amber got straight to the point. "So, after you called, I immediately started digging, and I might have information that could prove useful to your investigation—which I'm happy to share if you can keep me looped into the new case involving Travis."

"Very subtle, Amber," Noah said dryly. *Ever the journalist.*

"Subtlety is overrated. You should know that by now." She dropped into the chair across from him, every movement radiating the confidence of someone used to commanding rooms. "Nice to see you, by the way."

Lila hovered in the doorway, practically vibrating with excitement. "Remember when you two were engaged and actually liked each other? Those were good times."

"Lila," Noah warned, but Amber just laughed.

"Your brother and I still like each other just fine," she said, winking at Lila. "We just figured out we were better at being friends than sharing a bathroom."

"Yeah, but they say friendship is the best basis for a relationship," Lila pressed.

"Lila," Noah groaned at her misplaced nudging. "Stop."

Of course Amber thought Lila's machinations were hilarious, but the woman had a daft sense of humor so that tracked. But soon enough, Amber sobered to add, "As much as your brother is a great guy…we're about as good together as an egg and tuna sandwich. However…" she gestured to between her and Lila "…you and me? Never gonna stop being besties."

Amber returned to Noah. "In all seriousness, did you think I wouldn't come? That case was my first major story."

"The case that made your career," Noah recalled.

"It did," Amber agreed with an appropriate level of respect. "I still wish there'd been a better outcome for Travis's family. Maggie Longshadow deserves some closure."

He couldn't argue that point.

"You look good, fit," Amber said with an appreciative smile. "Glad to see you're still putting in time at the gym instead of getting soft on too many plates of beans and fry bread."

He chuckled. "You look good, too."

Amber grinned. "I know."

Noah shook his head with silent amusement. Same Amber that he remembered.

"So, Agent Thunderhawk of the BIA cold case task force. That's quite a step up from tribal police," Amber said with respect. "Impressive."

"And you're quite a step up from the local paper," he countered. "*New York Times*, *Washington Post*—you're doing all right for yourself."

"We both chased what we wanted." Her smile held a hint of their old intimacy. "Even if it meant chasing different directions."

Noah nodded. "Are you happy? Seeing someone? Or just chasing the next story?"

She ticked off her answers on her fingers because she was a smart-ass, "Yes. Kinda. And always."

He chuckled. One thing between them had always been their easy banter. The one thing he missed. The rest? Not so much.

"Okay, enough with the small talk. Tell me about Sophia Bennett. What's she like? I've been itching to get a meeting with Bennett for over a year, but she avoids the press like the plague. Something tells me she doesn't think much of journalists. Not that I'm surprised. Not many investigators ride with journalists. Internal bias and all that."

"I don't know her well enough to weigh in on that score, but she's good at what she does, that much I can tell." He hadn't told Sophia about calling Amber, and now he regretted that decision, but it was too late. He studied her face, reading the subtle tells he remembered so well. "What's this information you have?"

Amber glanced toward the doorway, lowering her voice. Thunder growled as dark clouds gathered in the distance, casting the kitchen in premature twilight. "I've been working on a story about drug trafficking moving into reservation territories in Montana. My source says there's a new player trying to establish routes through the state, using local kids as runners."

"And you think this connects to our victim?"

"Drugs and dead teenagers usually go hand in hand," she said grimly.

"How are they recruiting the kids?"

Amber shrugged. "A variety of ways, but they always know who to target—kids without great home lives, not a lot of connections to ground them and a need for love and acceptance. Group homes are an easy target, runaways, foster care kids."

He thought of Claire Redstone and her facility—and Sophia's reservations. "You remember Clear Skies?"

"Of course. Is Claire Redstone still running it?"

He nodded. "Me and Sophia paid a visit to the facility yesterday."

"How'd it seem?"

"Same as before—orderly, well-run." Noah drummed his fingers against the scratched surface of the table, a nervous habit he'd never quite broken. "The kids seem to be happy and healthy, which is a far cry from what I've seen in other places. Claire runs a solid facility. As far as I can tell, she remains an asset to the community."

"I remember her, the grandmotherly type."

"Do you remember Logan Crowe, a kid interviewed at the time Travis went missing?"

"Yeah, they were friends, if I remember correctly," Amber answered. "What about him?"

"Complete turnaround. He's helping Claire run Clear Skies. You wouldn't recognize the kid now. All grown up and respectable, and I attribute that to Claire's influence."

"Nice to hear a success story, kinda rare in those circles."

He nodded, returning to the original reason Amber showed up. "You got an outfit I should be watching for?"

"Not yet, but I'll let you know if I hear anything specific. What can you tell me about the young girl who was found?"

"Not anything until I talk to my partner, but there's also very little to tell even if I wanted to. Medical examiner hasn't released his findings yet."

"Can you arrange a meeting with Bennett?"

Noah didn't know how he felt about that. "I doubt she's going to be open to talking to the press about this case. It's too fresh." He pushed back from the table, needing to move. Outside, storm clouds were gathering over the mountains, matching his darkening mood. "Look, if I'm being honest, I probably shouldn't have called you. I'm sorry."

"But you did." Amber wasn't going to let him off the hook, not now. "Because you know I'm good at what I do. And because part of you never let go of Travis's case, either."

He couldn't argue her point. Amber had a way of getting information that he couldn't because she wasn't concerned with the evidence chain holding up in court. He felt that having the resources and ingenuity of an investigative journalist could be useful, but he wasn't sure if Sophia would agree.

"So, what do you say, Agent Thunderhawk? Want to compare notes? For old times' sake?"

Thunder rumbled in the distance as Noah weighed his options. Finally, he said, "It'll all depend on how my partner feels. If she's not good with your involvement, I can't rope you in. Got it?"

"Just get me a meeting… I'll get her to see that I'm a valuable asset to the investigation," Amber said with confidence. "I have contacts that the feds couldn't possibly reach."

"I'm sure that'll win her over."

Amber rose and walked to the door, her expression turning serious. "Noah? For what it's worth… I'm glad you called. I think we both need closure on this case."

Noah nodded, feeling what was unsaid between them. The Travis Longshadow case had left scars on everyone involved at some level. It was time to put this case to bed.

Thunder cracked overhead as Amber hurried to her car, the storm finally breaking. Noah watched from the doorway as the Mustang's taillights disappeared into the deluge, two red eyes swallowed by darkness.

He pulled out his phone, thumb hovering over Sophia's number. Better to tell her now, get ahead of it before Amber started making waves on her own. But the words of his old training officer echoed in his mind: *The moment you lose control of information in a case, you lose control of the case itself.*

Lightning split the sky, illuminating his mother's beadwork through the window. The delicate patterns threw shadows on the wall—interconnected, complex, like the web of relationships in Stone River. One pull of the wrong thread could unravel everything.

Before he could start the text, his phone buzzed: a text from Sophia. Speak of the devil.

Medical examiner's preliminary report is in. I'll pick you up in twenty.

The storm raged on, but Noah barely noticed the rain as he grabbed his keys. The ME's report would have to take precedence over his confession about Amber. He just hoped that decision wouldn't come back to bite them both.

Chapter 8

The medical examiner's office smelled of industrial cleaner and stale coffee, with an underlying sweet-metallic scent that Sophia had long ago learned to identify as death. She stood at the window, watching the rain turn to light snow flurries in the harsh fluorescent light of the parking lot. Her breath fogged the glass as headlights cut through the growing darkness of the building storm—Noah's truck pulling in.

The basement of Stone River's municipal building housed the ME's office, and like most basement offices, it felt removed from the world above. The fluorescent lights buzzed overhead, casting everything in a pallor that made even the living look half dead. Sophia had spent countless hours in offices like this one, waiting for details that would fuel her nightmares.

Dr. Marcus Walsh's office was exactly what she'd expect from a small-town ME: cluttered but methodical, with decades of case files lining metal shelves and anatomical charts yellowing on the walls. A skeleton hung in one corner, wearing a Santa hat that seemed wildly inappropriate given their reason for being here and the fact that it was only late September.

The man himself sat behind a desk that had seen better days, his wild gray hair standing up like he'd been running his hands through it all day. Dark circles under his eyes suggested he'd been working late, probably on their case.

Or maybe he just looked like that because the job took a toll—either way, the man wasn't winning any beauty contests.

She watched him shuffle papers, noting how his hands shook slightly. Not from age—this was something else. The weight of what he'd seen on that table, perhaps. Even seasoned professionals weren't immune to the horror of examining murdered children.

"Noah," Walsh said gravely as they entered, standing to greet them. "Been a while since you darkened my door. Sad to see a case like this bring you home."

"Hey, Doc." Noah's greeting was equally familiar, and Sophia noted how Walsh's presence seemed to put him at ease. "This is Special Agent Bennett from the FBI."

"Dr. Walsh," Sophia acknowledged, shaking his hand. His grip was firm and professional, but his eyes were kind behind wire-rimmed glasses.

Walsh nodded, his expression sobering as he pulled a file from his desk. It was thick—never a good sign. "Well, I've got an ID on your victim. Fingerprints matched a missing person report from six months ago." He opened the folder, revealing the photo of a young girl with bright eyes and a tentative smile. The kind of school photo parents used to tuck into wallets before everything turned digital. "Laramie Baker, sixteen. Reported missing from Bright Horizons Group Home in Missoula."

Sixteen. They were always so young. The girl in the photo looked nothing like the brutalized body they'd found, but there was something in her eyes—a wariness that spoke of someone who'd already seen too much of life's darker side.

"Any details in her file about her home life? Why she ended up in the group home?" Noah asked.

Walsh shook his head. "Nope, you'll have to get that from Missoula, most likely."

Sophia made a quick note on her phone to call social services for information on the girl and contact the original investigator into the missing person's case.

"The good news, if you can call it that," Walsh continued, pulling out a preliminary report, "is that she fought like hell at the end. The bad news is pretty much everything else." He spread several photos across his desk with the precision of someone who'd done this thousands of times. "Let's start with cause of death and work backward."

Sophia activated the digital recorder on her phone, though she knew every detail would be seared into her memory regardless. She liked to have multiple sources of documentation for her cases, even if some of the information was likely duplicated.

"Cause of death was blunt force trauma to the head," Walsh began, his voice taking on the clinical tone doctors used when delivering difficult news. "The fatal blow was delivered to the right temporal region with considerable force—we're looking at something heavy and curved, possibly a pipe or tire iron. Death would have been rapid but not instant."

He pointed to a close-up photo that made Noah shift uncomfortably beside her. "But that's just the end of a long list of injuries. Multiple fractures in various stages of healing— seven ribs, all fingers on the right hand, left ulna. Pattern suggests systematic torture over weeks, maybe months. The breaks were amateur work—violent but not precise. These weren't done by someone who knew what they were doing, just someone who enjoyed causing pain."

Sophia made notes, her handwriting sharp despite her churning stomach. "The fingers?"

"Broken one at a time, probably with pliers. Old technique, favored by people who want information or watched too many mobster movies." Walsh's mouth tightened. "I've found similar trauma patterns in cases involving cartel interrogations."

"You said she fought back?" Noah asked, his voice rougher than usual. "What kind of defensive wounds did you find?"

Walsh pulled out another photo. "Bruising on her forearms, broken fingernails—she didn't go quietly. Found skin under her nails, sent it for DNA testing. Bruising around her wrists and ankles consistent with restraints, probably rope given the fiber patterns in the skin. These were applied and removed multiple times over several weeks, based on the layering of contusions."

He paused, removing his glasses to rub his eyes. When he continued, his voice was softer. "Tox screen showed high levels of heroin and methamphetamine. Track marks on both arms, some fresh, some scarred over. No way to know if this was recreational use or abuse."

Sophia thought of the girl's photo, that tentative smile. How long after the photo was taken before the drugs had dulled that light in her eyes?

"There was also evidence of repeated sexual assault," Walsh continued, his clinical tone slipping slightly. "Some injuries were fresh, others older. I've detailed everything in my report, but—" He stopped, shaking his head. "It's not easy reading."

"What about the writing on her arm?" Noah asked. "Travis Longshadow's name."

"Marker pen, probably standard Sharpie. Written postmortem, roughly twelve hours after death based on skin absorption patterns. Though why she'd have Travis's name on her skin is your job to figure out."

"Time of death?" Sophia asked.

"Based on liver temperature and decomp, I'd put it between forty-eight and seventy-two hours before she was found. Weather makes it tricky to be more precise." Walsh handed them each a copy of his report. "I'll email you the full findings, including the DNA workup. But there's one more thing."

He pulled out a final photograph showing a close-up of the girl's ankle. "This tattoo—it's crude work, probably done with a homemade gun. Six months old at most, based on healing patterns. Matches the one you were asking about, Agent Bennett."

Sophia studied the image—a crude circle with a jagged slash. The same mark she'd been tracking across three states. "Any other tattoos or identifying marks?"

Sophia's mind immediately connected this case to her others: three dead girls in Idaho and two in Wyoming, all with the same crude brand. All Native, all between fifteen and seventeen, all found with high levels of drugs in their systems. The pattern was undeniable: someone was targeting indigenous girls, likely promising them escape from troubled situations, only to trap them in something far worse.

"I'll need to see everything from Bright Horizons," she said, already making notes. "Intake records, incident reports, visitor logs, staff records including any who left in the six months before Laramie disappeared. Also any surveillance footage they still have, though that's probably long gone."

Noah nodded. "I can reach out to Missoula PD, get their missing person report. Might be worth checking if any other kids went missing from that home."

"Good thinking. And we'll need her complete social services history, including where she was before Bright Horizons, any previous placements, family contact information." Sophia paused. "The brand usually shows up within the first month of captivity. They mark their property early." She returned to the medical examiner. "Anything else?"

Walsh answered, "Small cross on her left wrist, looks professional. Probably predated her disappearance. And this—"

He pointed to a scar on her collarbone. "Surgical pin from a childhood injury. Medical records confirm it was from a bicycle accident when she was eight."

Eight years old, still innocent enough to ride bikes and get into accidents. Eight years before whatever darkness had claimed her had started reaching out its tendrils.

"I'll have the full tox screen results tomorrow," Walsh said, gathering the photos. "And the DNA analysis should be back within the week. I've put a rush on it."

"Thank you, Doctor." Sophia tucked the report into her bag, its weight seeming far heavier than paper should be.

Walsh watched as they rose, adding, "I hope to God you find whoever did this because… This just ain't right."

Aside from acknowledging the statement with a short nod, there wasn't much to say. Cases like this always left a mark.

Outside, the patter of rain had let up, leaving the smell of wet pavement behind. Sophia closed her umbrella and stood in the parking lot, letting the cold air fill her lungs until the antiseptic smell of the ME's office faded. Each breath clouded before her face, disappearing into the darkness like ghosts. Noah waited quietly by his truck, giving her the space she needed. She appreciated that about him—he seemed to understand the weight of moments like these.

When she finally turned back, her mind was clear. She was good at this part—turning grief into action, horror into purpose. "We need to look into that group home in Missoula, see if there are any connections to Stone River. And we should talk to her family—"

"I have to tell you something," Noah said, then hesitated. "I did something you might not like."

Sophia studied him, noting the tension in his shoulders. Snow gathered in his dark hair, melting against the warmth of his skin. "Go on."

"I called someone about the case. A journalist named Amber Laughlin."

"Why would you do that?" Sophia cocked her head, curious.

"She's from Stone River, too. She wrote a piece about Travis Longshadow back when he was killed. I figured she was going to hear about it anyway, and it didn't seem right for her to hear it from anyone aside from me first—but I understand if you don't agree."

To his obvious surprise, Sophia smiled. "When doing my research on the Longshadow case, I ran across her piece. Actually, I'd like to talk to her. You saved me a phone call."

Noah blinked, unprepared for her response. "Really? She was under the impression you don't like the press."

"Oh, I think they're like locusts," Sophia said, matter-of-fact. "But even locusts serve a purpose. If she has information that could help us find who did this to Laramie Baker, I'll take it."

"You're not mad?"

"About you contacting her? No. But next time, run it by your partner first." She watched his reaction, pleased when he simply nodded, accepting the mild rebuke without defensiveness. "How do you know her, anyway?"

Noah's hesitation was brief but noticeable. "We used to be engaged."

"The plot thickens," Sophia chuckled, but something twisted in her chest. She wasn't the jealous type, but that could be because she'd never let anyone get close enough for her to care. However, she felt an unfamiliar twinge in her chest when she thought of Noah and his industrious journalist. "And are you still pining for your ex?"

His snort of laughter was immediate and genuine. "Hell no."

The relief that flooded through her was unexpected and,

frankly, inconvenient. Momentarily struck by her visceral reaction, she struggled to regroup until she was able to focus on
the case, dragging unpleasant details to the forefront of her
mind. On Laramie Baker's bright eyes in that school photo.
On the name of a long-dead boy scrawled on her skin when
her body was found.

"Right. Good. Then call her. Set up a meeting. Let's find
out if she's got something that can help our case."

"You sure?" Noah hesitated. "Amber can be…tenacious,
but she's good at what she does."

"Well, she's a good writer, I know that much for sure. She's
got a nose for news and a way with words. That's either a
recipe for disaster or a powerful ally. I guess we'll see where
your friend lands."

"If you're not okay with this…"

"Stop worrying," Sophia cut in, letting him off the hook.
"I trust you. If you feel that you had a good reason to loop her
in, I trust your judgment."

Something shifted in his gaze as he accepted her statement
with a nod, relieved to move on.

"Why'd you break up?" she asked suddenly.

Noah shrugged. "We both decided we're better as friends
than lovers. When our careers took us in different directions,
it was almost a relief to end things because it gave us an out
with no one ending up the bad guy."

"The cleanest breakup ever," she murmured with a half
chuckle. "Damn, Noah, are you a saint or something?"

"Definitely not that," he returned with a short shake of his
head. "Just never saw a need to make an enemy for no reason."

The rain started up again, landing in light dewy drops on
Noah's hair as he pulled out his phone. Lights from passing
vehicles created sparkles out of the raindrops on his skin.
His strong jaw stood out in moonlight. *Very handsome man.*

She sucked in a private breath, appalled at her thoughts. She had a murdered teenager to think about, a trafficking ring to unravel, a killer—or killers—to catch. Everything else was just noise.

But she couldn't quite ignore how his emphatic *hell no* had made her smile.

The medical examiner's preliminary report sat heavy in her bag, filled with clinical descriptions of torture and assault. Somewhere out there, the people who had done this to Laramie Baker were probably sleeping soundly, untroubled by their crimes. But not for much longer.

Back in their vehicle, Sophia pulled up her case files on her laptop while Noah drove. The rhythmic sweep of windshield wipers marked time as she cross-referenced details.

"In the past eighteen months, I've tracked six victims with that same tattoo," she shared. "All Native girls between fifteen and seventeen. All last resided in group homes or foster care. All found on reservation land."

"You think the traffickers are deliberately using tribal lands as dumping grounds?"

"I think they're exploiting jurisdictional gaps." Sophia pulled up a map dotted with red markers. "Look at this pattern—Crow, Northern Cheyenne, Wind River. The victims are taken from cities, moved through the trafficking network, then disposed of on reservations. Local law enforcement gets overwhelmed, evidence gets lost between agencies…"

"And families never get answers," Noah finished grimly.

"Laramie fits the pattern perfectly. Started at Bright Horizons in Missoula, disappeared six months ago." Sophia studied the medical examiner's preliminary report. "Same signature—the tattoo, the torture, drugs in their system. But this is the first time they've left a message. Why Travis's name?"

"Definitely doesn't make sense," Noah said with a frown. "On the surface, there doesn't seem to be a connection."

"But there has to be." Sophia closed her laptop, watching rain dance on the windshield. "Someone was meant to see that name. The question is…was it a message for you specifically or for someone else who might be connected to the original case?"

Noah was quiet for a long moment, processing. "We need to talk to Bright Horizons. Find out if they have any connection to Clear Skies."

"Already on it." Sophia pulled out her phone. "I've got a contact at the Montana Department of Health and Human Services. Let's see what she can tell us about the funding and staffing overlaps between these facilities."

The storm intensified as they drove back to Stone River, but Sophia barely noticed. While her mind should've been solely focused on the case, her thoughts kept wandering to Noah and his journalist.

She believed him when he said he wasn't pining for his ex, but Sophia had to wonder if the same were true for the woman. She found it difficult to understand why any woman in her right mind would cut someone like Noah loose.

Sophia and relationships were a sour mix of failed nonstarters, the failure of which might be pinned squarely on her chest like a scarlet letter F. There seemed a pattern from the exit interviews. *Cold-hearted bitch* came up a lot. One had to assume that if a similar sentiment kept popping up, there had to be some truth in it.

It wasn't that she didn't want a deep connection with someone—it was that when things started to get cozy, she got distant. If backpedaling were an Olympic sport, she'd medal in gold.

And, thus, she had a list of past lovers who probably had

nothing nice to say about her. Which made her real curious about Amber Laughlin.

She could almost hear her hardest Quantico instructor, Patricia "The Dragon" Grogan barking at her. *Jesus, Bennett, get your shit together and stop worrying about stuff that's none of your damn business. Now get in line!*

Her mind snapped back into focus with the muscle memory of a soldier with PTSD, flashbacking to their time in a foxhole during heavy combat.

Whoever was running this trafficking ring knew the system inside and out and knew exactly how to make vulnerable girls disappear into the spaces between jurisdictions. And now they were getting bold enough to taunt investigators with a message.

That usually meant one of two things—they were getting careless or they had reason to be completely confident in their power to operate without consequences.

Either way, Laramie Baker's death had just become the key to unraveling something much bigger than a single murder.

Chapter 9

The early morning commuter flight from Great Falls to Missoula gave them just enough time to review Laramie Baker's file. Her story was depressingly familiar—caught with prescription pills at sixteen, no parents in the picture, no extended family who could care for her. The system had written her off as just another troubled Native teen, making her the perfect target.

"Single incident of possession," Sophia noted, scanning the documents. "Adderall, not her prescription. But the courts used it to push her into Bright Horizons rather than juvenile detention." Sophia flipped through the file, adding, "Oh, and some misdemeanor marijuana possession and drug paraphernalia charges peppered in there for color. To be honest, pretty mild if you ask me. I've seen much worse." She closed the file, frowning. "But she was very pretty."

"Nothing more dangerous than being pretty without protection," Noah said, disgusted. "Add in the fact that no one would look for her if she was gone, she's practically a gift-wrapped offering to an organized group of predators."

"Her social worker tried advocating for alternative placement, noting Laramie's good grades and clean record before this, but was overruled by the judge."

Noah's expression darkened. "I'd be willing to bet that judge has a history of going hard on anyone who isn't white.

Systemic racism is hard to root out, but it's sure as hell easy to see if you know what you're looking for."

Sophia nodded, hating that Noah was right. She'd seen enough to know that sometimes justice wasn't blind and the system was inherently flawed, but it was all they had to work with.

They landed, picked up the rental car and proceeded straight to Bright Horizons. Morning sun glinted off buildings like fool's gold. Somewhere in that gleaming facade, someone had looked at a lonely sixteen-year-old girl and seen nothing but profit.

Bright Horizons sprawled across its grounds like a dated institutional campus—all weathered brick and institutional windows, the kind of place designed to warehouse problems rather than solve them. Where Clear Skies maintained its facade of clinical efficiency, this facility had the worn-down look of a place running on minimum funding and maximum profit margins.

The grounds were unkempt, dead patches of grass between cracked sidewalks suggesting no one cared much about appearances. A rusty basketball hoop hung askew in what passed for a recreational area. The message was clear—this wasn't a place meant to rehabilitate; it was a place meant to contain.

Sophia felt Noah tense beside her as they approached the entrance. "Different aesthetic than Claire's operation."

"This feels like a prison," she said quietly. "I hate it already."

The lobby wasn't much better than the outside. The furniture was serviceable but worn, no expense wasted on luxury or frivolity. The receptionist at the desk looked like she hated life and her job. Given the surroundings, Sophia didn't blame her.

Both Sophia and Noah flashed their credentials, but Sophia spoke for them. "We have an appointment to speak with Director Rafael Delgado."

The woman's gaze swept their credentials, and she immediately typed a message into her computer. Seconds later, she cast a short smile that definitely didn't reach her eyes, gesturing to the closed door down the hall. "Director Delgado is ready for you."

"Thank you," Noah murmured, following Sophia down the carpeted hallway that smelled like an old person's house.

Director Rafael Delgado met them in a corner office with floor-to-ceiling windows overlooking the mountains. He was younger than Sophia expected, maybe early forties, wearing an expertly tailored suit that spoke of serious money. His handshake was firm but calculated, like everything else about him.

The juxtaposition between the facility's modest appearance and Delgado's flair for fine things was jarring.

"Agents," he said, gesturing to leather chairs. "I was devastated to hear about Laramie. We've been cooperating fully with local law enforcement since she was first reported missing."

"And yet no one thought to contact federal authorities when she disappeared," Sophia noted, watching his face. "Given the statistics on missing indigenous youth…"

"We followed standard protocols." Delgado's smile remained pleasant, but his eyes hardened slightly. "Laramie was a challenging resident who chose to leave our program. There's only so much we can do. It's not like we can tie our residents to their beds. That kind of thing is frowned upon." He said with a wink. It was clear that he meant it to be lighthearted, but it landed wrong for Sophia.

"Laramie Baker was brutally beaten, tortured, sexually assaulted and then killed. I hardly find now an appropriate time for levity, Director Delgado," Sophia returned sharply.

Delgado had the grace to appear chastised, offering a stiff apology. "Of course. I'm sorry if I offended you. It's a defense mechanism to find humor in challenging situations. We're all devastated by Laramie's death, and we're eager to help in any way we can."

Sophia accepted Delgado's apology with a nod before continuing. "Prior to her running away, had she expressed anything that might indicate why she didn't want to stay?" she asked.

"Not specifically. Like many of our residents, Laramie was resistant to authority. Despite our best efforts, some young people simply aren't ready to accept help." He pulled a file from his desk. "As you can see, Laramie pushed against the structure here at Bright Horizons. She had a history of acting out."

Sophia studied the documentation.

The incident reports painted a different picture than what was in her original case file. "These behavioral citations seem excessive for minor infractions," Sophia noted. "Writing her up for insubordination because she questioned why boys had longer recreation time?"

"Strict documentation helps maintain order," Delgado said smoothly. "It may seem small to you, but to juveniles who've had little to no structure in their lives, it's about teaching accountability."

"Laramie was a beautiful girl," Sophia stated, switching gears.

Delgado frowned. "And?"

"What safeguards do you have in place to protect pretty girls from predators that might be hiding in your staff? How many male security guards/counselors do you have?"

"What are you implying?" Delgado asked, his gaze narrowing slightly. "Because it sounds like you're accusing my staff of inappropriate behavior with female residents, which I can assure you doesn't happen."

Noah jumped in. "Statistically, it *does* happen. We just want to know what you're doing to protect vulnerable young residents from harm at the hands of those in authority."

"We've never had a single complaint in that regard," Delgado answered coolly. "I think our record speaks for itself. Does that satisfy your concerns?"

Sophia smiled. "Thank you. Actually, we're going to need your security footage from the night Laramie ran away."

Delgado sighed, leaning back in his chair. "Unfortunately, we don't have the server space to hold onto footage past a month. That footage is long gone. However, I can tell you there was nothing on the footage that would help. Laramie knew where the blind spots were, and she used them. None of the footage showed Laramie sneaking off the grounds. We've since purchased additional cameras to mitigate that weakness."

Convenient. Sophia kept the quip behind her teeth, but Delgado's smug attitude made her teeth grind. Did that make him guilty? Maybe not of being responsible for Laramie's death but certainly of being an asshole.

"We'd like to interview your staff," she said. "Anyone who worked directly with Laramie."

"If you think that's necessary, though I should mention that several key staff members have moved on since Laramie was here. Natural turnover in our field, as I'm sure you understand."

"Interesting," Sophia murmured as she stood. "Director Delgado, in my line of work I've interviewed countless group home directors, and in my experience, a high turnover in a facility usually indicates a problem with management."

Delgado's professional demeanor frosted over but his smile remained. "Very interesting," he returned. "Now, if you'll excuse me, I have another appointment scheduled. My assistant, Letty, will take you to where you need to go on campus. If there's anything else you need, don't hesitate to call."

And that was the politest way of saying, *Get the hell out of my office before I have you thrown out* that Sophia had ever heard, but that was okay. If he was guilty, maybe she'd rattled him. If he was innocent but offended, too bad. She wasn't here to make friends.

As they left, Sophia noticed cameras tracking their movement—were those the new cameras Delgado had mentioned? Maybe Delgado was telling the truth about the blind spots missing Laramie's exit, or maybe he was lying and covering his tracks. It could go either way. One thing was for sure— Sophia didn't like him.

But she didn't like Claire, either. Maybe it was Sophia's bias poking its head into the case again.

Noah surprised her with his observation. "Delgado is a peacock who likes to spend money on himself but seems to be a miser when it comes to his facility."

"Yeah, I was thinking the same."

"But being a jerk doesn't mean he's a criminal," Noah said. "On the surface, Bright Horizons is a bust. We've got nothing to tie the facility to any wrongdoing and no obvious reason to dig into Delgado's background aside from a cursory check, which I can tell you right now, is not going to show anything. No judge in the world will sign off on a warrant to grab computers or servers with so little to go on."

Sophia knew that as well. She couldn't put her finger on it, but something about Delgado made her skin crawl. She would like to think it was more than just her personal bias against group homes causing it.

They pulled away from Bright Horizons, leaving its institutional facade and carefully maintained veneer of legitimacy behind. But Sophia couldn't shake the feeling that they'd just scratched the surface of something much darker. The question was—would they find enough evidence before someone else ended up with a crude tattoo and a death sentence?

She glanced at Noah's profile as he drove, seeing the same determination she felt. Whatever was happening between these facilities, whatever connection led to Laramie's death, they would uncover it.

They had to.

Chapter 10

The lobby of Rivers Edge Luxury Apartments gleamed with polished marble and brass, a far cry from the institutional fluorescents of Bright Horizons. Noah watched James Kleppins approach through the glass doors, noting how the security guard's uniform strained against his middle, how sweat already darkened his collar despite the sharp cold in the air.

"What's this about?" Kleppins asked, eyes darting between their badges. "Am I in trouble?"

"Have you broken any laws we should know about?" Sophia's voice held that deceptive calm that made people want to fill the silence. She could hold a master class in how to make people trip on themselves to spill their guts. Noah had seen this tactic work before—that ability to make suspects uncomfortable enough to talk, even when they knew they should be keeping their mouths shut.

"No, of course not." Kleppins wiped his upper lip. "I just—I don't work at Bright Horizons anymore. Haven't for months."

"We'd still like to ask you a few questions." Noah pulled out Laramie's photo, the same school portrait that had been in her file. Young, hopeful, alive. "Do you remember this girl?"

"No, I—" Kleppins started to say, then stopped as recognition flickered across his face. More sweat beaded on his forehead. "Maybe. We had a lot of girls come through."

"This one was special," Sophia said. "Laramie Baker. Director Delgado described her as particularly troubled."

"Right, right." Kleppins nodded too quickly. "That's what I meant. Troubled kid, like most of them there."

Noah noticed how the guard's hands kept moving—straightening his tie, adjusting his belt, never still. "Funny, because a minute ago you said you didn't remember her at all."

"Look, it was months ago." Kleppins' voice took on a defensive edge. "You try keeping track of dozens of messed-up teenagers."

"We talked to other staff members," Sophia said. "They remembered Laramie quite clearly. In fact, they had very different descriptions of her behavior than what you just gave us."

Color rose in Kleppins's face. "Maybe I'm mixing her up with someone else."

"A pretty girl like Laramie?" Noah pressed. "She's the kind that catches people's attention, right?"

Something dark passed behind Kleppins's eyes. "What exactly are you implying?"

"We're not implying anything," Sophia said smoothly. "We're trying to understand how a girl in a secure facility managed to disappear, only to turn up dead hundreds of miles away."

"What do you mean?" Kleppins asked, his tongue darting to wet his lips. "She's dead?"

"Beaten, tortured and sexually assaulted before she was murdered," Noah supplied. "So you can understand why we're asking anyone who might've known Laramie if there's something they might remember."

"Well, I'd like to help, but I don't remember anything about the kid. She was like all the rest. They all start to blend, you know?"

"Even the pretty ones?" Sophia asked.

Kleppins met Sophia's inquiring gaze. "Even the pretty ones."

The words hung in the air between them. Outside, clouds gathered over the mountains, threatening another storm. Noah watched Kleppins struggle with something internal, some weight pressing down on his conscience.

Before he spoke again, Kleppins cleared his throat, his eyebrows working as he swallowed. "Look," he said, his voice losing its defensive edge, replaced by something that sounded almost like grief. "I'm real sorry about that girl. No one deserves to go like that. But like I said, I don't have anything to say about her time with the facility. I didn't have any dealings with her to my recollection, and if I did, they couldn't have been all that bad because I don't remember. Know what I mean?"

"We understand," Noah said. "Why did you leave Bright Horizons? Better pay here? Or was there something else?"

"Personal reasons." Kleppins straightened his tie again, a nervous tell. "Nothing to do with any of this."

"James." Sophia leaned forward slightly. "If you're afraid of someone, we can protect you. Whatever you saw at Bright Horizons—"

"I didn't see anything!" The words burst out too loud, making all three of them glance toward the lobby where the apartment manager pretended not to be watching. Kleppins lowered his voice. "Look, I'm sorry about what happened to that girl. Really. But I can't help you."

"Can't?" Noah caught the word choice. "Or won't?"

Fear flickered across Kleppins's face, there and gone so fast Noah might have missed it if he hadn't been looking. The guard's hands trembled slightly as he wiped more sweat from his forehead. "You don't understand," he said finally. "Some things…it's better not to know. Better not to ask questions."

"Better for whom?" Sophia's voice remained gentle but insistent. "Not better for Laramie."

Kleppins flinched. "I have a family, too. A daughter about her age." His eyes found Laramie's photo again, and something broke in his expression. "I just… I can't. I'm sorry."

The silence stretched between them, heavy with things unsaid. Noah thought about Travis Longshadow and his buried case. How many people were carrying secrets that poisoned them from the inside or cost them their life?

"What did Delgado have on you?" Noah asked suddenly.

Kleppins's head snapped up. "What?"

"Your hands shake when you mention his name. What did he have on you?"

"Nothing." But Kleppins wouldn't meet their eyes. "He was just my boss."

"A boss you were afraid of," Sophia noted. "A boss worth running from?"

"I didn't run," he denied, shaking his head. "I just…needed a fresh start. That's all."

Noah studied the man before them—middle-aged, overweight, probably counting the days until retirement. Not a bad person, necessarily, just someone who'd looked the other way when looking closer meant facing dangerous truths. And whatever he was scared of, it was bad enough to keep his mouth shut.

"If you change your mind," Sophia said, holding out her card, "if you decide that knowing what happened to Laramie is worth more than whatever Delgado is holding over you— call us. Day or night."

Kleppins took the card with shaking fingers. "I wish… I wish things were different." He straightened his tie one last time. "But I can't help you. I'm sorry."

"Well," Noah said as they walked to the car, "that was interesting."

"He knows something." Sophia's voice held absolute certainty. "Did you see how he reacted when you mentioned Delgado blackmailing him?"

"Yeah." Noah started the engine, letting the familiar rumble settle his thoughts. "Question is, what's got him so scared he won't talk even with federal protection on the table?"

"Something bigger than one dead girl." Sophia buckled her seat belt as Noah pulled out of the parking lot. "Something systemic."

The first drops of rain hit the windshield as they merged onto the highway. They'd both seen Kleppins's fear, his obvious knowledge of something he refused to share. But without someone willing to talk, they were spinning their wheels.

"So that's three former employees, zero useful information," he said.

"Not exactly zero." Sophia flipped through her notes. "Kleppins's reaction to Delgado's name was worth noting. And he practically ran when offered federal protection."

"People don't run from nothing."

"No, they don't." She closed her notebook.

The rain intensified, matching Noah's darkening mood. Another witness too scared to talk, another thread leading nowhere. But something about Kleppins's fear nagged at him—that nervous tie-straightening, the trembling hands, the way he'd looked at Laramie's photo with what seemed like genuine regret.

"Pizza?" Sophia suggested, reading his mood. "Before we head back?"

The storm intensified as they navigated through Great Falls's streets, past the historical downtown where brick buildings from the railroad era stood sentinel against the darkening sky. Lightning flickered in the distance, highlighting the refineries on the outskirts of town.

"Tell me something," Sophia said, breaking their comfortable silence. "How many cases like this have you worked? Where everyone knows something, but no one will talk?"

Noah thought about it as he turned onto Tenth Avenue. "Too many. Especially on the reservations. People learn early that staying quiet is safer than speaking up." He caught her questioning look. "Not because they don't want justice. But because justice doesn't always protect the ones who help it along."

"Like Kleppins and his daughter."

"Maybe." Noah pulled into Mario's parking lot, the neon sign casting red shadows through the rain-streaked windshield. "Man's terrified, but not just for himself."

"Makes me wonder what he witnessed at Bright Horizons that was worth threatening his family over." Sophia unbuckled her seat belt but didn't move to get out. "The way he looked at Laramie's photo…"

"Like he was seeing a ghost," Noah finished. "Or his own kid."

They sat for a moment, listening to the rain drum against the truck's roof. The smell of garlic and tomatoes wafted from the pizzeria, but Noah's appetite had faded as he thought about Kleppins's trembling hands, his nervous tells.

"You know what bothers me most?" Sophia asked. "His reaction when we offered protection. Most witnesses jump at federal protection if they're just scared of normal retaliation. But Kleppins? He acted like we couldn't possibly protect him from whatever he's afraid of."

The implications of that settled between them like a physical weight. Noah thought about all the patterns they'd seen so far—the missing girls, the trafficking network, the wall of silence they kept hitting. How high up did this thing go?

They settled into a corner booth where they could watch the door. Some habits you couldn't break, even off duty. But as they debated toppings (Sophia insisted on extra cheese, Noah argued for pepperoni), he felt some of the day's tension start to ease.

And now he was also thinking about this introduction between Amber and Sophia.

Noah had no worries that Sophia couldn't handle herself, but he didn't know how he felt about Amber and Sophia working together. Felt weird in a way. Not because he wanted to get back together with Amber, but because Amber wouldn't hesitate to spill his worst traits if she thought it would score points with her new favorite FBI agent.

And he was starting to really like Sophia—and maybe not only in a professional way. But he wasn't about to make things awkward by crossing a line.

Stick to the case, Romeo.

"You think Bright Horizons is connected to Clear Skies in some way?" he asked, needing a quick redirect.

"Two facilities, same basic setup, both dealing with troubled teens no one's looking for too closely?" Sophia shook her head. "I don't know, but if they were, it would make sense. Almost a perfect network of supply, you know? But just because it makes sense doesn't mean it's happening. Plus, there's a five-hour distance between the two facilities. That alone makes it difficult to connect the two."

"Well, even if we're right, we can't prove anything without someone willing to talk." The frustration that had been building all day edged into his voice. "And everyone we interview either knows nothing or is too scared to say what they know."

"Hey." Sophia's hand found his arm, warm through his sleeve. "We'll find another way in. The best part about guilty people? They usually find a way to rat themselves out eventually. There's no such thing as a perfect crime."

The simple touch grounded him, reminded him he wasn't doing this alone anymore. Being home again, returning to the case that'd been his first real big crime—and the one that haunted him—was messing with his head. But he wasn't that twenty-five-year-old rookie anymore. He had countless wins under his belt. He was a solid investigator. And now he had Sophia Bennett at his side, picking up the pieces with him. That was no small thing.

For now, though, they had pizza waiting and a long drive back to Stone River ahead of them. One step at a time. That was how you built a case that would stick.

But what would they find when it was all said and done?

His task force colleagues had already closed cases that netted big fish. He wasn't afraid of casting his net, but the risk wasn't small when you were dragging in a marlin. You could get skewered while you tried.

Chapter 11

After a full day of paperwork and setting up interviews, Noah had arranged for Amber to meet him and Sophia at the Red Feather for dinner. He wasn't thrilled about this idea, but Sophia was on board and seemed eager to put a face to the woman behind the byline.

Now as he leaned against the worn leather booth, watching the two women size each other up like prize fighters before a match, he realized he might've just facilitated the worst idea in history.

The late afternoon sun slanted through the windows, catching the golden highlights in Sophia's burnished strawberry-blonde hair and the sharp intelligence in her green eyes. He'd have to be blind to miss that she was an attractive—hell, beautiful—woman. Okay, so maybe he'd noticed right away that she had the kind of looks that turned heads wherever she went, not that she seemed to notice or care unless the attention involved a body count. But he wasn't some opportunist Chad who leered at attractive women, assuming every woman was fair game. There were rules against this sort of thing for a reason, and he supported those reasons.

Still, something magnetic about her presence drew people in, himself included.

There was something comforting about the familiar sounds of the diner as it hummed with local patrons, the sound of clinking silverware and low-key chatter blending into background noise. No matter how long it had been since returning home, there were some things he could always count on remaining the same.

News of the dead girl had spread through Stone River like wildfire, and seeing the FBI agent with Noah and his ex-fiancée would give the gossip mill enough fuel to run for weeks. Small towns kept score in ways a big city could never.

In a way, Noah was the proverbial big fish in a small pond because he'd gone and made something out of himself in ways that most never managed, making him a favorite topic of conversation.

Amber slid into the booth across from them in a fluid movement. "I can't tell you how excited I am to finally meet you," she said directly to Sophia, practically ignoring Noah, which was fine by him. It was fascinating to see Amber appear starstruck by an FBI agent.

"Pleasure's all mine," Sophia returned, playing the social niceties game. "You've got quite a way with the pen."

"You've read my work?"

Sophia nodded. "It caught my attention."

"In a good way?"

Noah cut Amber a look. *Enough already.* He paused long enough to accept the menus from the waitress, then said, "Okay, so introductions aren't really necessary, but Amber Laughlin meet Special Agent Sophia Bennett."

Amber caught the waitress before she left, returning the menu. "I don't need this, hun. All I need is one piping hot order of chicken fried steak, if you wouldn't mind," she said with a charming smile.

"How about you?" the waitress asked Noah and Sophia. "Chicken fried steak platters all around?"

"Sure," Sophia said, and since it was easier to agree, he nodded, too.

The waitress went on her way, and it was back to business.

Sophia didn't waste time on more small talk, going straight to the heart of why they were meeting. "Why are you so invested in helping with our case?"

A smile tugged at Amber's lips, appreciation flickering in her eyes at Sophia's directness. "Travis Longshadow's story launched my career. Every journalist dreams of the story that puts them on the map—he was mine." She shrugged, unapologetic. "But in this industry, you're only as good as your last assignment. Newspapers are cutting back on their freelancers, magazines even more so. I need something that will set me above the competition. When Noah called me about the newest case with a connection to Travis's, I knew I had to chase it down. Plus, everyone loves a cold case comeback, especially one that pulls at the heartstrings. Missing indigenous youth, corruption, possible trafficking ring? It's journalistic gold."

"You're an opportunist," Sophia surmised with an expression that confirmed what she already suspected. "Is that all?"

"Is it being opportunistic to chase down compelling stories?" Amber shot back, not the least bit cut by Sophia's statement. "We all have bills to pay."

"Don't get me wrong, your naked honesty is refreshing," Sophia said. "I don't think I would've trusted some bullshit answer about how you feel the need to make a difference. For you, it's about ambition. I can respect that."

"Both statements can be true. I want to write stories that make a difference, but you can only be altruistic for so long before the power company starts sending you pink notices."

"Fair enough," Sophia said.

"But while I care about success, I also care about my stories. When I dig into something, I'm committed to finding the truth."

Noah shifted uncomfortably, remembering how Amber had thrown herself into Travis's case fifteen years ago. She'd been relentless, digging up leads he'd missed, pushing when he wanted to step back. Her drive had been one of the things he'd loved about her, but when he realized they both loved their careers more than each other, he knew it was time to end things. Fortunately, Amber had agreed.

If she hadn't been a writer, fate might've made Amber a damn good investigator.

"Last question, does the fact that your ex-fiancé is leading the investigation have anything to do with your interest in the case?" Sophia asked, her voice neutral but her eyes sharp.

Amber's laugh was genuine enough to pinch his ego. "Noah? Please. We both moved on years ago. This isn't about putting the band back together again—it's about justice. And a damn good story."

"Okay, you've made your point," Noah groused, shooting Sophia a look. "Are you satisfied yet?"

Sophia chuckled, her amusement doing something to soften the jab to his ego. "Yeah. She's cool."

"My turn," Amber said, leaning forward. "Why agree to meet now when you've been dodging my calls for over a year?"

"Because now you might be useful."

Sophia didn't pull punches or pretend to be anything other than what she was—ruthless and to the point. He liked that about her, but he could see how that might rub people the wrong way.

"Damn, girl, you're hardcore, but I like it," Amber said, leaning back. She tapped the Formica table with her fingernail before proposing, "Let's work together for mutually beneficial purposes. Would you be willing to keep me in the loop in exchange for information I may have that could help the investigation?"

"If you have information that may help, I could just compel you to share what you know," Sophia said.

"And as a journalist, I have a legal right to protect my sources. You can throw paper at me all day long, it's not going to do anything but waste time you could've spent chasing leads. Working together seems more efficient, don't you think?"

"In my experience, journalists can't be trusted with sensitive information," Sophia countered.

"You can trust me."

"Why?" Sophia's bald question would've sent a lesser person running. Not Amber.

Amber's gaze swiveled straight to Noah. "Because he trusts me, and you trust him."

The tension in the booth crackled with competitive energy, and neither woman was willing to give ground.

Noah fought back a smile as he witnessed the verbal sparring. He'd tried to warn Sophia about Amber's tenacity, but clearly she could hold her own.

The waitress appeared with their drinks, her eyebrows lifting slightly at the charged atmosphere before retreating wisely. Noah wrapped his hands around his glass, content to observe. He knew better than to interrupt when two skilled interrogators were at work.

Sophia took her time sipping her water, making Amber wait before she said, "If I agree to this, do I have your word that you won't publish one word until the investigation is finished?"

"Do I get exclusive information—holding nothing back? I don't want the sanitized investigation CliffsNotes. I want it all," Amber countered. "If you get a call, after Noah, I want to be next to know about it. I want to be in the trenches with you."

"Like an embedded journalist behind enemy lines?" Sophia supplied with an arched brow. "You know I can't guarantee your safety."

"Just adds to the spice of the story," Amber said, undeterred, but Noah didn't like it.

"Wait a minute, that's not a good idea," he said gruffly. "We don't know what we're dealing with—you're not trained for this kind of thing, Amber."

"Calm down, Noah. I know how to take care of myself. I've learned a thing or two since we were together. Don't worry."

But Amber's assurances didn't lessen his anxiety. The liability of having a journalist on their tails, trailing their every move? He didn't think Isaac would clear that request.

Sophia read his mind. "Noah's right, you can't go on every call, but I promise to keep you in the loop. If your information proves useful, you'll have the access you need for your story. However, make no mistake...the players in this game are dangerous. There's a lot less heat involved taking out a journalist rather than a cop. Know what I mean? In their eyes, taking out a civilian is far less risky than two federal agents."

"I'm aware of the risks," Amber said, holding firm. "I'm meant to write this story. Nothing will change my mind about that. We can work together or not...but I'm writing this story either way."

Noah knew Amber wouldn't budge.

Sophia seemed to sense the same and relented with a shrug as if to say, *It's your funeral, lady*, adding, "Fine. But if you burn us for a headline?" She leaned forward, voice dropping. "I'll make sure your career never recovers. Are we clear?"

"Crystal." Amber's triumphant smile was short as she went straight to business. "There's a drug trafficking network operating across three states that might be responsible for that tattoo on your victim." She pulled out a thick manila folder, the kind Noah knew meant sleepless nights and endless cups of coffee. "I first caught wind of the drug network when I was writing a piece for *Vice* on Montana state prisons."

Sophia's expression didn't change, but Noah caught the slight shift in her posture—the predator scenting prey. "Go on."

"I was interviewing inmates, getting information on suspected abuses within the system, when one of the inmates said they had information on guards dealing drugs within the prison."

"Did they have proof?" Sophia asked. "Inmates will say just about anything, especially when they're trying to impress a pretty journalist. Doesn't make it true."

"I thought the same, but they gave me the name of a missing person's case. Said she was running product for the network that feeds into the prison."

"What'd they want in exchange for the info?" Noah asked, interested.

"That's the sad part—they didn't want anything. The girl, by the name of Ursula Bowen, went missing from the Crow reservation two summers ago." Amber paused to pull a grainy black-and-white photo from her stack of paperwork and hand it to Sophia, "The girl was the inmate's cousin."

Noah's stomach tightened as he recognized the girl. The case had crossed his desk briefly before going cold. "Ursula Bowen, sixteen, with a history of minor criminal offenses, was listed as an at-risk runaway," he recalled with a frown. "Her missing person's case is still open."

"Not anymore," Sophia corrected him with a grim look. "Bowen's body was found a year ago." She met Noah's gaze. "And she had the tattoo. She's one of the cases that popped up when I started doing a search on the tattoo recorded in postmortem exams."

Noah was shocked to hear about Bowen's case. He would've thought someone would've mentioned it to him when her body was recovered, but the leadership in his previous department… Well, it was safe to say they didn't run as tight a ship as Isaac Berrigan.

The food arrived, momentarily pausing their conversation. Noah watched Amber tuck into her chicken fried steak with familiar enthusiasm while Sophia picked at hers thoughtfully.

"What information were you able to find on the dirty guards?" Sophia asked.

Amber's regretful expression didn't bode well. "Not much. The minute I even mentioned the possibility of in-house corruption, I was sent packing, and I was refused access to the inmate who'd told me about the drug network within the prison."

Sophia didn't look surprised, and neither did Noah. Corruption was a cancer that could spread anywhere.

"Do you remember the name of the inmate?" Sophia asked.

"Of course. I take meticulous notes." Amber pointed to a name on a piece of paper. "Randall Johnson, incarcerated for second degree manslaughter. He broke into a house in Hardin thinking no one was home, only to find a little old lady firing a shotgun at him. Lucky for him, she was practically blind and missed him by a mile. He tackled the woman, broke her hip in the fall and then punched her in the face, shattering her orbital bone so badly she needed reconstructive surgery. Sadly, after surgery, she died from complications. She was eight-nine."

"Damn." Noah whistled, shaking his head. "That's a shit sandwich."

"Was he on drugs when he committed the crime?" Sophia asked, curious.

"He had a history of drug offenses," Amber confirmed.

"And he suddenly had an attack of conscience about his misguided cousin?" Sophia asked.

"I can't speak to his motives, but even hardened criminals usually have a weak spot for someone," Amber said, shrugging. "Maybe Ursula was his."

Sophia nodded, satisfied with Amber's intel. "I'd like to see your research," she said. "All of it."

"Sure." Amber's eyes gleamed with that familiar intensity Noah remembered. "But not here. Too many ears in a small-town diner."

Noah caught Sophia's slight nod of approval. Both women understood the value of discretion, especially in a place like Stone River where walls had ears and secrets rarely stayed buried. "Fair enough," Sophia said, returning to her plate, though Noah could tell her thoughts were far from food.

Not Amber, though. Business concluded, Amber was already stuffing another bite into her mouth, dancing a little in her seat with joy. "Mmm, I swear no one makes chicken fried steak like the Red Feather. God, I've missed this." She paused and dabbed her mouth with her napkin, a gesture that didn't quite hide her satisfied smile. "I think this is the beginning of a beautiful partnership."

Noah wasn't so sure about that. Having Amber involved complicated things in ways he couldn't quite articulate. But watching these two strong-willed women with him on the case? He just hoped they were all ready for whatever ugly truths they might uncover.

Chapter 12

The Montana night air hit Sophia like a slap, shocking after the warmth of the diner. Stars pierced the darkness overhead, impossibly bright compared to DC's light-polluted skies. She pulled her jacket tighter, her boots clicking against worn asphalt as Noah walked her to her car.

Professional courtesy, that was all this was. She'd seen enough small towns to know the social rules: a local boy makes sure the city girl gets to her car safely. Nothing more.

"Well," Noah said, hands stuffed in his pockets as she unlocked her rental, "that was interesting."

"Your ex is…unexpected." Sophia kept her tone neutral, leaning against the driver door instead of getting in. The cold metal pressed through her jacket, grounding her. "Smart, though. I can see why you trust her."

"Amber's good at what she does." His breath fogged in the air between them. "Sometimes too good. She doesn't always know when to back off, and that's what worries me. I don't want her getting hurt by getting in over her head."

"She's smart. I have a feeling she knows when to pull back to protect her ass," Sophia said. "She'll be okay."

The parking lot was nearly empty now, just a few trucks still lined up at the far end. Music from the diner drifted out faintly, some old country song about lost love and regret. How fitting.

Sophia found herself searching for something to say that would extend this moment without seeming obvious. She was good at reading people—it was part of her job—but Noah Thunderhawk remained frustratingly opaque. Professional, competent, clearly carrying old wounds from the Travis case, but there was something else there. Something that made her want to dig deeper. Get closer.

Which was exactly why she needed to get in her car and drive away.

"With that said, we should probably discuss ground rules for working with Amber," she said instead, her investigator's mind providing a convenient excuse. "Maybe over drinks?"

The words were out before she could stop them.

She watched Noah's expression shift just slightly and immediately backpedaled. "But it's late, and we've got an early start tomorrow. Another time."

She was an idiot. The Red Feather was literally right there, the only bar in town, and she'd just made things awkward by suggesting drinks when they'd just left the place. *Way to go, Bennett.*

"Yeah, early start," Noah agreed, but he didn't move away. The crisp autumn air carried the scent of woodsmoke from somewhere nearby, reminding Sophia that this wasn't just any small town. This was Noah's home, filled with his history and his memories. Including those with Amber.

A gust of wind cut through the parking lot, and Sophia suppressed a shiver. "Well, good night then."

"Good night, Agent Bennett." There was a hint of something in his voice—amusement, maybe?—at the formality of using her title.

"Sophia," she corrected automatically, immediately wishing she hadn't. They'd already covered this at breakfast, but somehow it felt different in the dark, standing close enough that she could see the stubble darkening his jaw.

"Sophia," he repeated softly, and damn if her name didn't sound different when he said it like that.

She forced herself to move, opening her car door with perhaps more force than necessary. "See you tomorrow."

Noah waited until she was in the car before stepping back, and she caught a final glimpse of him in her rearview mirror as she pulled away. A solid presence in the gathering dark, he watched until she turned onto the main road.

The drive back to the Whispering Pines took less than five minutes, but it was enough time for Sophia to thoroughly berate herself for that awkward drink suggestion. She was better than this. Smarter. She didn't get tangled up in personal complications during cases, and she certainly didn't get attracted to colleagues.

Back in her room, Sophia went through her usual security routine. Sweep the bathroom and closet. Check the window locks. Test the chain on the door. Old habits from years of hunting predators who sometimes decided to hunt back.

The hotel room felt smaller tonight, almost claustrophobic. She kicked off her boots and retrieved the bottle of cheap Merlot she'd bought at the gas station mini-mart that morning. Not exactly high-class, but it would do. She poured herself a generous glass, opened her laptop and settled cross-legged on the bed.

The case files glowed on her screen: photos of the dead girl, the tattoo, Travis Longshadow's old case notes that Noah had finally sent over. She should focus on those.

Instead, her mind kept circling back to the way Noah's shoulders had tensed when Amber mentioned their past relationship.

"Stop it," Sophia muttered to herself, taking a long sip of wine. She didn't have time for…whatever this was.

But as she scrolled through autopsy reports, her thoughts drifted. Noah was different from the usual cops she worked with. Most of them either resented her presence or tried too hard to impress her. Noah did neither. He was just…himself. Solid. Dependable. The kind of partner who had your back in the field without making a big deal about it.

The kind of man who walked women to their cars on cold nights, not because he thought they needed protection, but because it was the right thing to do.

Sophia took another drink, grimacing at the wine's acidic bite. She was usually better at compartmentalizing. It was a survival skill she'd learned early in the foster system—don't get attached, don't let people too close, focus on the goal. Those rules had served her well in her career, allowing her to move from case to case without emotional entanglement.

So why was Noah different?

Maybe it was seeing him with Amber. Their history was evident in a hundred small ways—shared glances, inside jokes, the way they unconsciously leaned toward each other when speaking. They had the kind of ease that only came from real intimacy.

And yet, neither was interested in getting back together— that much was abundantly clear.

Sophia's relationships never lasted long enough to develop that kind of shorthand. Her longest relationship had been six months with another agent, which ended when he suggested she might want to consider a less demanding position if she wanted things to work between them.

She'd shown him exactly what she thought of that suggestion by taking a promotion that put her in a different field office. Now that guy was forever in her phone contacts as Fragile Ego Ex.

The laptop screen dimmed, and Sophia realized she'd been staring at the same paragraph for ten minutes. With a frustrated sigh, she pulled up Noah's personnel file instead. She'd reviewed it before because she always vetted potential partners thoroughly, but now she found herself looking at the personal details she'd previously skimmed over.

Forty years old. Never married. No children. Distinguished service record with tribal police before joining the BIA task force. Multiple commendations for work on trafficking cases. The River Rock case had been particularly impressive—she remembered reading about it when it broke.

But who was the man behind the badge? Did he have a favorite movie? What were his comfort foods? Was he afraid of spiders? What were his pet peeves?

"This is ridiculous," Sophia muttered, closing the file. She was acting like a teenager with a crush, not a federal agent with over a decade of experience. Besides, office romances never worked out; she had plenty of evidence to support that conclusion. Plus, she was pretty sure there were rules against messing around with interagency partners. And if there weren't any rules on paper, it was certainly frowned upon by superiors. Her planned trajectory was higher, not lower, on the promotion scale.

No. Whatever this attraction was, she needed to shut it down. Hard.

Her wineglass was empty. She hadn't noticed drinking it all.

She rinsed the glass in the bathroom sink, watching the red wine residue swirl in faint pink down the drain. A glance in the mirror showed her what she already knew—she looked tired. The kind of bone-deep exhaustion that came from constantly maintaining barriers, keeping people at arm's length.

Her mother's face flickered in her memory—or what she remembered of it. Sometimes, she wasn't sure if her memories were real or constructed from the few photos she'd managed to keep through various foster homes. Would her mother approve of the woman she'd become? The choices she'd made?

"Oh, Bennett, get over yourself," she told her reflection firmly. She was not going to spiral into childhood trauma just because a handsome colleague had her off-balance. She was better than that.

Back in the main room, she changed into yoga pants and a soft T-shirt, then spread her mat on the floor. Exercise always helped clear her head. As she moved through her usual routine, she forced herself to think about the case logically.

Fact: Noah was a good investigator with deep ties to the community.

Fact: Those ties could be valuable for the investigation.

Fact: Amber's journalism background and previous research could provide crucial leads.

Fact: Any personal complications would compromise the investigation.

Conclusion: Maintain professional distance at all costs.

Simple. Clean. Like solving an equation.

Except nothing about this case was simple. Dead girls with mysterious tattoos. Cold cases suddenly heating up. Group homes with too-perfect reputations. And now Noah Thunderhawk, with his quiet strength and careful kindness, throwing her meticulously maintained equilibrium off-balance.

Standing in warrior pose, Sophia allowed one final speculation: Noah was probably an excellent romantic partner—thoughtful, loyal and committed. She could see it in the way he still carried guilt over Travis's case, in how he worried about Amber's safety even years after their relationship ended.

But she wasn't the relationship type. She was more like a

wasp…solitary, focused and dangerous when provoked. Better at stinging than nurturing.

Moving to downward dog, Sophia exhaled slowly. Her job required absolute focus. Getting distracted by what-ifs and maybes wasn't just unprofessional—it was dangerous. She'd seen too many cases go sideways when emotions clouded judgment.

The timer on her phone chimed, ending her workout. She rolled up her mat, tucked it away in the corner, and went through her nighttime routine with military precision. Teeth brushed. Face washed. Doors checked one final time.

Her service weapon went on the nightstand within easy reach. Another habit born from experience that threats didn't always announce themselves with a convenient warning.

The bed was too soft, the kind of mattress that tried too hard to be comfortable and ended up feeling like a stale marshmallow. Like this whole evening, she thought wryly. Trying too hard to find meaning in normal social interactions.

Tomorrow, she'd do better. Keep things strictly professional. Focus on interviewing Randall Johnson at the prison and following up on Amber's leads about the drug trafficking connection. That was what mattered, not how Noah's eyes crinkled slightly at the corners when he smiled or how his presence made her feel oddly safe despite her ingrained distrust of everyone.

Sophia reached over and turned off the lamp, plunging the room into darkness broken only by the faint glow of streetlights through the curtains.

Her phone buzzed on the nightstand. She glanced at her phone, seeing that she'd gotten another email from her supervisor back in DC.

UPDATE REQUESTED: Montana case connection to Idaho trafficking network? Need preliminary assessment ASAP.

Sophia sighed but reached for her laptop again. Isaac might be running his task force with military precision, but her boss had his own demands. She typed a quick response:

Possible connection to Ursula Bowen case (Montana, 2022). Same tattoo signature. Meeting local BIA task force agent tomorrow to interview prison source re: drug connection. Will update after.

Another buzz. This time from the forensics lab:

Preliminary results—Soil samples from the victim's clothing: Traces of fertilizer compound consistent with agricultural use Mineral content suggests riverbed origin Full analysis pending

She flagged that for tomorrow's discussion with Noah. The riverbed detail might help narrow down where the girl was killed versus where the body had been dumped.

Three more emails demanded her attention, updates on other cases she was technically still handling back in DC, a request for her testimony in next month's trafficking trial in Oregon and a reminder about mandatory sensitivity training that was already overdue.

The job never slept. Never took a night off. Never asked if you had other plans or needed a break. It was probably why she'd chosen it—harder to feel lonely when you were never truly alone, always connected to the next case, the next victim, the next pursuit.

Her phone buzzed one final time. A text from Amber:

If you're heading to Montana State Prison tomorrow, let me know if you need anything else from my research. Or I could tag along. Just a thought.

Sophia started to reply, then decided it could wait until morning. She wasn't Amber's handler; that was Noah's headache now. She had to admit, though, that the journalist's drug trafficking angle might be their best lead so far.

In the quiet, she could hear the distant rumble of trucks on the highway, heading somewhere else, carrying other people's stories.

That was what she was here for, to uncover stories. To find justice. Not to wonder what kind of romantic partner Noah Thunderhawk might be or whether she was missing out on something by keeping everyone at arm's length.

She was what she was—a wasp, not a bee. Solitary. Focused. Dangerous.

Sleep came slowly, and when it did, she dreamed of stars over Montana, impossibly bright and frustratingly out of reach.

Chapter 13

Noah's phone vibrated against his hip for the third time as he climbed into his truck. Amber. He let it go to voice mail, knowing exactly what she wanted. She'd been texting since dawn, pushing to join them on the drive to Montana State Prison.

Even after all these years, her persistence was both admirable and exhausting.

Sophia was on board to let Amber be involved, but he wasn't ready to let her tag along. Besides, Amber had to understand that even if she claimed to understand the risks, he wasn't about to put her in harm's way just so she could get her story.

The early morning sun wrapped Montana in crystalline light that made everything sharp and clear, like fresh-cut glass. Noah watched Sophia's rental pull up beside him in the tribal police parking lot, her red hair catching fire in the sun. She stepped out, already moving with that focused energy he was starting to recognize.

"Ready?" she asked, coffee cup in hand.

"Just about." His phone buzzed again. "Mind if we take my truck? Driving helps me think."

"You going to get that?"

"No. It's Amber."

"Ah, yeah, she texted me last night. I didn't answer, either."

He sighed, silencing the call. "She can hold her horses. If you give her an inch, she'll take a mile, and I'm not ready for that yet."

Sophia nodded, already moving toward the passenger side of his truck. "Then let's go before she shows up anyway."

The drive to Montana State Prison would take about three hours, cutting through some of the state's most beautiful and unforgiving country. They left Stone River behind, the morning sun burning off the last traces of valley fog as they headed west. Noah settled into the familiar rhythm of the road, letting the miles unspool beneath them.

Sophia spent the first hour on her laptop, reviewing everything they had on Randall Johnson. "Three prior convictions for drug trafficking," she said, breaking the comfortable silence. "All involving meth distribution on tribal lands."

"Pretty common story," Noah admitted. "My cousin Michael's rap sheet looks about the same. Some people just never find what they need to get out of their own way."

"How'd you do it?"

"My dad," Noah admitted without reservation. "As I mentioned, he was a tribal cop, too. A damn good one, too. Everyone remembers my dad being one of the good guys in a place where law enforcement is sometimes a bad word."

"Why is that?"

"Poverty and addiction make for bad judgment," Noah answered grimly. "I've seen good people be destroyed by the false hope drugs provide in the moment. When you've got nothing to work toward, no hope of being anything better, morality slips away. And cops aren't immune to temptation so, you can do the math on that."

"You said that your dad was killed on the job. What happened?"

"A domestic gone wrong. Worst kind of call there is. You

show up trying to help and then, when you go to arrest the son-ofabitch beating the snot out of his woman, she goes and turns on you." He hated the sequence of events that led to his father's death. Thinking about it always made his chest tighten. "She probably never meant to kill anyone, but it happened anyway. So, instead of hauling off her drunk husband to sleep it off in a cell, she was arrested for manslaughter. She's still serving time, but it doesn't bring my dad back. The irony?" He chuckled darkly. "She went to school with my dad. I can guarantee you, my dad never in a million years would've thought someone he knew like that would be the death of him."

Sophia frowned in commiseration. "I'm sorry. That must've hurt even more."

Noah shrugged. "My dad was gone. Didn't really matter to me how it happened. After I got through the anger stage of my grief, I realized I wanted to be a cop like him. The People need hope for something better. That's always what my dad used to say, and I realized he was right."

Sophia let a respectful silence follow his admission as the truck ate the miles, the scenery passing by in a colorful blur.

The late morning sun caught the frost clinging to the fence posts along the highway, making them glitter like diamond-crusted bones. Sometimes, he took for granted how beautiful Montana really was—especially when most of his time was spent in an office. The opportunity to be back in the field was another reason he'd pushed hard to get a position on the task force.

The prison rose from the valley floor like a medieval fortress, all cement walls and razor wire glinting in the sun. Noah had been here before, interviewing inmates who might have information about reservation crimes. The place always left him feeling hollow.

Warden Mitchell Hayes met them in his office, a man whose

carefully pressed uniform and rigid posture screamed career corrections officer. His handshake was firm and professional, but his smile never reached his eyes.

Noah thought that career correctional officers lost bits of their soul the longer they stayed in the career. There was something so bleak about prison life that he couldn't help but wonder if the cement walls had the power to leach all of the joy out of a person's soul, whether they were incarcerated or paid to be there.

"Agents," Waden Hayes said, gesturing to the chairs in front of his desk. "How can I help the Bureau of Indian Affairs and the FBI today?"

"We're here about one of your current inmates—Randall Johnson, DOB 03-09-85," Sophia said, getting straight to the point. "We've come by some intel that he may have information relevant to an ongoing trafficking case."

Something flickered across Hayes's face—so quick Noah almost missed it. "Randall Johnson, let me check." He paused, tapping into his computer, scanning for the inmate. Then, his expression shuttered as his mouth turned down. "Johnson was killed six months ago. Stabbed by another inmate during breakfast."

"Stabbed? How'd that happen?" Noah asked. "Aren't there security protocols in place to deter inmate violence?"

Hayes chucked as if Noah were naive. "We try our best, but when you lock a man up for years on end, sometimes they lose the veneer of civility—that's if they'd ever had it to begin with." Curiosity piqued his next question, "What's your interest in Johnson?"

"Like we said, an ongoing trafficking case," Sophia answered smoothly. "Forgive me for pointing out an odd coincidence…we were told that Johnson provided information to a journalist about drugs coming into the prison through the guards, and now Johnson is dead. See how that seems a little convenient?"

Hayes leaned back in his chair. "I assure you, Agent Bennett, there was nothing convenient about it. These incidents create mountains of paperwork. Anytime there's an act of violence within the prison, it has to be documented, safety protocols examined, and new practices put into place. It's a pain in the ass and a disruption to the flow of a well-oiled machine."

"Someone died on your watch. Don't you think that warrants more respect than a statement that their death screwed up your routine?" Sophia challenged.

Hayes shrugged, patronizing Sophia with a short answer. "Of course, but we see a lot between these walls. Different kind of jungle than you federal agents are used to, if you know what I mean."

"We'd like to see the incident report," Noah interjected smoothly.

"Of course." Hayes's agreement came abruptly as if he just wanted to get them out of his office. He quickly printed a copy and passed it over. "Everything's in order. Perpetrator was identified and dealt with. We do our best to avoid these types of things but it happens, unfortunately."

Sophia studied the report. "Says here it happened in the cafeteria. Security footage?"

"Technical issues that week. Camera was down for maintenance."

"All the cameras?" Noah asked.

Hayes's jaw tightened slightly. "The relevant ones."

"That's another convenient coincidence," Sophia murmured with a pointed look. "Along with the timing. Gotta tell you, Warden Hayes…it doesn't look good. One could almost say it looks retaliatory. Like someone wanted to send a message to anyone else thinking of talking."

"Have you read Johnson's file? He was a liar, a thief and a drug addict. He could have told me the sky was blue on a summer day, and I still wouldn't have believed a word he said," Hayes said. "That's just the reality of prison life. Inmates lie. All the time. For any reason. Am I sorry he died? The politically correct answer—of course. The honest answer—I wish he hadn't been killed on my watch. But I don't really think the world is worse off without him. One less drain on the state teat."

"A humanitarian at heart," Sophia quipped derisively.

Hayes leaned back in his chair, exhaling loudly. "Is there anything else you need?"

"Even if we did, it doesn't seem likely you'll have it," Sophia returned.

Noah felt the room in the temperature dip. Hayes had been going through the motions, but Sophia was poking the bear, needling him.

"You know…your journalist? She isn't exactly known for her journalistic integrity—and frankly, I find it hard to believe that two federal agents would put much store in anything a journalist would say when we've all been burned at some point or another by the media."

"Not all journalists lack integrity," Noah said.

"Well, we can agree to disagree—and Amber Laughlin? If I had my way, she'd never step foot in my prison ever again. That *Vice* piece she ran created problems when there weren't any." Hayes shuffled some papers on his desk with the agitation of a man irritated by people he deemed unworthy of his time. "Johnson was just her latest attempt to stir up trouble."

"I guess we'll never know because Johnson is dead," Sophia said flatly. "Along with his allegations about guard corruption involving a drug network that may be connected to a string of dead Native teens."

Hayes went very still. "I don't know anything about dead teens, but I can tell you, my guards are clean."

"Maybe, maybe not," Sophia said.

"I've had about enough of this bullshit. What are you implying, Agent Bennett?"

"I'm not implying anything. I'm stating facts. An inmate makes allegations about corruption. Months later, he's dead. Security cameras meant to document the attack malfunction. Records are anemic at best." She leaned forward slightly. "You have to admit, it doesn't look good."

"What doesn't look good," Hayes said carefully, "is federal agents coming into my facility making baseless accusations. Johnson was a violent offender with a history of causing trouble. He got into a fight. He lost. End of story."

"We'd like to see your safety records," Noah said. "Statistics on inmate deaths due to violence over the past five years. Particularly any that occurred shortly after inmates made similar allegations."

The temperature in the room seemed to drop ten degrees. The last traces of Hayes's smile vanished. "That would require considerable time and resources to compile. Without a warrant—"

"We can get one." Sophia's voice was cool and professional. "Along with authorization to interview every guard who was on duty that morning. Every inmate who witnessed the incident. Review all communication logs, visitor records—"

"Then I suggest you get that warrant." Hayes stood, making it clear the meeting was over. "Now, if you'll excuse me, I have a facility to run. My secretary can show you out."

"One more thing," Noah said, remaining seated. "The inmate who killed Johnson. Damien Reynolds. Where is he now?"

"Transferred," Hayes said shortly. "To a maximum security facility in Wyoming."

"When?"

"A week after the incident."

Noah nodded slowly. "Would you happen to have his transfer paperwork?"

Hayes's expression could have frozen hell. "With all due respect, Agent Thunderhawk, until you come back with a warrant, this conversation is over."

"Fair enough." Noah stood, matching Hayes's rigid posture. "Thank you for your time."

As they walked out, Noah noted how every guard they passed seemed to be watching them. Not obviously, but with the kind of careful attention that suggested their conversation with Hayes was already common knowledge.

"They're nervous," Sophia murmured as they approached the exit.

"Good," Noah replied quietly. "Nervous people make mistakes."

The Montana sun hit them like a physical force as they stepped outside. But it was nothing compared to the heat in Sophia's eyes as she turned to him.

"I don't like him."

Noah's response was warm with sardonic humor. "I don't think he likes you, either."

Sophia shot him a look, but a brief smile curved her lips before she said, "He's an egomaniacal jerk, but the question is, is Johnson's death connected to our case or is Hayes just covering his ass about unsafe prison conditions?"

Noah stared out at the razor wire glinting in the sun. "Both, maybe." He drew a deep breath. "We need to know more about Johnson. Family, friends and anyone who might have visited him here. We also need more background on Ursula Bowen."

Sophia nodded. "Let's see if Johnson still has connections in the area."

"Worth a shot," he agreed, starting the engine, watching Sophia pull out her phone to make notes. Working with her was like dancing with a live wire—dangerous, unpredictable but somehow exhilarating. And he had a feeling they were just getting started.

As they pulled away from the prison, the sun caught the razor wire one last time, making it sparkle like Christmas tinsel. But Noah couldn't shake the feeling that somewhere in those files Hayes wouldn't show them, somewhere in the dead man's desperate accusation, lay a truth that would burn a lot brighter—and a lot more dangerously—than morning frost on steel.

Chapter 14

The directions to Randall Johnson's mother's house took them south from Billings toward the Crow Reservation. The late morning sun had given way to heavy clouds that pressed down on the prairie like a lid, turning the late September landscape into watercolor shades of brown and gray. If she believed in omens, the broiling of ominous clouds barreling down on them would've put her nerves on edge.

Thankfully, she didn't believe in any of that.

She studied the case file open on her lap while Noah drove, his hands steady on the wheel as they navigated I-90 South. The silence between them was comfortable now, the kind that came from growing trust rather than awkwardness. She was hyperaware of that ease and how dangerous it could be—only because she'd never actually experienced anything like it before. Sharing space with someone had always felt as if one of them was trespassing, which had usually contributed to the eventual end of all of her relationships.

And speaking of ending...

"I have to question Amber's judgment for letting a guy like you go," she said, voicing a private thought without thinking. Heat crawled up her neck, but she didn't haul her words back. She risked a glance his way. "I mean, I'm just saying, from what I can tell, you're a good guy. Are you, like, a terrible kisser or something?"

Noah chuckled ruefully at her question, answering, "I like to think I'm decent in that department. No one's complained so far."

"Well, some people are too polite to say something like that to someone. Not me, though. If some guy comes at me like a Saint Bernard flopping his tongue around, I'm going to call him out." His laughter coaxed a small smile from her. She added, "Although, I have a feeling you're pretty good at that, too."

"Yeah? How so?"

"Just a gut instinct, I guess." *Because you listen, and you pay attention*, which were hallmarks of a good lover. "Not that it matters, just making casual conversation."

"Conversation about my kissing skills," he mused. "Interesting."

She shot him a quick look. "No, seriously, I don't mean anything by it. I probably shouldn't have said anything. Sorry."

"No need to apologize. Ask anything you like."

That openness was exactly the thing that drew Sophia and made her want more. Talking to a man in their field who didn't posture, choke on machismo and flex like a rooster in the yard was an anomaly that she couldn't resist. "Okay, did you love her?"

He didn't pretend confusion at her question, didn't play games—another point in his favor. Not that he needed any more points. "I thought I did," Noah admitted. "But I think if I'd truly loved her, it would've hurt a lot more when we parted ways. If anything, I was a little relieved. Amber was a lot to deal with."

That she could believe. Sophia was starting to like this woman. "Strong women are hard to handle."

But Noah shook his head, correcting her assumption. "It wasn't that she was strong. We just didn't complement each other the way two people who are aligned should. I don't have anything against a woman who knows her own mind. I prefer it."

Noah's calm and reasonable assessment gave Sophia pause. Was that her problem? She'd never found someone who complemented her personal relationship style? Or was she just difficult to relate to? Was she unlovable? She chewed her bottom lip without thought until she realized the tiny tell gave away more than she was comfortable sharing.

Get your head straight. Sophia roused herself from the errant direction of her thoughts. "We'll want to turn off at Crow Agency," she said, checking the GPS coordinates. "His mother's place is about twenty minutes from there."

Noah nodded, eyes focused on the road ahead. "You said she was a teacher's aide?"

"Yeah, at Crow Agency School until retiring five years ago." Sophia flipped through her notes. "Regular visitor to the prison until about three months before Randall's death. Then suddenly, all her visits stopped."

"Right around when he started talking to Amber about corrupt guards," Noah noted.

"Exactly."

The mountains loomed in the distance, their peaks lost in the heavy clouds. A sign welcomed them to the Crow Indian Reservation, the tribal seal bright against the faded blue background.

"What's your read on Hayes?" Sophia asked, curious about Noah's take on the prison warden.

"I've met him briefly before. Career bureaucrat protecting his territory," Noah shared. "But there was something else there today. The way he jumped to defend his guards before we even made accusations. Seemed a little too defensive. If there's one thing I know about prison wardens, it's that nothing happens on the block that they aren't aware of. The question is, if there's a dirty guard network, is he purposefully looking the other way or is he on the take, too?"

"My thoughts exactly." Sophia closed the file, watching a hawk circle overhead. "He was awfully quick to discredit Amber's journalism."

"No one in law enforcement likes a journalist," Noah said with a snort. "They have a tendency to stir things up and muddy the waters, even if nothing's going on. I don't necessarily blame him for his opinion on Amber, but that combined with the other stuff… Yeah, he's acting suspicious."

"Are you going to share what happened at the prison with Amber?"

"At some point. She'll just badger me until I do."

"She's tenacious."

"You have no idea." A hint of fondness crept into his voice, and Sophia stamped down the flicker of…something…that rose in response. Not jealousy. She didn't do jealousy.

The gravel road leading to Sarah Johnson's place snaked through the grasslands like a river, each bend revealing more of the blinding beauty of the reservation. Small houses dotted the landscape, most with pickup trucks parked outside, each separated by enough distance to give the illusion of isolation.

The Johnson house appeared around the final curve—a modest single-story with vinyl siding gone chalky from sun exposure. Wind chimes made from copper pipes hung from the front porch, their hollow music carrying across the yard. The Johnson place could've been plucked from any reservation in the area. The commonalities carved by hard times, a lack of precious resources and a fierce sense of pride left little room for creative differences.

Noah had always been aware of his privilege in that respect.

His father had made a decent living to provide for his family. Not everyone was so lucky.

Two vehicles sat in the gravel drive: a weathered Ford F-150 and a newer model Subaru Outback.

"Someone's home," Noah said as he parked behind the Subaru.

Sophia nodded, gathering her notes. The wind had picked up, and the approaching storm system made the air feel heavy with anticipation. She'd interviewed enough grieving parents to know the weight of these moments—how a simple knock could shatter whatever fragile peace they'd managed to construct around their loss.

They were halfway to the front door when it opened. A woman emerged onto the porch, her silver hair pulled back in a braid, her face lined with the kind of weathering that came from both age and sorrow.

She appraised them with a hard stare that missed nothing. "You're cops. What do you want? There isn't nothing here for you to take or threaten me with, so state your business and get going."

"Mrs. Johnson," Sophia said as they reached the porch steps. "I'm Special Agent Bennett with the FBI, and this is Agent Thunderhawk from the Bureau of Indian Affairs. We'd like to ask you some questions about your son."

"My son is dead." The words fell like stones.

"We're sorry for your loss," Noah said, his posture as straight as his gaze was keen. "We recently learned of his death. Would you mind talking to us about him?"

She eyed both of them with open suspicion. "Why?"

Sophia and Noah shared a look before Sophia replied, "Before Randall died, he told a journalist that there were guards dealing drugs through a network that may be responsible for the death of several teens, all of whom were tattooed with a specific tattoo. We're investigating those deaths. We went to speak to Randall but discovered he'd been killed in an altercation with another inmate."

At that, the woman scoffed, her gaze wintry. "As if that were the truth. My boy was murdered—and not by another inmate. By the guards."

"Why do you believe that?" Noah asked.

"Because he'd been begging me for months to get him transferred. I tried and tried to get his good-for-nothing lawyer to get him out of there, but the dumb woman stopped taking my calls. I was in the process of trying to find a different lawyer when I got the call that he'd been killed."

"According to the visitor logs, you stopped visiting Randall a few months before he died... Any particular reason for that?" Noah asked.

"I didn't stop visiting—they stopped letting me see him. Always some excuse why his visiting privileges had been revoked, but I know it was because they didn't want him talking to anyone on the outside. I was onto them, and I said as much to that sonofabitch Warden Hayes. Trying to tell me my son was making his own trouble, breaking prison rules... That was nothing but lies. And then he was dead. You tell me that they didn't kill him to shut him up."

Sophia felt this woman's anguish and could see how it'd hardened her. She also didn't doubt that Sarah was telling the truth as she knew it, but there was no way they could verify her story. The prison could make the revocation of visitor privileges look legit on paper, even if it wasn't.

The hard-eyed woman's gaze welled for a split second—as if that was all she could allow of her grief—before spitting out, "Good for nothing, the lot of you. My Randall was a good boy. He didn't deserve what he got."

Sophia knew never to speak ill of a mother's son, no matter

if that son was a dirtbag who'd rob her blind just to feed his drug habit. Treading cautiously, Sophia asked, "Did Randall ever tell you that he feared retaliation for what he'd shared with the journalist? Did he write it in a letter or anything like that?"

Sarah took a minute to sniff back tears, shaking her head. "Randall was dyslexic and hated to read or write. Said it gave him headaches. I'd visit him to put money on his books. That's when he told me he was scared someone was going to jump him for talking. It's that journalist that put him in danger. My boy's blood is on her hands."

Sarah's accusation hung in the air between them. Sophia kept her expression neutral, though her mind was already cataloging the implications. If Randall had been expressing fear before his death, there might be prison records, requests for protective custody, and transfer applications.

"When exactly did Randall start saying he was afraid?" Sophia asked, keeping her tone gentle but firm.

"March." Sarah's response was immediate. "Right after that woman came sniffing around. Talking about guard corruption, acting like she cared about what happened on the reservations, like she gave a damn about Native kids going missing. Got my boy all worked up about his cousin Ursula, made him think he could do something about it." Her voice cracked slightly. "Should've told him to keep his mouth shut."

"Did Randall ever share with you how he thought the guard corruption and the missing kids were connected?" Noah asked.

Sarah shook her head. "Just that he thought Ursula got mixed up with someone from the prison and got killed for it. Who knows if it was true, though. No way to prove it."

"Can you tell us about Ursula and Randall's relationship?" Sophia asked.

"She was his second cousin. Though Randy was more like an uncle to her really. She was only sixteen when she disappeared." Sarah's expression softened slightly at the mention of the girl. "Used to come around here all the time when she was little. Randy would give her piggyback rides, teach her to fish. Even after he got in trouble with drugs, Ursula never looked at him different. She was a good girl."

"When's the last time you saw her?" Noah asked.

"Summer, four years ago, right before everything changed. That's when she started running with a rough crowd from Hardin." Sarah frowned, something dark crossing her expression. "There was this older boy she was seeing…"

"You remember his name?" Sophia asked.

"Tommy, Tommy something. Drove a black pickup with chrome rims. Real flashy for these parts. Started showing up that July, always hanging around her. By August, she was different. Distant. Then in September, she was just…gone."

"Did Randall ever mention Tommy when he talked about the drug network?" Sophia pressed gently.

"Not by name. But in March, when that journalist got him worked up, Randy started talking about how it was all connected. Said Ursula wasn't the only girl going missing. Said these men, they'd pick out vulnerable girls, get them hooked on drugs first. Use the pretty ones to recruit others." Her hands clenched in her lap. "Said by the time anyone noticed they were gone, it was too late."

"Did Ursula have other friends who went missing? Anyone else she was close to before she changed?"

"Yeah, there was another girl, Melissa White Bear. Those two were thick as thieves growing up." Sarah's voice softened with memory. "Then in early summer, Melissa just disappeared without a trace. That hit Ursula hard, they'd been best friends since grade school. She started pulling away from everyone, missing school, you know that kind of thing. Then in July, that's when Tommy showed up. Acting all concerned about her, like he understood what she was going through. By September, Ursula was gone, too."

Noah shared a look with Sophia before Sophia asked, "Is it possible this Tommy guy worked for the prison by any chance?"

Sarah shrugged. "I don't know. Maybe. He must've made good money somehow to own a fancy car, but I couldn't tell you much about that."

"If the prison didn't allow you to visit, how'd you get information from Randall?" Noah asked with a frown.

"When my squawking got too loud, they allowed one three-minute call," Sarah admitted. "But I could tell they were watching him because he had to pick his words real careful. Probably had someone standing over him the whole time."

Sophia nodded, processing the information. "Did Randall mention Melissa White Bear at all?"

"In our last phone call," Sarah admitted. "Said he'd figured something out about Ursula and Melissa." Her hands trembled slightly. "A week later, he was dead."

Was this useful information or just speculation from a grieving mother? It was easy to spout conspiracy theories but difficult to prove them.

"Did Randall mention any specific threats?" Noah asked. "Names of guards or other inmates?"

Sarah's eyes narrowed. "If I had names, you think I wouldn't have brought charges on someone? I didn't have nothing but a dead boy that everyone wrote off as a dead-beat. Now you show up asking questions…" She shook her head. "It's too late now."

"Mrs. Johnson," Sophia said carefully. "We believe there's sufficient evidence to suggest your son's death wasn't random. But to prove that, we need to know everything he told you. Even small details could help us find out what really happened."

The wind picked up, rattling the copper chimes. Sarah wrapped her arms around herself, looking suddenly older and more vulnerable. "He said something about packages coming in through the laundry. Said one of the guards—a woman— was the connection to the outside. But he never gave me a name. Said it was safer for me if I didn't know."

Sophia felt Noah tense slightly beside her and knew he was thinking the same thing she was. A female guard. That narrowed things down considerably.

"Besides the journalist, did anyone else come to see you about Randall in those last few months?"

Sarah's expression shifted, just slightly. "Some woman. Said she was from a prisoner advocacy group. Wanted to help with his appeal." She snorted. "Never saw any paperwork, though."

"Do you remember her name?"

"Claire something. Didn't catch the last name." Sarah's mouth twisted. "Pretty lady, older. Talked real nice, like butter wouldn't melt. But something about her…" She shrugged. "Randall didn't want to see her again after that one visit."

"Did this Claire leave a card or any contact information?" Sophia asked, though something in her gut told her they'd never find a trace.

"No." Sarah let out a harsh laugh. "All these people wanting to 'help' my boy, and now he's dead." She fixed them with a hard stare. "You know what the prison told me? Said he died quick. Clean knife to the kidney. But I don't believe them. My boy had bruises all over his body. Looked like he'd been through a grinder. You can't tell me that was from a single fight in a cafeteria."

"How'd you know about the bruises?" Noah asked.

Sarah lifted her chin with open defiance. "I requested to see the body, wanted to make sure it was my boy and not some random person they claimed was him. It was my right as his next of kin. They weren't happy about it, I can tell you that much, but I made them do it anyway."

"Good for you," Sophia said, impressed. "The woman guard, the one handling packages, would you recognize her if you saw her photo?"

Sarah's expression closed off immediately. "I told you what I know. My boy is dead, and looking at pictures won't bring him back." She stepped back toward her door. "Now if you'll excuse me, I got things to do."

"Mrs. Johnson…" Sophia pulled out her card. "If you think of anything else—"

"I won't." But Sarah took the card anyway, tucking it into her pocket with hands that trembled slightly. "Just…if you do find out who killed my boy, make sure they suffer." Her eyes met Sophia's, filled with a mother's raw grief. "Make sure it wasn't for nothing."

The door closed with a quiet finality. Thunder rolled overhead as they returned to the truck, the wind whipping up dust devils in the yard.

"Do you think she knows more than she's saying?" Noah asked once they were inside.

"Not sure, but I do know that's a woman eaten up by grief."

Back in the truck, Sophia reviewed her notes. "So, Randall starts drawing attention to guard corruption and drug trafficking right after learning his cousin Ursula disappeared. Then he gets killed when he tries to expose it."

"And both Ursula and her friend Melissa vanished after getting involved with this Tommy character," Noah recounted. "A guy who shows up in an expensive truck, grooms vulnerable girls, likely gets them hooked on drugs so they're more easily controlled…"

"Then they disappear into the trafficking network," Sophia said. "Human trafficking is so insidious and interconnected that those girls could've been used for sex, as drug mules or collateral with other networks."

Noah agreed. "If Randall could identify specific guards involved in both the drug trade and the trafficking operation, that would've made him too dangerous to keep alive."

"And who's going to ask questions about the death of an inmate that the rest of society has written off?" Sophia returned with a knowing look. "No one."

"Exactly. They're almost the perfect victims."

Sophia buckled up. "Thankfully for us, there's no such thing as a perfect crime. They've screwed up somewhere… We just have to find it."

Chapter 15

The road stretched endlessly before them, Montana's vast landscape rolling by as Noah navigated the highway. Sarah Johnson's revelations were still flipping through his mind, especially the connection to another potential victim.

"Any mention of a Melissa White Bear in your trafficking cases?" he asked, glancing at Sophia.

She frowned, opening her laptop. "I have every name memorized, and Melissa White Bear isn't one of them," she answered, tapping through her notes to verify. "But we're only seeing the tip of the iceberg with these victims."

She sighed, and something in that small sound made Noah want to reach across the console between them. He didn't.

"Human traffickers have an endless supply of throwaway teens," she continued. "The system writes them off—if they're old enough to run away, they must be old enough to take care of themselves. That's why no one notices when they disappear."

"You were in the foster care system," Noah said quietly, showing he'd done his homework.

"Yep." Sophia's exaggerated "p" sound cut at something inside him, like he could sense the raw wound she was determined to downplay.

Noah caught her profile as she stared out the windshield. The weak afternoon light caught in her hair, turning it to fire.

He had a fairly good idea of who Sophia was as an investigator, but it was the woman behind the badge who endlessly fascinated him. Everything about her was a mix of professional polish and raw integrity that left no room for games and politics—and he admired the hell out of that quality.

But what he felt for her was so much more than that, and he'd be lying if he said it wasn't.

"Everyone talks about 'saving the children' until it comes to actually doing it," Sophia said finally. "Foster kids get broken in ways most people can't fathom. Makes them perfect targets for predators who manipulate pain for profit."

The edge in her voice made him wonder what she'd seen, what she'd survived. He wanted to ask, but she was already moving on, shoulders straightening as she pulled herself back behind that stoic professionalism.

"I can run the inmate ID for Randall's alleged killer while you drive," she said, efficiently changing topics. The message was clear: conversation over.

Noah followed her lead, despite the lingering questions. "Hayes handed over that incident report awfully quickly," he said. "Almost like he wanted us to have it."

"Either he's hiding nothing, or he's trying to make us think this angle's a dead end." Her fingers flew across the keyboard, the rhythmic tapping filling the cab. Noah found himself catching sight of her hands, noting how delicate and strong her fingers were—a perfect analogy for the woman herself.

"Huh. That's interesting," she said suddenly, breaking his reverie.

"What've you got?" He leaned slightly closer, catching the faint scent of her shampoo—something clean with a hint of vanilla.

"Reynolds's ID number from the report—MT7749321—

isn't showing up in the system." She frowned, eyebrows drawing together. "Let me try archived records."

"Could be a clerical error," Noah suggested, merging onto the interstate.

Sophia shot him a skeptical look. "In a prison death report? Those are triple-checked." She reached for her phone, her sleeve brushing his arm as she moved. "I'm calling Wyoming State Penitentiary."

Noah listened as she made the call, her voice taking on that crisp, authoritative tone she used with officials. Goddamn, it was sexy how she commanded respect without effort.

"No record of any transfer under that ID," she reported. "And they have no inmate named Damien Reynolds listed, period."

Their eyes met briefly. "So, either Reynolds doesn't exist—" Noah began.

"—or someone created a very convenient scapegoat for Johnson's death," Sophia finished. The synchronization of their thinking no longer surprised him. "Someone knew enough prison protocol to create a plausible-looking number but didn't have enough pull to make it valid in the system."

Noah pulled out his phone, putting it on speaker. He had connections that might help, and he wanted Sophia to witness this particular call.

"Judge Martinez's office," a familiar voice answered.

"Jenny, it's Noah Thunderhawk. Is she available?"

"Noah! Hold on, she just finished a hearing."

A moment later, Judge Elena Martinez came on the line. "Noah, what kind of trouble are you stirring up now?"

He couldn't help but smile at her tone. "Need some guidance on accessing prison records without a warrant. My partner and I have concerns about an inmate death at Montana State."

"Hayes giving you trouble?" The judge's voice sharpened.

"You could say that."

"That man's been sitting on his throne too long," Elena said. "The AG's office has been looking for an excuse to audit that place. Give me twenty-four hours."

After ending the call, Noah caught Sophia studying him, something like admiration in her eyes. The look warmed him more than it should have.

"Good connections," she noted with open respect in her gaze.

"Judge Martinez was the first prosecutor to give me a win when I was still with the tribal police. She knew my dad, came to his funeral." He paused, aware he was sharing personal details he rarely mentioned to colleagues. "She's solid."

They fell into discussion about the mystery inmate and how to access Johnson's real cause of death. The easy back-and-forth between them felt natural now, their thoughts aligning without effort.

"We need to compare the medical examiner's report against the prison's incident report," Sophia said, tucking a strand of hair behind her ear.

Noah tracked the movement, distracted by the simple gesture. What was he doing? Where was his head? "Prison deaths fall under state jurisdiction," he said, forcing his attention back to the case. "The ME's office in Helena would handle it. But if Johnson's death triggered an internal investigation, those reports would be separate."

"And harder to access without that warrant Hayes wants us to get." Sophia's fingers stilled on her keyboard. "I've seen this pattern before in Arizona. They split the paperwork trail into fragments, making it nearly impossible to piece together."

"Unless we can prove a civil rights violation," Noah suggested. "That would give us federal jurisdiction."

"We'd need more than a suspicious ID number and a missing transfer record."

Noah drummed his fingers on the steering wheel, ideas forming. "What if we track it from the Wyoming end? Every interstate transfer requires specific documentation. If Hayes filed fake transfer papers…"

"That's federal wire fraud," Sophia said, her eyes lighting up. "And that opens doors we don't need a warrant for."

Their minds were working in tandem again, building on each other's thoughts. Noah found this intellectual connection more intimate than any physical attraction he'd felt before.

"Should we let Amber dig into Hayes while we work official channels?" he asked.

Sophia considered this, her lip caught between her teeth in concentration. "She's already got prison sources," she said finally. "But we need to stress keeping things quiet for her protection."

"Controlling Amber's like attempting to harness a hurricane," Noah said with a small smile.

"Feed her the prison leads," Sophia suggested. "Let her chase those paper trails while we focus on the Melissa White Bear connection."

Noah glanced at her, surprised. "Why hand off the prison lead?"

"When chasing people this bad, it's easy to get distracted by more bad guys."

He nodded slowly, seeing her point. "So, Melissa White Bear could be our second potential victim connected to Johnson, but we still have nothing connecting either of them to Laramie or Travis."

"Exactly. Hayes might be dirty, but he's not our target."

"So, our prison trip was a waste of time?" Noah felt irritation rising.

"Not necessarily," Sophia said. Her hand touched his arm, the contact brief but electric. "If Johnson connects to our case, we've laid the groundwork for getting answers."

Noah grunted, frustrated but seeing her logic. "I'd still love to see Hayes get caught in his own net. The man thinks he's God."

Sophia chuckled, the sound unexpectedly warm. "Oh, I agree he's trash, but we can't dilute our resources. If Hayes is dirty, we'll hand it off to another department. Our priority is the trafficking victims."

His father used to say every lie had a weak spot—you just had to be patient enough to find it. Noah wondered what weak spots they'd uncover as they dug deeper into this case.

The highway stretched before them, endless and empty. Yet somehow, with Sophia beside him, methodically working through evidence and theories, Noah didn't feel alone in this pursuit. Their professional rhythm had become something deeper, more intuitive—a connection he wasn't ready to name but couldn't ignore, either.

And, despite every alarm bell clanging in his head, he wanted more.

Montana's vast skies darkened as afternoon faded toward evening. They still had miles to go, but in the quiet space of the truck cab, with the steady presence of a partner who thought like he did, Noah felt something he hadn't experienced in years: the comfort of being truly in sync with another person.

The realization was both reassuring and terrifying. What was he supposed to do with these feelings?

Felt like trouble waiting to happen.

Chapter 16

The diner materialized like a mirage through the Montana dusk, its neon sign buzzing against the darkening sky. Rose's Truck Stop was the kind of place that served breakfast and coffee all day, strong enough to strip paint. Sophia's stomach growled, reminding her they'd skipped lunch during the prison visit.

"Hungry?" Noah asked, already signaling to turn in.

"Starving." She glanced at her watch and noted it was nearly seven. The drive back to Stone River would take another two hours. "Good call, pulling off here." One of the things she was beginning to appreciate about Noah was his quiet observation and decided action. He didn't make a big deal about what was needed, he just evaluated and acted. If more people were like Noah, the world might be a better place.

The parking lot was half full, mostly semis and a few dusty pickups. Inside, the diner smelled of coffee and grilled onions. A tired-looking waitress led them to a booth by the window, where headlights from passing trucks swept across their faces like searchlights.

"Coffee?" the waitress asked, already pouring.

"Please," they said in unison.

Sophia wrapped her hands around the mug, letting the warmth seep into her fingers. Her jaw ached. She'd been clenching it for hours, a bad habit her dentist warned would eventually crack a tooth. Consciously, she relaxed the muscles, rolling her shoulders to release some of the day's tension.

"You okay?" Noah asked, doctoring his coffee with cream. "It's been a long day. I'm definitely feeling it."

"Yeah, this job can and will eat at you. That's something they don't share when you're a bright-eyed cadet just eager to make a difference in the world. The things we see, get exposed to… It takes a toll eventually."

The waitress returned. Noah ordered meatloaf. Sophia went with a turkey club, too drained to think about choices.

As they waited, her mind wandered to an old case. "Three years ago, I was working probably one of the saddest trafficking cases of my career. I mean, all cases of human trafficking are awful, but when the victims are the smallest, most vulnerable…it just sticks with you."

"What happened?"

"We ended up at a women's facility in Arizona. Turns out the guards were trafficking inmates' kids." She took a sip of coffee, bitter and strong, hating the memory. "By the time we uncovered it, four little girls were dead. The youngest was barely two."

"That's disgusting." Noah's expression darkened. "Did you get them?"

"Some. Not all." The failure still burned. "Two guards disappeared before we could make arrests. Still looking."

"Maybe it's not right to admit this, but I admire your ability to compartmentalize when you've got something like that case in your memory. Is that case why you pushed Hayes so hard?"

"Yeah, probably. Corruption within any branch of law enforcement rubs me the wrong way. We're supposed to be the good guys. If not us, who's going to do the right thing when there's so much bad out there?"

"I get it, trust me, I do. When you've been in law enforcement fields long enough, inevitably you're going to run up against people who abuse their power."

She met his eyes across the table. "What about you? I got the sense that there was something personal in there for you, too."

Noah was quiet for a long moment, turning his coffee cup in slow circles. "Yeah, it's my cousin Michael. The one I mentioned? He did time here. Short stint, three years for possession with intent to distribute, got out in a year and a half for good behavior. He said some things about what went on inside, but…" He shrugged. "He was using heavily back then. Hard to separate truth from drug paranoia."

"And now?"

"Now I'm wondering if he was more lucid than we thought."

Their food arrived, steam rising in the fluorescent light. Sophia hadn't realized how hungry she was until the first bite hit her stomach. "Tell me about him," she said. "Michael."

Noah's fork paused halfway to his mouth. "Why?"

"Because you get this look when you talk about him, and I want to get to know you better."

He smiled slightly. "Should I be flattered or worried?"

She smiled with a hint of teasing. "Depends on what I learn about you."

He chuckled, taking the bait. "Fair enough." He took a bite and chewed thoughtfully. "As a kid, Michael was…bright. Really bright. Could've done anything he wanted. But our dads died within a year of each other, mine in the line of duty, his in a drunk driving accident. He started acting out by junior high, and in high school, he just went off the rails. Started using and dealing. Classic story."

"You were close?"

Noah sighed. "I'm considerably older than him, but he always felt like one of my little brothers. I'm the oldest of five, so having a younger cousin around didn't feel any different than having another brother. I tried to look out for him, but Michael was always diving into trouble headfirst." His smile turned wistful. "But loyal. The kind of kid who'd take a beating for his friends without hesitation."

"Sounds like someone worth saving."

"Yeah." Noah's voice roughened slightly. "Just wish I'd tried harder when it mattered."

Sophia recognized the weight in his words, the same guilt she carried over cases that went sideways, lives she couldn't save. Without thinking, she reached across the table, touching his hand briefly. "We can't save everyone."

His skin was warm under her fingers. She pulled back quickly, but something had shifted in the air between them.

"No," he agreed quietly. "Even if we wish we could."

"Does he still live in Stone River?"

"Yeah, in subsidized housing on the reservation. Thankfully, my aunt Twylla was able to get Michael into one of the apartments because of her connections to the tribal administrative office. Otherwise…he'd have to live with my aunt and that wouldn't be good for either of them."

"Is Michael abusive to his mother?" Sophia asked.

"No, but he's unpredictable when he's using."

Most addicts were. "Do you still talk with Michael?"

"Not so much in recent years. My sister Lila keeps me up on current events, but I've been too busy with work to keep up with Michael's ups and downs. I can't say that I tried real hard to keep in touch, though. Watching Michael slowly kill himself was just depressing."

"Does that make you feel guilty?" Sophia probably shouldn't have asked, but she had an overwhelming desire to know more about what made Noah Thunderhawk tick.

He chuckled ruefully. "That hot bulb you got me under is starting to burn."

"Sorry," she said, blushing. "I shouldn't stick my nose into your personal business."

"It's okay, I don't mind sharing with you. I'm just not used to opening up about that stuff. It feels a lot like standing in your underwear in the town square on a cold night."

She smiled, appreciating his ability to remain open when she found it to be such a challenge.

Outside, a semi's air brakes hissed in the parking lot. The sound seemed to break whatever moment had formed, and they both returned to their food. But the silence was different now—comfortable like they'd crossed some invisible boundary between colleagues and…something else.

"Your turn," Noah said, surprising her.

"My turn?"

"Fair's fair. I shared my tragic family story. What's yours?"

Sophia studied him over her coffee cup, weighing how much to reveal. "Parents died when I was eight."

"That's rough. Must've been hard."

She almost deflected into her standard response when people got too personal. But something about the way he looked at her, patient and undemanding, made her want to give him a real answer.

"Car accident. Dad fell asleep at the wheel coming home from a late shift. Mom was with him." The words felt rusty from disuse. "I was staying with my grandmother that weekend. When the dust cleared, it was apparent she couldn't keep me—early stages of dementia. So, into the system I went."

"That's rough."

Putting it into words somehow bleached the horror of that moment from her history. The terror and bewilderment of a small girl being told to throw her clothes into a garbage bag and being torn from her life without a second thought as to how it would traumatize her was hard to articulate in a way that conveyed the bland, bureaucratic cruelty of it.

She still remembered screaming, trying to claw her way out of the social worker's arms, pleading with her grandmother to save her, and the poor woman being helpless to stop what was happening.

In her child's mind, she'd hoped and prayed her grandmother would just miraculously appear and rescue her from the hell that'd become her life, but the door never opened with her gran on the other side.

Years later, she discovered that her grandmother had died in an assisted living facility six months after Sophia had been folded into the foster care system. Fate was an unkind bitch at times.

She swallowed the sudden lump in her throat. "It is what it is." She forced a shrug. "Made me good at my job. You learn to read people fast in foster care, figure out who's safe, who isn't. Useful skill for hunting predators."

Noah nodded, understanding in his eyes rather than pity. She appreciated that. If there was one thing she couldn't stand, it was pity. She'd rather swallow razor blades than suffer that look pointed her way.

"Is that why you specialize in trafficking cases?" he asked. "Protecting kids who can't protect themselves?"

"Something like that." She smiled slightly. "Plus, I'm too stubborn to quit once I sink my teeth into something. Just ask my supervisors."

"Now that, I believe." His answering smile made something warm unfurl in her chest.

The waitress appeared with their check. Noah reached for it, but Sophia was faster.

"My turn," she said. "You can get the next one."

She realized what she'd implied only after the words were

out. But Noah just smiled that quiet smile of his, and some-how that was worse than if he'd commented.

Back in the truck, the night pressed close against the win-dows. Sophia's gaze drifted toward Noah as he drove, his pro-file outlined against the dash lights. He was measured with his words and actions, but there was nothing uncertain about the way he handled the truck on the dark mountain roads. She wondered what else he did with that kind of quiet confidence.

Stop it, she told herself firmly. They had a case to solve. Dead girls who deserved justice. She couldn't afford distractions.

But as another set of headlights swept past, illuminating the cab, she caught him glancing her way. Their eyes met briefly before both looked away.

Too late, a small voice whispered. She was already distracted.

The miles stretched ahead, dark and full of possibilities she wasn't ready to name.

The truck's heater hummed steadily as Noah navigated the winding mountain roads. They passed a sign for Stone River—eighty-five miles. The moon hung low over the mountains, casting everything in silver light. Sophia studied the strong line of his jaw, the way his eyes seemed to catch every detail of the road ahead.

"Tell me something," she said, surprising herself.

"About what?"

"Something real. Not about the case. Not about work." She wasn't sure why she was asking, except that the night felt somehow separate from their normal lives, as if being in this truck together created its own pocket of reality.

Noah was quiet for a moment, then, "I used to want to be a musician. Played guitar in a band during high school. We were terrible."

Sophia laughed, genuinely surprised. "What kind of music?"

"Whatever was popular. A lot of Pearl Jam covers. My sister Lila still has blackmail videos somewhere."

"I can't picture it."

"Good. Let's keep it that way." But he was smiling. "Your turn."

"I…" She hesitated, then decided to match his honesty with her own. "I collect Russian nesting dolls. The really intricate hand-painted ones. Started in my second foster home—the mother was Russian. She gave me my first set before they sent me back."

"How many do you have?"

"Seventeen sets. All different styles, different artists." She rarely told anyone about this hobby; it felt too personal and too revealing. "They're the only thing I've kept from those years."

"What appeals to you about the nesting dolls?" he asked.

She took a minute to think about her answer. "I don't know. Maybe that there's always another little doll hiding underneath. Like the layers of a fractured person, getting smaller and smaller as you dig deeper."

"Is that how you feel about yourself?"

Heat rushed to her cheeks, and she was grateful for the dark. She forced a laugh. "It's not that deep, Noah. I just like the dolls. I think they're cute—and they're the only thing I collect. I figure I can allow myself one stupid collecting habit."

"I get it," Noah said without ruffling at her sudden defensiveness. "I collect rare coins. Expensive hobby. My dad got me started."

That piqued her interest enough to settle her exposed nerves. "Yeah? Why coins?"

"My dad said that he liked to collect the coins because it reminded him that even things that seem out of style can still hold value. When he died, I took up the hobby as a way to remember him. Now, it's a relaxing way to let my mind rest."

"Do you go to antique stores or something to find the coins?" she asked, interested.

"No, most of my searches are online now. It's such a niche market that it's hard to find coin shops anymore."

Sophia nodded, enjoying learning such a personal little tidbit about Noah.

They drove in silence for a while, the road unfurling before them like a black ribbon.

A deer bounded across the road, forcing Noah to brake sharply. Sophia's hand shot out instinctively, bracing against the dashboard. When they recovered, she realized Noah's hand had moved to protect her, arm stretched across her chest like a barrier.

He pulled it back quickly, but the warmth of the gesture lingered. "Sorry," he muttered. "Force of habit."

She released a shaky breath. "Don't apologize." It felt odd to be cared for in the way that Noah instinctively did for the people in his life. An unfamiliar yearning clawed up her throat until she forced it back down. "It's all good."

Their eyes met again in the darkness, and neither looked away immediately this time. Something electric crackled in the space between them, dangerous and tempting.

A truck roared past in the opposite direction, high beams flooding the cab with harsh light. The moment broke, but Sophia could still feel her heart racing. From the near miss with the deer, she told herself firmly. Nothing else.

But as Stone River drew closer, she found herself wishing the drive was longer. In the morning, they'd be back to business—following the threads of the case wherever they led. For now, though, she let herself exist in this quiet space with Noah, where boundaries blurred, and possibilities felt endless.

Just for tonight, she told herself. Just for these few hours.

The lie tasted bitter, but she swallowed it anyway.

Chapter 17

The morning sun hadn't yet crested the mountains when Noah pulled into the River Bend Apartments parking lot, though calling them apartments was generous. The two-story complex sagged under years of neglect, its brown siding bleached to the color of old bones. Empty beer cans and cigarette butts littered the cracked pavement, a testament to lives lived on the edge of desperation.

Noah sat in his truck, something heavy in his chest. He remembered how Michael used to be—all quick smiles and quicker wit, the kind of kid who could light up a room just by walking into it because he was funny and thrived as the center of attention. That was before the shadows crept in, before the drugs found a way into that gaping wound left behind by the father who'd taken out two innocent lives on a drunk ride home one cold winter night.

Uncle Joseph had had demons that only grew stronger with a bottle of Jack. Noah could never understand how two brothers could be so different. Joseph had been a mean drunk but desperately repentant once sober. With the hangover, promises to be better always followed.

He remembered his dad being so patient with his brother, even when everyone else in the family had grown tired of Joseph's bullshit.

Noah remembered one time when he had gone with his

dad to settle Uncle Joseph during one of his drunken rages. He'd been angry for the destruction Uncle Joseph had left in his wake, for his aunt Twylla's tears and his cousins' white-faced fear that made them look like small barn owls. His dad's counsel from that night stuck with him.

Something to remember, son...what you see is the addiction acting out, not the person. That's not my brother, that's a man being eaten alive by demons. We can't see them, but he fights them every day of his life. Just because a battle is silent doesn't mean it's not hard.

The conversation with Sophia about Michael had haunted him all night. Lying in his childhood bed, staring at the ceiling while his mother's wind chimes sang their hollow song outside, Noah realized he couldn't keep avoiding this. Not just for the case, but for all the promises he'd made and broken over the years.

Unit 22B. Second floor, end unit. Noah climbed the metal stairs, each step groaning under his weight. A torn garbage bag leaked something dark and sticky down the concrete. The whole place reeked of poverty and forgotten dreams.

He knocked twice, sharp and professional, though his heart hammered against his ribs. Movement inside—shuffling feet, a muffled curse. The door opened on a face that hit him like a physical blow.

Michael looked old. Not just aged but worn down to bare bones and yellowed skin. His eyes were jaundiced and cloudy with more than just sleep. Track marks dotted the insides of his arms like a constellation of failures. What had begun with methamphetamine seemed to have progressed to even harder drugs.

But when he recognized Noah, that old smile flickered to life, a ghost of the boy he'd been. "Well, shit," Michael said, voice rough as gravel. "The prodigal cousin returns."

He scratched absently at his forearm, skin flaking under his yellowed nails. "Mom send you to check up on me?"

"Can't I just want to see my favorite cousin?"

Michael's derisive chuckle basically said *bullshit*, but he stepped back, gesturing Noah inside with an exaggerated bow. "Well, come on in, then."

The apartment was a single room with a kitchenette, everything touched by the diseased hand of addiction. Fast food wrappers covered every surface. Unwashed dishes grew forests of mold in the sink. The bed was just a mattress on the floor, sheets gray with age and God knew what else.

The sour smell of unwashed bodies and filth stung Noah's nose.

"You look good," Michael said, dropping onto the mattress. His smile turned sharp and mildly resentful. "All cleaned up in your fed clothes. Making the family proud. *Agent* Thunderhawk." He made a sound like a crowd roaring with applause. "The shining star of Stone River. How proud we all are."

Noah ignored the dig and leaned against the wall, careful not to touch anything. "How you been, Michael?"

"Oh, you know. Living the dream." He gestured to the squalor around him. "Got my own place, no responsibilities, plenty of time to pursue my…hobbies." His hands shook as he reached for a pack of cigarettes. "But you didn't come here for a family reunion. What do you want, Noah?"

The question hung between them, heavy with years of missed calls and broken promises. Noah watched his cousin light the cigarette, remembering summer days when they were kids, back when Michael followed him around like a second shadow.

He knew bringing up Travis would take a sledgehammer to any perceived niceties, but it had to be done. "Look, I know you're not going to like this, but I need to talk to you about Travis," Noah said carefully.

Michael went very still, the cigarette burning forgotten between his fingers. "What for?"

"You might've heard about the female body found on the mountain…"

"Yeah, I heard something. What's that got to do with Travis?"

"His name was written on her body."

Confusion seemed to war with the general disordered nature of Michael's drug-soaked brain. "Why?" Then he thought better of his question and shook his head vehemently. "You know what, forget it. I don't want to talk about it."

"Yeah, well, the case is back open, and I don't have a choice but to talk about it," Noah said. "And you were Travis's best friend. I have to ask—"

"Jesus Christ." Michael stood abruptly, agitation sharpening the chip on his shoulder. "That was fifteen years ago, man, and now you want to talk about Travis? That's some bullshit. Hell, I don't remember much about last week, and you want me to remember details about a lifetime ago? Give me a break."

"If there was anything—"

"I said I don't remember." Michael's brittle voice cracked under the strain, and sweat started popping along his hairline. He wiped at his forehead, rubbing the sweat on his dirty jeans.

Noah forced himself to stay calm, even as guilt churned in his gut. "What happened, Michael?"

"I don't know."

But Noah didn't believe him. Why hadn't he pressed Michael back when Travis's case first opened? Had he been afraid to learn that his wayward cousin had something to do with Travis's death?

"If you know something… I need you to tell me now, Michael," Noah implored his cousin. "If you're scared—"

"Scared? Hell yeah, I'm scared—and you should be, too. You think that badge is going to protect you? It won't."

"Protect me from who?"

Noah scratched his arms harder, leaving red welts. "You're an idiot, man. That's all I got to say."

"Michael, work with me. Do you know what happened to Travis?" Noah pressed, starting to run out of patience. "If you know something…"

"I don't know nothing!" Michael shot back, his gaze darting as if he were afraid someone was listening to their conversation. The paranoia was textbook junkie behavior, but something in his cousin's face made Noah's cop instincts buzz.

"I can protect you—"

Michael's bark of laughter wasn't a good sign. Noah felt Michael's tenuous grip on hospitality slipping. Should he keep pushing or back off?

Within that heartbeat of indecision, Michael shared something in a tone that sounded pulled from behind iron gates. "You know that place, Clear Skies? You know the one they send the messed-up kids to?"

"Yeah. Of course. What about it?"

"Travis said…" Michael swallowed hard. "He said something wasn't right there. Said kids would go in and come out different. Or not come out at all." He scratched his arms again, harder. "I told him he was crazy. Told him to leave it alone. But he wouldn't. And then…"

A car backfired outside.

Michael jumped, nearly dropping his cigarette. "You need to go," he said suddenly. "I shouldn't be talking about this. They watch, you know. They're always watching."

"Who's watching, Michael?"

But his cousin was already retreating into himself, that brief moment of clarity swallowed by whatever demons rode his blood. "Doesn't matter. Nothing matters. You should go. Tell Mom I'm fine. Tell her…" He trailed off, staring at nothing.

"Let me help you, man," Noah said, stepping forward, but Michael flinched and backed away.

"Don't," he said. "Just…don't pretend you care now. It's too late for all that, you know? I'm not that little kid that you have to try and save. That ship sailed a long time ago. You gotta go—and don't bother coming back, okay?"

The words hit like body blows, each one true enough to draw blood. Noah forced himself to breathe through it. "Michael…"

"Too late." Michael's smile was all broken glass. "Way too late, cousin."

Noah knew he should push harder and ask more questions. But looking at Michael—trembling, scratching, drowning in whatever darkness had claimed him—he couldn't do it. Not today.

For just a moment, something flickered in Michael's eyes— a glimmer of that bright kid who'd followed Noah around, who'd dreamed of being just like his big cousin. But it died as quickly as it came.

"Some things can't be fixed, man," Michael said. He turned away, retreating down the short, dingy hallway toward the bathroom. "Go home, Noah. Go back to your perfect life and your perfect job. Leave the past where it belongs."

Noah stood there for a long moment after Michael slammed the bathroom door shut. Everything in him screamed to stay, to somehow make this right. But you couldn't save someone who didn't want saving.

Outside, the morning sun had finally crested the mountains, painting the world in shades of false gold. Noah sat in his truck, hands trembling on the wheel, while Michael's words echoed in his head.

What had Travis seen at Clear Skies? Noah shifted with discomfort at the question. He'd already interviewed Claire Redstone, once when Travis's body showed up, and recently with Sophia. Clear Skies was a dead end.

So why would Michael say that?

Michael was the definition of an unstable witness. Any intel from Michael would have to be seriously vetted before being taken at face value, but that didn't mean there wasn't something worth chasing.

He blew out a short breath, frustrated and angry that he couldn't do more to help Michael, but his focus had to be the case, not his cousin's addiction.

Noah started the engine, trying not to see the disappointed face of his father in the rearview mirror. Sometimes, being a good cop meant being a bad cousin. He just wished knowing that made it hurt less.

A memory surfaced: Michael, at fourteen, bouncing on his toes as he explained his latest scheme to make quick money. Back then, that restless energy had seemed like ambition and drive. Now, it just looked like a kid's desperate attempt at being the man of the house when he had no idea what that meant.

Michael had only been nine when Uncle Joseph died. The bewildered kid was suddenly supposed to be in charge? That was too much pressure to put on a child, but their culture sometimes perpetuated generational trauma without even re-alizing it.

Maybe Michael never had a chance.

Noah pulled out his phone, thumbing through his contacts until he found his aunt Twylla's number. He should tell her about Michael's deteriorating condition. The yellowed eyes and skin suggested liver problems, serious ones. But what would telling her do except cause her more worry? She'd already tried everything to help her son, including a stint at that fancy rehab center in Idaho that had cost her entire savings.

Still, he couldn't shake his father's voice: *That's not my brother, that's a man being eaten alive by demons we can't see.*

Noah hit Dial. The phone rang three times before his aunt's tired voice answered.

"Noah? Is everything okay?"

"Just checking in. Stopped by to see Michael."

A long pause. "How bad?"

"He needs medical attention, Auntie. His eyes are yellow. His skin, too."

She exhaled slowly. "I know. Tried to get him to go to the clinic last month. He wouldn't." Her voice cracked slightly. "Says he's fine. Always says he's fine."

Just like Joseph had, right up until the end.

"Thank you for checking on him. I know he probably doesn't seem like he cares, but he's always looked up to you," she said, her soft voice warming. "He's a good boy with a good heart."

Poor Aunt Twylla, always trying to protect Michael. "How's Lynette?" he asked, trying to ease the sting of his call.

"Oh good, very good. She's working in Missoula now for some fancy doctor. She wants to go back to school and get her nursing degree, but for now she's doing medical billing. I'm very proud of her. She helps me out some when she can, but times are hard for everybody these days. The cost of living is eating everyone alive. Just the other day, I was looking at the price of cheese—"

"That's great news," he said, knowing he needed to cut off his auntie or she could go on like this for hours. "Lynette was always a smart girl. Tell her I said hi for me the next time you talk."

"I definitely will."

Noah hesitated to bring up anything Michael said about Travis, but something was nagging at him. "Auntie…did Michael ever mention anything to you about Clear Skies? As in, something bad happening there?"

"Oh, Noah, I love my boy, but his mind isn't right. Claire is a blessing to our community. You know that. Whatever he said, it was the drugs talking, not him."

His aunt confirming what he suspected should've been a relief, but that nagging feeling remained. "Thanks, Auntie," he said, ending the call with the promise to keep in touch, though he knew that was likely just courtesy. He loved his auntie, but he barely had time to call his mother, much less extended family members.

The sun had risen, burning away the last traces of morning mist.

In the harsh light, the River Bend Apartments looked even more decrepit, a collection of broken dreams and broken people, all trying to survive one more day.

Should he share with Sophia what Michael said? Would Sophia's bias cloud her judgment?

Maybe they'd been too quick to back off Claire Redstone. Every instinct told him they needed to dig deeper, but this time through Logan Crowe. People who turned their lives around usually loved talking about their redemption stories. And Logan had been close to Travis in those final days.

Noah pressed Dial. Sophia answered on the first ring.

"I'm heading back now," he told her. "But I think we need to take another run at Clear Skies. Not through Claire this time—through Logan Crowe."

"What changed your mind?"

"I went to see my cousin Michael. He remembered some-thing about Travis noticing problems there. Could be noth-ing but…"

"But even paranoid junkies get it right sometimes," Sophia finished. "We'll leave as soon as you get here."

Noah ended the call, taking one last look at Michael's win-dow before pulling away. Some demons you couldn't fight for other people.

That was just the sour truth of life.

Chapter 18

If Noah was still bothered by his visit with his cousin, he didn't show it. Sophia respected his professionalism when this case rubbed against personal bias. It was a skillset not many could master. Not that she ever had to deal with that issue. Some might say there was a benefit to being alone in the world—no one held her loyalties.

If anyone could lay claim to the lone wolf syndrome, it was Sophia. Hell, she didn't even know the name of her nearest neighbors, and she preferred it that way.

But Noah's stoicism in the face of something that had to be really painful, watching a family member struggle with addiction, only made her admire him more.

Except with that deepening respect came an unexpected and unwelcome feeling—attraction.

It was one thing to understand why you were single and another to wonder why someone as handsome, accomplished and smart as Noah didn't have someone waiting for him at home. Because he absolutely should.

Noah was the kind of man who should have an amazing woman to share his life with, maybe even a few kids because he'd probably make a great father.

The ephemeral memories she had of her own father were wispy and thin as if drawn on vellum but she remembered his laugh—deep, throaty and warm—like a hug made into sound. A lump rose in her throat. See? This was why she didn't go there.

Sophia was grateful when Clear Skies came into view. It gave her overactive brain a chance to latch onto something else.

"Looks like Claire Redstone's Buick isn't in the parking lot," she noted. "That's good luck for us."

Noah offered a short nod. "Let's go see what Logan has to say when Claire isn't in the room," he said, exiting the truck.

They walked into the reception lobby and found Logan talking with the receptionist with an easy but professional demeanor. He looked up as soon as the door jingled and smiled with uncertainty when he saw them.

"I'm sorry, did you have an appointment with the director today?" he asked with an apologetic expression.

"No, no, this is an impromptu visit," Noah assured him, attempting to put Logan at ease.

Logan relaxed as he shared, "Oh, that's a relief. For a second I thought I'd accidentally overlooked a meeting. Claire's not actually here today. She had a state funding review in Helena. but maybe I can help with whatever you need. Has there been a break in the case?"

"Actually, that works out perfectly as we came to speak to you," Sophia said, matching Logan's smile. "Would you mind taking a minute?"

"Me? I guess, sure," Logan agreed with a quizzical smile. "Anything to help."

"Do you have someplace we could talk that's more private?" Sophia asked, maintaining her calm and approachable smile. Logan was doing a good job of appearing unthreatened by their visit, but Sophia didn't trust anyone not to turn on a dime—no matter if they started out with welcoming smiles.

"Of course," Logan said, quickly ushering them into a small

office that clearly served as a generic workspace. The desk was too neat, the walls too bare to be a place where any one person spent serious time. A temporary space, then. Interesting.

As if reading her mind, Logan explained, "Sometimes we have students who need a quiet space to do their work, so we set up this area."

Sophia smiled. "Very considerate."

"Coffee?" Logan offered, already reaching for a carafe. His movements were smooth and practiced as he displayed the kind of social grace that came from years of making others comfortable. No wonder Claire trotted out Logan like a prized pony. Without knowing his backstory, you'd never guess the kid had started off as a little thug-in-training. "Just brewed fresh, I promise."

"Please," Noah said.

Sophia declined with a small shake of her head. Too much coffee made her jittery, and she wanted to be as sharp as a tack.

"So." Logan settled behind the desk, hands folded loosely. "What can I do for you?"

Sophia let Noah take the lead. In their previous interaction, Logan had responded better to Noah, probably due to their shared history. She could learn more by watching than talking.

"Just following up on a few things," Noah said easily. "If you don't mind, I'd like to revisit your friendship with Michael and Travis."

"Oof. That's a painful chapter to revisit."

Sophia nodded in understanding but remained silent, encouraging Logan to continue.

"Right, so, I can't say I was anyone's friend back in the day." Logan admitted ruefully, rubbing his forehead in thought. "Pain makes people act out and do stupid things. Travis was a good kid, and I didn't treat him like I should've."

"Meaning?" Sophia asked, intrigued.

"Like Claire already told you, I came to Clear Skies as a messed-up kid. I was lying, stealing—on my way to landing in prison for sure, but she helped turn my life around. Without her... I don't know where I might've ended up."

"Claire seems to have a sterling reputation around town," Sophia acknowledged with a faintly held smile, beginning to feel a little annoyed at how saintly the woman came across. No one was that perfect, and Sophia didn't trust anyone who appeared to be. "Can you elaborate about what you mean about how you treated Travis?"

"I'm embarrassed to admit it—but I was a bully," Logan admitted, his cheeks flushing. "I...was hurting on the inside and I said and did things I'm not proud of. I was friends with Michael first, and Michael brought Travis around. I think I was jealous and afraid that I might lose my friend, so I tried to pit Michael and Travis against each other in the hopes that Travis would take off."

Noah frowned at this information. "I don't remember you saying any of that during the original investigation."

"No, I probably didn't. I was a scared kid who didn't know how to be honest with myself or others." Logan had the grace to look ashamed by his admission. "I should've been more forthcoming, but I knew how it looked. I was a bad kid with a reputation, and there were plenty of people who probably could've said that I bullied Travis. I would've been your number one suspect—so I kept my mouth shut. But that doesn't mean that I didn't want whoever hurt Travis to get caught. Like I said, I was scared."

Sophia shared a look with Noah, likely sharing the same thought.

Noah sipped his coffee from the insulated paper cup before saying, "So, why tell us this now?"

"Because you're asking, and I'm ready to be honest. I've

had lots of therapy and not just the kind where you sit and tell a therapist your deepest, darkest secrets. Meditation, yoga, prayer, you name it, I've probably tried it. But as Claire says, healing can come in all sorts of ways, and I've embraced them all. I used to be afraid my past would incriminate me, but now, I know I've changed. I have nothing to hide, and I want to be honest."

Sophia had strong feelings about the supposed healing of sharing deeply held trauma—it didn't make it go away, it just morphed into something else less recognizable. At the very least, Logan hadn't pointed to the sky with some trite *I owe it all to God* sentiment that would've tested Sophia's ability to remain professional.

"I know it's uncomfortable, but can you tell us more about those last few months before Travis died?" Noah said.

Logan's fingers tapped once against the desk, the nervous tic so slight most people would miss it. But Sophia wasn't like most people.

"That was a rough time," he said slowly. "I was using pretty heavy. To be honest, my memory's not the best from that period. I have spots in my memory that are just blank. Doc says it's trauma-related, the brain's way of protecting us."

"But you remember Travis was a good kid," Sophia noted. Not accusatory, just observant.

Logan's smile flickered. "Some things stick with you, even through the haze. Travis was…different. Didn't fit in with the usual crowd. Quiet."

"How so?" Noah asked.

"He noticed things. A real people-watcher. Maybe that's what made people pick on him, made them nervous." Logan shrugged, though a subtle frown pulled on his brows. "Man, it hurts to think of that time in my life. Makes me thankful I'm not that person anymore."

"You were part of Lionel Redhorse's crew, right?" Noah recalled.

Sophia remembered the name from Travis's file, a person of interest who'd been interviewed and ultimately let go from lack of evidence. But even fifteen years ago, Redhorse's rap sheet had been robust.

"I ran with him," Logan admitted. "But like I said, I wouldn't say I was anyone's friend back then."

Sophia said, "Are you still in contact with Lionel Redhorse?"

"Absolutely not."

The definitive answer left no room for misinterpretation, but Logan doubled down in case there was any doubt. "Pretty much after what happened to Travis, he went his way, and I went mine. I hate to say it because I know it sounds corny, but Travis dying… It changed me. Might've been the only way that I would've seen a path toward changing my ways."

"Realizing your own mortality can go a long way toward creating change," Noah said, shooting a glance Sophia's way. Did he believe Logan's redemption story, or was he suspicious of the miraculous turnaround like Sophia?

Maybe it was her bias raising its ugly head again, but she didn't believe people truly changed. A leopard couldn't change its spots and all that.

A shadow passed over Logan's expression as he paused to sip his coffee. "I wish I could help more, but like I said, I was pretty far gone back then. Claire helped me turn things around, get clean. Everything before that is pretty fuzzy."

"Tell us about that," she said. "How Claire helped you."

Something warmed in Logan's eyes at the mention of Claire's name, as if he were eager to sing her praises. "She saw something in me when everyone else had given up. Gave me structure, purpose. A job when no one else would take a chance on me." He gestured to the building around them. "Now I get to help other kids the way she helped me."

"Must be rewarding," Sophia said. "Seeing them transform the way you did."

"It is." But something shifted in his expression, subtle, like a cloud passing over the sun. "Though not everyone wants to be helped. You can't save them all. I think that's the hardest part of the job—accepting that everyone has to walk their own path."

Sophia frowned, still stuck on one particular point in Logan's story. "If by your own admission, you bullied Travis... why'd he stick around?"

Logan sniffed, going very still, his expression faltering as he shared, "I... I think he stayed because of Michael. They were tight back in the day, and Travis was loyal. I mean, that's just a guess. Honestly, I don't know. I wish..." He hesitated, then changed gears. "Yeah, I guess we'll never truly know. All I can say for sure... Travis was a good guy, and he didn't deserve what happened to him."

"Which was?" Sophia queried, her senses sharpening to a pinpoint.

Logan sensed her energy change and quickly clarified, "Him dying, of course. Good people shouldn't die young. That's all."

A knock at the door made them all turn.

A teenage girl stood in the doorway, shifting nervously from foot to foot. "Sorry to interrupt, Mr. Crowe, but the new kid's having another incident."

Logan stood smoothly. "Duty calls. Unless there's anything else...?"

"We're good for now," Noah said, standing as well. "Thanks for your time."

The morning had warmed considerably by the time they

reached their vehicles. Birds sang in the pine trees, the sound almost too cheerful for the weight settling in Sophia's gut.

"Well?" Noah asked.

"He says all the right things," Sophia answered.

"And you don't believe him?"

"Let's just say… I have a hard time swallowing his ultimate redemption story hook, line and sinker. Maybe that makes me a jaded bitch, but I can't shake the feeling that he's hiding something."

"It could be survivor guilt," Noah supposed with a thoughtful frown. "He has to wonder sometimes how fate chose him to live and not a good kid like Travis. Those kinds of thoughts can mess with your head."

"Maybe." Sophia wasn't convinced. "But he was awfully vague about those last few months before Travis died. I don't care what he said about the drugs blotting out his memory. Unless he had a cerebral hemorrhage, he couldn't have afforded to do the amount of drugs necessary to damage the memory center of his brain."

"What do you mean?"

"Drugs are expensive," Sophia put it bluntly, "and something tells me Logan wasn't some trust fund kid."

Noah chuckled at her dry comment, confirming, "No, he wasn't."

"Exactly, so that leads me to believe that his memory isn't as damaged as he likes to say it is, which then leads me to my next question…what's he not telling us?"

"You make a solid point," Noah said, his step matching hers.

"And another thing…this place gives me the creeps. Everything about it is too damn perfect. Reminds me of a model home. Something dressed up for show to hide the fact that it has no soul or personality. A place to groom Stepford children or something. This place feels like the fake smile of a person who stopped taking their antidepressants."

Noah wasn't entirely on board with her opinion. "I don't know about that. Claire runs a tight ship. You can't assign negative karma points just because they like a tidy and orderly environment."

"There's tidy, and then there's militant," Sophia said, scanning the perfect grounds. "Even the grass isn't allowed to express itself here. Have you ever seen a yard so impeccably maintained? Not a single dandelion anywhere."

"Look, I'm not saying you're wrong, but I don't exactly see it the same way," he said, but added, when she started to ramp up, "However, I agree with you about something being off. I can't put my finger on it, but it's there. I just don't want to go making accusations that could end up hurting good people if we're wrong."

"Noah." She stopped to stare at him. "I'm not a rookie. You don't have to school me on procedure."

"I'm not trying to school you. I'm just concerned that you're coming in a little hot because of your personal history," he warned.

A sharp retort bubbled on her tongue, but Noah spoke up again before she could fire back.

"I trust your gut. If you say something feels off, I believe you. All I'm saying is…let's handle this the right way so that if we have to make an arrest, it's an airtight case."

That simple logic blew the hot air from her balloon. He wasn't telling her to calm down or downplaying her concerns, he was just trying to make sure they did everything by the book. She acknowledged him with a short nod, realizing he was right.

It wasn't like her to let her feelings run the show, but this case was starting to creep under her skin in ways she hadn't expected. Drawing a deep breath, she took a minute to regroup just as another thought came to her.

"Maybe he's sleeping with her," Sophia suggested, causing Noah to grimace. "What? You know it happens. The misplaced gratitude causes people to think they feel a certain way and then temptation takes care of the rest."

"God, I hope that's not the case," Noah said with a subtle shudder at the thought. "But I get the impression he thinks of Claire as more of a surrogate mom than a lover—however, now I need brain bleach to get that image out of my head."

Nothing made Sophia squeamish anymore—she'd seen too much at this point. "Maybe so." She opened the passenger door but didn't get in. She needed to clarify something. "I understand people get nervous talking about their past when it wasn't the best, but something about his reaction when you asked about Travis…it wasn't just discomfort. It was fear—and I'm not just saying that because I have a bias against immaculate group homes."

Noah was quiet for a moment, processing. Finally, he nodded, showing his willingness to see where her hunch could lead. "So, what's our next move?"

"We need to know more about Logan's transformation. Employment records, arrest history, anything that shows what was really happening in those months before Travis died."

"Should be easy enough. Stone River is too small to hide much," Noah said. "I can make some calls."

They climbed into the truck, and Noah pulled out of the parking lot, handling the big vehicle with that understated masculine energy that Sophia couldn't ignore.

She grew up in Texas. Every boy she ever knew had a truck at some point in their life. She'd never been one to go weak in the knees at the sight of a man behind a four-wheel-drive gas-guzzler.

But there was something about the way Noah handled himself that made her mind wander to places best left alone. Lord only knew her thoughts in that direction weren't professional. But they sure as hell felt damn personal.

And that was a problem.

Chapter 19

The old case files spread across Noah's desk like a paper autopsy, yellow pages filled with details that haunted dreams, including witness statements, crime scene photos and time lines that led nowhere. Fifteen years of dust and regret, all laid bare under harsh fluorescent lights.

The case minutiae staring back at him felt like a rubber stamp with the word FAIL slamming down on his past investigative skills. Most days, he wasn't one to drown in regret, but from the start, this case had burrowed beneath his skin like a burr under a wolf's pelt.

You're a goddamn hypocrite, Thunderhawk, getting after Sophia for making things personal when this case is nothing but personal for you.

He'd been staring at Logan Crowe's original witness statement for twenty minutes. Details, memories and chaotic snippets echoed in his head, making it difficult to hold onto a single train of thought. Drawing a deep breath, he tried again to focus, hoping Sophia couldn't sense the turmoil in his head.

When he finally wrangled his thoughts, something stood out in Logan's original statement. On the surface, the statement was typical for a teenager—vague on details, heavy on attitude, but there was something else, something that didn't quite fit with the polished, redemption-story version of Logan they'd just interviewed.

"You've been reading that same page for ten minutes." Sophia's voice cut through his concentration. She leaned against his desk, two fresh cups of coffee in hand. The bitter scent of station coffee filled the air between them. "What are you seeing?"

Noah accepted the cup, letting the warmth seep into his hands. "Logan told us he was using heavily during that time, that his memory was fuzzy from drugs."

"Right." Sophia settled into the chair beside his desk, close enough that her knee brushed his when she leaned forward to look at the file. "You're not buying it?"

"Look at this." Noah pointed to the original statement. "This interview was conducted at 8:00 a.m., forty-eight hours after Travis went missing. Logan's answers are detailed, specific. Times, places, what people were wearing. Not the kind of recall you'd expect from someone deep in addiction."

Sophia's eyes narrowed as she read. "Could have been coming down, his mind starting to function again?"

"That might explain him being coherent during the interview, but would he remember so many details about what happened if he was high while they took place? It seems unlikely. I've interviewed enough addicts to know the patterns. They either can't remember anything, or they remember too much—trying to prove they're reliable. This…" he tapped the page "…this reads like someone who was clearheaded and careful about what they said. Even purposeful. Like reciting something scripted."

"And today he claimed not to remember anything from that period." Sophia took a sip of coffee, thinking. "To play devil's advocate, I feel compelled to point out that people's memories do fade over time. Details become less clear as time goes on. Maybe he really doesn't remember anymore, even if his memories were clear at the time."

"True. But why lie about being high?"

"Maybe there's something specific he doesn't want us to realize he remembered." Sophia set her cup down, reaching for the original time line they'd constructed. "What else did he say in that first interview?"

Noah flipped through the pages, finding the key section. "He claimed he was at home all evening, hadn't seen Travis in days. But look at this statement from my cousin Michael, taken two days later."

Sophia leaned closer, reading where he pointed. Her hair brushed his shoulder, carrying the faint scent of something floral. Noah forced himself to focus on the words, not the warmth of her presence.

"Michael puts Logan at the Cut Bank River that afternoon, same place they found Travis's body." Her voice sharpened with interest. "Did anyone verify Logan's alibi?"

"That's just it, his mother backed up his story, said he was home all night, said something about getting a night pass for good behavior, even though technically, he was in the custody of Clear Skies at the time for juvenile delinquency charges. But I remember interviewing her. She was…" Noah searched for the right words. "Nervous. Like she'd been coached on what to say. Honestly, I just chalked up her behavior to being apprehensive about talking to the cops."

"And protecting her son."

"Maybe. But Logan wasn't even a serious suspect at the time. We were focused on Lionel Redhorse and his crew." Noah rubbed his temples, fighting a headache. "I should have pushed harder. I was so certain that Lionel was somehow the culprit that I ignored anything else that I thought was a waste of time."

"Hey." Sophia's hand touched his arm briefly. "You can't rewrite the past. But we can figure out if he's lying now."

Noah nodded, grateful for her steady presence. This case made him doubt every decision he'd ever made, but Sophia's focus helped him stay grounded in the present. "There's something else." He pulled out another file—tribal police records from the months before Travis's death. "I've been going through Logan's arrest record. Minor stuff mostly—drunk and disorderly, possession of drug paraphernalia. But look at the gaps."

Sophia studied the dates. "Nothing between March and June that year. Right before Travis died."

"Exactly. If he was using as heavily as he claims, there should be more contact with law enforcement. Instead, it's like he dropped off the radar completely."

"Or someone was protecting him." Sophia's expression turned thoughtful. "When did he start at Clear Skies?"

"According to his records, he was admitted as a resident three months before Travis's death. Hired on as maintenance staff two years later." Noah leaned back, studying the pattern of dates. "Claire Redstone's perfect success story."

"Little too perfect, maybe." But Sophia's tone was careful, neutral. She knew how he felt about Claire and Clear Skies's reputation in the community.

"I don't know." Noah stood, needing to move. The small office felt suddenly claustrophobic, the weight of old mistakes pressing in. "Claire's helped a lot of kids over the years. I don't know of anyone in this town who's ever said a bad word about her. It doesn't make sense to even look her way for any of this—even if Logan turns out to be involved."

"I'm not saying she hasn't done good work." Sophia watched him pace, her expression unreadable. "But good works can hide a lot of sins. You know that as well as I do." Her voice gentled as she added, "You and I have both been doing this job too long to ignore the fact that good deeds can be an effective cover hiding something more sinister."

Before Noah could respond, his phone buzzed. Amber. He showed Sophia the screen.

"She's been digging into Randall Johnson's prison death," Sophia said. "Might have something."

Noah hesitated. Bringing Amber deeper into the investigation felt risky, but they needed every lead they could get. He hit Accept, putting the phone on speaker. "Tell me you've got something good," he said by way of greeting.

"Buddy, it's practically Christmas." Amber's voice crackled with excitement. "I've got proof your mystery inmate Damien Reynolds never existed. Not just in Wyoming—anywhere. The ID number they gave you? It's real, but it belonged to a prisoner who died of cancer six years ago."

Noah and Sophia exchanged looks. "They recycled a dead man's ID number?"

"Exactly. Sloppy work for a cover-up, but it proves someone falsified those transfer records. And here's the kicker— I found a connection between one of the guards on duty the day Johnson died and a trucking company that operates routes through Montana, Idaho and Wyoming."

"The same states where trafficking victims have been found with the tattoo," Sophia said quietly.

"Winner winner, chicken dinner." They could hear Amber typing in the background. "I'm still tracing the money, but there's definitely a connection between your most recent vic and Ursula Bowen, suggesting that the trafficking network was working some kind of angle through the prison system."

"I would love to nail Hayes to the wall for some kind of corruption," Noah muttered. "Good work, Amber. All right, send us everything you've found out so far. We'll get the paperwork started for warrants on Hayes's prison records."

Sophia nodded. "That tattoo is going to be the one thing that trips them up. So far, it's our best lead." She leaned forward to add, "Yeah, real good work. If you're not careful, you might just change my opinion on journalists."

"Ha! My plan is working. No, but seriously, whatever's happening behind those concrete walls...it needs to stop. They're just kids, for chrissakes."

Noah fell silent, digesting the enormity of the situation. "You hear rumors of sex parties involving kids in the Hollywood scene, and then you find out the stories are real, but you're not surprised because rich people think the rules don't apply to them but when you find out this shit is happening in the blue-collar sector? It makes you feel like nowhere is safe from this kind of corruption." Shaking off the darkness, he added, "Hey, Amber, be careful out there. Don't stick your neck out so far that you get it chopped, okay?"

"Stop being such a worrier. I've got security measures in place." Her voice softened slightly. "But thanks for caring. I'll be in touch."

After the call ended, Noah leaned back in his chair, mind moving in dizzying circles. "We need to lay this out—all of it. There are too many pieces on the chessboard to see our next move."

"We've basically got two cases colliding with each other with one shared element but no real lead as to how they're connected. We haven't found a lead to Travis from Laramie aside from his name on her skin, but Laramie is connected to the other victims by the shared tattoo."

"You thinking whiteboard?" Sophia was already moving, marker in hand. Her efficiency in anticipating his needs gave him that familiar warmth he was trying to ignore.

"Time line," he confirmed. "Let's map everything we know

for sure against what people claimed. We'll start with Travis's case and then move onto what we know about Laramie."

They worked methodically, Noah reading from files while Sophia created a detailed time line. Her handwriting was precise and analytical—time, date and witness statements in careful columns. The whiteboard slowly filled with a spider's web of connections.

"Look at this gap," Noah said, tapping five months of silence on the board. "Just like Logan's sudden drop off police radar before Travis died. Another period where someone slips completely off the radar."

"Except this time, we know why." Sophia's voice held a controlled anger as she added details beneath the time line. "The progression tells a story," she continued, pausing to digest their fact puzzle. She rubbed her chin in thought as she mused out loud. "They're using these kids for something... but what specifically? Drug mules? Sex slaves? Recruiters?"

"Quite possibly all of the above," Noah returned grimly. "Juveniles are the easiest to fly under the radar and the easiest to make disappear." He studied the timeline. "The question remains, why leave Travis's name on Laramie? That's the piece that doesn't fit the pattern. The other victims didn't have messages left with their bodies."

"Someone's trying to tell us something," Sophia said quietly. "Or warning us off. Maybe an informant from the inside?"

The whiteboard gleamed under harsh lights, two time lines of tragedy connected by invisible threads they were still trying to unravel. Sometimes, seeing it laid out so clinically made the horror of it more stark, not less.

"I'm still stuck on this." Sophia circled the gap in Logan's arrests. "If he was using at that time as heavily as he claims, there should be a paper trail. Addicts don't just stop getting caught. They make stupid mistakes when high and end up attracting attention."

"Unless someone was protecting them." Noah pulled out the old newspaper articles he'd collected—yellowed clippings from the *Stone River Gazette*. "Here—coverage from when Travis disappeared."

Together, they spread the articles across his desk. The headlines screamed tragedy: BODY OF LOCAL TEEN FOUND IN RIVER. But the smaller details caught Noah's attention now—quotes from witnesses he'd forgotten about, perspectives that time had blurred.

One article quoted Alanna Yuctah, Travis's English teacher: "He seemed troubled those last few weeks. Distracted. Like something was weighing on him."

Another mentioned Travis had spent time researching something he wouldn't talk about at the library. The librarian had noticed him making copies of old newspaper articles, but couldn't remember what they were about.

"Why didn't we follow up on this?" Noah wondered aloud, frustration creeping into his voice.

"Because you were focused on Redhorse's crew," Sophia said gently. "It made sense at the time."

"Did it? Or was that just the easy answer?" He stood abruptly. "I need coffee. Real coffee, not this station sludge. You want to grab lunch?"

Sophia checked her watch. "It's almost two. No wonder my stomach's eating itself."

When they arrived, the Red Feather was busy with the late lunch crowd, but Martha steered them to a quiet booth in the back. Noah automatically ordered a double-patty cheeseburger and fries, needing comfort in the form of grease and carbs. Sophia surprised him by ordering the same.

"What?" She caught his look. "I enjoy a good burger, too."

"Just wondering where you put it all." The words slipped out before he could catch them.

She chuckled a warning, "Careful, Thunderhawk. That's dangerous territory."

He deserved that. "Sorry. Professional respect only, I promise."

"Liar." But there was warmth in her voice.

They were both dancing around whatever this was between them, neither willing to cross that line first. But the yearning to know more about Sophia, the woman, not just the badge, was starting to gnaw on him. She was a mystery that beckoned even as he tried to ignore the pull. It wasn't like him to be so distracted. Wasn't his style, and he didn't like the way it made him feel off-balance.

Shake it off, redirect.

Noah pulled out the files they'd brought, spreading them on the table between their coffee cups. "Let's look at Michael's original statement again. I want to compare it with what he told me yesterday."

Young Michael's words stared up at him, clear and coherent—so different from the broken man he'd become. Guilt bobbed in Noah's throat for not being there for his cousin, but even if he'd known what Michael would become, was there anything he could've done to change it?

He had to stop fixating on his guilt with Michael. Shoving his personal feelings into a deep, dark place, he refocused on the present, more than grateful to have Sophia's steady presence grounding him with purpose.

If nothing else, they made a good team professionally. But he'd be a liar if he didn't admit to wondering if there could ever be anything more between them than the job.

It was stupid to even wonder.

Chapter 20

The October sun painted Stone River in watercolors, turning the mountains into waves of gold and amber as fall dug its claws deeper into Montana. Saturday. Technically, Sophia had the weekends off. But what was she going to do in a town where she knew almost no one, and the one person she knew was a colleague?

She stared out her hotel window, coffee growing cold in her hands as she watched the town come alive below. After nearly two weeks here, she still felt like an outsider looking in—except, increasingly, when she was with Noah.

Not that this feeling was foreign. She'd never found a place that resonated with the idea of home. It wasn't a hard line to decipher why she felt that disconnect, but there were definitely times when she felt that distance more than others.

She envied Noah's easy way with people that familiarity afforded. His name opened doors, whereas she was immediately met with distrust unless Noah was standing beside her like some good luck totem in her pocket.

Ah, Noah... He really was a good man. Why couldn't she meet someone like Noah out in the wild? Or on one of those useless dating apps she'd briefly entertained after one too many glasses of wine on a weekend off?

Oof. That'd been embarrassing. All it had taken was three immediate pornographic messages from complete strangers to make her delete the apps with extreme prejudice and swear off drinking more than one glass of Pinot by herself ever again.

She knew all the reasons why messing around with a colleague was a recipe for a bad idea. It was also likely why she was drawn to the concept like a drunken moth heading straight for the destruction of the glowing bulb.

She'd teased him about his kissing style—so inappropriate—and yet, the question had lingered in her mind. Was his kiss as lush as his beautiful mouth suggested? Or was he stingy and tight, all business with those sensual lips?

Sophia sucked in a tight breath, mortified by her unruly thoughts.

She was the best in her field—countless commendations and certificates of merit lined her office back in DC—so why the hell was she mooning over a coworker like some love-sick teen with her first crush?

Because she was human.

And, if she was being honest, she was lonely. When was the last time she'd felt a man's arms around her, holding her tight, reminding her that she could be soft in the right hands?

Somehow, she'd girl-bossed her way straight into celibacy. That hadn't been the plan, but it sure ended up being the outcome.

Maybe she could talk to Amber and get the inside scoop on the enigmatic man.

No, don't do that, a voice warned. *Keep it professional.* The last thing she needed was more reasons to get distracted by the angular cut of Noah's jaw and how that rigidly maintained physique looked hard enough to stop a bullet.

But despite that excellent advice, she remembered how he'd looked at her over case files yesterday, how his voice softened when he talked about his family, how his presence made her feel…not safe exactly, but something close to it.

Yet that safety felt wrong, like she was holding something in her hands that didn't belong to her. She didn't know how to handle the prospect of a man who wasn't toxic in some way. Hell, in this scenario, she was the toxic one—Noah should steer clear of the hot mess that she was.

Her phone buzzed. Speaking of danger. Rousing herself, she read Noah's text message.

Thought you might want to see more of Stone River than police stations and diners. Weather's perfect for hiking if you're interested. No pressure. No big deal. Just offering.

Like the devil himself had just orchestrated a temptation of the highest order, Sophia's thumb hovered over the screen, paralyzed by two distinctly different feelings. She should say no. Keep the lines clean and distinct.

But the idea of getting out of this hotel room for some fresh air, stretching her legs and resting her mind if only for a day was a stronger draw than her good sense chirping in the background about being professional.

An offer to go hiking isn't inappropriate, a voice whispered. *Say yes.*

She sucked in a tight breath and texted, Where and what time? before she could change her mind.

His quick response made her grin: Give me an hour. Dress in layers and wear good shoes. I'll pick you up.

She chuckled softly, ignoring how her cheeks felt flushed. As if she'd never hiked before. Did he think she would show up with Jimmy Choos on her feet?

Sophia set down her phone, aware her heart was beating slightly faster. This wasn't a date. It was just two colleagues taking a break from a difficult case. That she'd packed her hiking boots was just good planning, not kismet.

Still, she took extra care with her ponytail, ensuring it was secure enough for hiking but not severe, and curled the ends for a little whimsy. The woman in the mirror looked back at her with knowing eyes. *You're in trouble, Bennett.*

Noah's truck pulled up exactly on time. He'd changed, too—worn jeans, hiking boots, a flannel shirt that made him look more like a local and less like a federal agent. The transformation suited him but didn't help quell the flutter in her stomach when she met his welcoming smile.

"Ready for the five-cent tour?" he asked as she climbed in.

"Depends. Are we talking tourist traps or the real Stone River?"

His smile was warm enough to chase away the morning chill. "Thought I'd show you my favorite hidden oasis. A place I used to go when life got too heavy." He pulled away from the hotel, heading toward the mountains. "Unless you'd rather see the world's largest ball of barbed wire."

"That's not really a thing, is it?"

"Guess you'll never know now."

The drive took them through parts of Stone River she hadn't seen yet—past small houses with Halloween decorations already up, children's bikes abandoned in front yards and lives being lived in the shadow of their investigation. Then the town fell away, replaced by pine trees and winding roads that hugged the mountainside.

Noah handled the truck with easy confidence, telling her stories about growing up here—learning to fish in the streams they passed, camping with his siblings, the time his brother David convinced their youngest sister, Lila, a mountain lion was stalking them during one of their overnighters.

"If you haven't had a hysterical ten-year-old little sister refusing to sleep in her own tent unless you do a complete perimeter search three times, you're lucky."

She knew it was probably one of those memories Noah remembered with annoyance, but she'd give anything to have those kinds of stories make up the bulk of her childhood. Her memories were *Dateline* fodder. "Must be nice," Sophia said with a short smile. "Having roots like that."

Noah glanced at her, reading something in her tone. "Yeah, it is." He navigated a sharp turn. "Unfortunately, took leaving to appreciate what I had, but then I guess that's how it goes for most things."

"When I left Texas, I never looked back," Sophia said. Putting that state in her rearview mirror had felt liberating. She remembered packing her meager belongings into the beat-up car she'd purchased with her own money and driving away with the biggest grin on her face. "Nothing but pain and bad memories for me in that place."

"Texas isn't much to look at anyway," he said, coaxing a smile out of her. "Not when you're surrounded by the majesty of Great Spirit here in Montana."

She chuckled, enjoying the pride in his voice at his native land. "It's definitely gorgeous here," she agreed, casting a curious glance his way. "Do you believe in God?"

Noah chuckled, admitting, "Probably. I mean, I don't go to church if that's what you're asking, but at the end of the day, I believe in a higher power—even if this job makes me question that belief every day."

Like everything about Noah, his answer resonated enough to send a warning down her spine. "I probably shouldn't have asked," she said, knowing she was crossing a line. "That question was too personal—"

"You can ask me anything."

His immediate permission humbled her, sucking whatever derisive quip she would've had at the ready right from her mouth. With each day, she liked him more, and that was an emotional entanglement she hadn't seen coming.

They passed a sign marking the boundary of the Blackfeet Reservation, the tribal seal proud against the weathered wood. Noah grew quieter, more contemplative. Sophia understood— this wasn't just his home, it was his heritage. The weight of that responsibility showed in the set of his shoulders.

The trailhead appeared suddenly, just a small gravel turn-out and a worn path disappearing into the trees. No signs, no markers. The kind of place you had to know to find.

"Most tourists stick to the state park trails, as they should," Noah said, pulling on a light jacket. "This one's mostly locals."

"How lucky am I that I get my own personal tour guide?" Sophia said, her smile widening. The easy camaraderie between them only made it harder to resist the urge to flirt. "I'm going to make all the girls jealous."

Noah chuckled but didn't take the bait. Instead, he motioned for her to follow with a warning, "Watch your step—the terrain can be tricky."

The trail started gently enough, winding through stands of aspen trees whose leaves whispered secrets in the morning breeze. Noah set an easy pace, not trying to prove anything. Sophia appreciated that. She was fit—FBI training saw to that—but he had the advantage of knowing this territory.

They walked in comfortable silence for a while, falling into an easy rhythm. The air was crisp, carrying the scent of pine and distant snow. Sophia's thoughts began to settle, the constant churn of the case quieting slightly.

"What do you think so far?" Noah asked as they paused for water.

Sophia guzzled from her water bottle before answering, something about the mountain air making honesty easier. "It's amazing. It's so different from where I grew up. Houston was all concrete and humidity. Here…" She gestured to the vista of mountains and valleys spreading below them. "It feels ancient. Like the land remembers things we've forgotten. Makes me feel small but in a good way."

"That's what the elders say." Noah's voice hinted at something deeper—respect, maybe, or longing. "That the mountains hold memories. Stories." He smiled slightly. "Course, they also say not to hike alone because of the skinwalkers, so take it with a grain of salt."

"Skinwalkers?"

"Shapeshifters. Bad medicine. Old stories to keep kids from wandering too far." But something in his tone suggested he wasn't entirely dismissing the legends.

Huh. Somehow, catching a glimpse of Noah's hidden superstition only made him more appealing instead of less. Normally, that would've given her the *ick*, as they called it, which would've helped smother this inconvenient crush that seemed to be forming against her will.

However, when it came to Noah, there was no ick in sight. *Damn it.*

The trail steepened, requiring more focus. Sophia found herself studying Noah as he moved, the fluid grace that came from knowing this landscape in his bones, the way he automatically offered a hand at tricky spots without making assumptions about her capabilities. It was…attractive. Dangerously so.

"Almost there," he said after another twenty minutes of climbing. "Worth the effort, I promise."

The overlook, when they reached it, stole her breath. Stone River spread below them like a miniature diorama, the morning sun turning the valley into a painting. Mountains marched away to the horizon, peaks still touched with last week's snow. The reservation lands stretched east, a patchwork of shapes that seemed to hold meaning if you knew how to read them.

"This is where you come to think?" Sophia asked, understanding now why he'd brought her here.

"Used to. After Travis died…" Noah walked to the edge, hands in his pockets. "Spent a lot of nights up here, trying to make sense of it. Watching the lights down there, knowing his killer might be somewhere in that valley."

Sophia moved to stand beside him, close enough to feel the warmth radiating from his body. "Must have been hard, carrying that weight in a town this small."

"Everything's harder in a small town. Everyone knows everyone. Their histories, their secrets." He turned to look at her, something shifting in his expression. "Makes it difficult to be objective sometimes."

"That why you left?"

"Partly." His voice roughened slightly. "Partly because I needed to prove I could be more than just John Thunderhawk's son. The guy who couldn't solve Travis's case."

The vulnerability in his admission made something twist in Sophia's chest. Without thinking, she reached out, touching his arm lightly. "You were what, twenty-five when Travis died? A rookie tribal officer with limited resources trying to solve a murder that's turning out to have layers we're still uncovering."

"Doesn't make dealing with my failure easier." But he didn't pull away from her touch.

They stood like that for a moment, the wind playing with Sophia's hair, the sun warm on their faces.

"Thank you," Sophia said finally. "For showing me this place."

Noah's smile was soft, private. "Thanks for letting me."

She should've pulled back. Should've cracked a joke or something to loosen the invisible mesh drawing them together, but wild horses couldn't have torn her away from that moment.

Noah's lips, soft and gentle, brushed across hers with a tender invitation, a silent question that she answered by opening her mouth and inviting him to taste her more deeply.

With nothing but nature all around them, Sophia sank into Noah's touch, losing herself to the safety of his presence. Nothing mattered beyond this moment.

When they finally pulled apart, Noah's dark eyes held hers, mirroring the realization that they'd crossed a line along with the certainty that neither regretted it.

"Not like a Saint Bernard," she murmured with a subtle tease as she held his gaze.

"Like I said, no complaints," he returned with the same gentle amusement in his tone. He sobered. "Are you okay?"

"Yeah," she answered, nodding. "Ready to head back?"

"Not really, but I guess we better," he said, squinting against the bright sun. "I doubt you'd enjoy hiking this trail in the dark."

The walk back down was quieter, both of them lost in thought. That kiss changed things. It was impossible to go backward after something like that, but Noah didn't seem overly pressed about the situation, so maybe she shouldn't be, either.

Except she was. She couldn't escape the feeling that she'd somehow corrupted a good man.

"You sure you're okay?" Noah asked, picking up on her silent vibration of growing anxiety. "You're real quiet and yet, somehow, very loud."

"I'm sorry," she blurted out.

"For what?"

"For kissing you. I know it was inappropriate, but I… It was the moment, I guess. Blame it on being out in nature. Birds, bees, you know, the whole primal thing."

His chuckle took her by surprise.

She glanced at him sharply. "You think this is funny?"

"A little."

Sophia narrowed her gaze. "Clarify."

"We're adults. We'll deal with it. Yeah, it's not ideal. I don't suggest we broadcast what just happened, but we're both consenting adults, and as far as I can tell, we both enjoyed it. So let's not waste energy beating ourselves up."

Solid advice. Was it really that simple? Relief bubbled up from somewhere deep inside as she smiled up at him. "Okay, then. I guess we'll just deal with it—whatever it is."

"That's the plan."

The rest of the hike was relaxed, their laughter light as they allowed themselves to enjoy an afternoon without the pressure of the case or expectations on their shoulders. It was, quite possibly, one of the best days in Sophia's most recent history.

It wasn't until they reached the parking area that reality crashed back in.

The sound of broken glass crunched under their boots. Noah's truck sat alone in the turnout, the driver's side window shattered. Glittering shards carpeted the ground like fallen stars.

Training kicked in. They approached carefully, scanning the area for movement. The brick lay on the driver's seat, heavy and brutal. Black ink stained one side, the message clear and deliberate:

YOU'RE NEXT

Noah reached for his weapon, but Sophia already knew they were alone. Whoever had done this was long gone, leaving only destruction and a distinct threat behind.

"They must've followed us," she said, frowning, her mind already processing the implications. "They waited until we were on the trail and then left us this little calling card."

Noah grunted in agreement, but his body was tight with anger.

Sophia studied the brick, the precise lettering. Not a rushed job. Someone had taken their time, wanting the message to be clear. Professional.

"Hey, there's an upside to this," she said, catching Noah's confused look. "This means we're getting close to something. Close enough that someone's worried."

That hint of wry humor was enough to loosen some of the tension radiating from Noah's frame. He drew a deep breath and released it before grabbing his cell and calling it in.

Sophia kept looking at the message, the black letters against red clay. Warnings that started with property damage usually escalated to personal violence quickly.

The sun that had seemed so warm earlier now felt harsh and exposing. She fought the urge to step closer to Noah, to seek the comfort of his presence. *Stop it.* That kind of thinking got agents killed.

Using a forensic kit he kept in the truck, Noah bagged the brick and brushed the shards of glass off the seat so they could sit without getting glass in their behinds. They both knew there was no point in dusting the truck for prints. The backlog for forensics would have some tech laughing in their faces if they bothered with the request.

"So much for a quiet Saturday," Sophia said with a sigh, mildly perturbed that the quiet intimacy of their moment had been shattered by the reality of their job.

The brick sat between them like a promise, its message clear: someone in Stone River had secrets worth killing for.

And they were getting too close to uncovering them.

Chapter 21

The shattered window turned every gust of wind into a whistle as Noah drove them back to Stone River. Glass crunched under his feet with each bump in the road, tiny reminders of how quickly peace could shatter into threat. He kept checking his mirrors, cataloging every vehicle in their vicinity, though he knew their messenger was long gone.

The brick sat between them in an evidence bag, its message threatening against the red clay. YOU'RE NEXT.

Three hours ago, he'd been looking forward to showing Sophia his favorite spot in the mountains. Now that sanctuary felt tainted, marked by someone who'd been watching, waiting for them to be vulnerable.

"You're grinding your teeth," Sophia said. She hadn't stopped scanning their surroundings since they'd found the window, but her voice was steady, professional. Like this was just another day at the office.

"Sorry." Noah rolled his shoulders, trying to release the tension cording his neck muscles. "Just trying to figure out who could have followed us up there. That trail isn't exactly on Google Maps."

"Which could mean it was someone local," Sophia said. "Someone who knows the area well enough to know how to stay hidden."

The implication hung between them. He couldn't articulate

how much he hated the idea that someone in his hometown might be the enemy. Maybe it was naive of him to believe that he knew most of the townspeople well enough to feel no one would do this, but he was struggling.

"I should have been more careful," he said finally. "That trail… It's not exactly a secret, but it's not somewhere tourists stumble onto, either. I didn't think…"

"Don't." Sophia's voice was kind but firm. "This isn't on you. If you're going to blame yourself, you'll have to blame me, too. I should have been more aware. I let my guard down."

He chuckled ruefully, realizing they were both tugging on the right to claim ownership of the situation. "Okay, how about we both treat the situation the same—someone committed an act of malicious mischief trying to scare us off the job, which we both know isn't going to happen."

"Sounds like a decent plan," she agreed, flashing him a smile that tickled his stomach as she pulled her pony tail into a severe knot, all traces of the relaxed woman from their hike erased. He missed her already, that softer version who'd melted into his arms and made him feel like he owned the world and anything was possible.

Before this moment, he'd been pressed about his attraction to Sophia. Now? He didn't care. He liked her. A lot. Denial was useless, and it used up precious energy he needed to spend on the case. When he framed it that way, it was much easier to put in its place.

"For what it's worth and despite my impending insurance claim," he said, "I'm glad we did this."

A ghost of a smile touched her lips. "Yeah. Me, too."

They passed the reservation boundary sign, its tribal seal watching their return with ancient eyes. Noah remembered his father's words about intuition, about listening to that quiet voice that whispered warnings. Was he being too cavalier about the situation with the brick? Or maybe too reckless about his attraction to Sophia? He supposed he'd just have to wait and see how it played out before he'd know.

"We need to call Amber," Sophia said, already pulling out her phone. "If someone's making threats, we're getting close to something. The prison connection, maybe. I don't like the idea of her being in the cross fire."

"The prison warden certainly has enough ties if he chose to use them in a criminal way," Noah said. "Though it feels pretty sloppy for someone as high up the chain as Hayes."

"I agree. At this point, I doubt Hayes even knows we know about the identity swap within his prison. We should keep it that way until we're ready to pull the trigger. Big fish have a way of swimming away from danger."

Noah nodded, then cursed as his truck hit a pothole, sending more glass skittering across the floorboards. The wind whistled through the broken window, carrying the scent of pine and snow from the mountains.

"Hey, I know you're staying with your mom, but given what just happened, maybe you ought to get a hotel room." Sophia's tone was light, but her eyes never stopped scanning their surroundings. "I'm concerned that you might be putting your family in danger by remaining there."

Noah quickly realized that Sophia was right. "I'll start calling around, see if there are any vacancies."

"I'm not trying to play travel agent, but my hotel has good security, interior corridors, cameras. I'm on the third floor, and there's a vacant room next door. Having you nearby would also be an added security measure for both of us. Safety in numbers, I have your back, you have mine."

Noah forced a chuckle to hide the way his thoughts skidded into unprofessional territory. "You suggesting we have a sleepover, Agent Bennett?"

"I'm suggesting we be smart about this." But there was a hint of color in her cheeks that hadn't been there before. "Unless you'd rather explain to your mother why someone's trying to kill you."

She had a point. His mother would immediately rally the entire family, turn it into a production. And Lila would never let him hear the end of it.

Still… "Won't it look suspicious? Both of us at the hotel?"

Sophia wasn't messing around, countering, "I don't care what it looks like. I care about keeping us both alive long enough to solve this case."

Noah watched a truck pass them going the other direction, automatically cataloging details—late model Ford, mud on the plates, single male driver. Nothing inherently suspicious, but everything felt threatening now.

"You're right," he said finally. "I don't like the idea of my family in danger because of this case."

"For what it's worth, I'm sorry. I know you probably didn't expect this case to become so complicated that you'd have to put distance between yourself and family."

"Risk comes with the job. My family understands that better than most. It'll be okay."

They rode in silence for a while, both lost in thought. Noah couldn't stop replaying the morning, the easy conversation on the trail, the way Sophia's eyes had lit up at the view, how natural it had felt showing her pieces of his world. Their kiss. Now all of it felt tainted by the threat left in his truck.

His phone buzzed. Amber.

"Put her on speaker," Sophia said.

Amber's voice filled the cab, tense and focused. "One of my sources says there's chatter about a big shipment coming through next week. Drugs, maybe people, too. Whatever you stirred up, it's got people nervous."

"Any idea about the route?" Noah asked, but he already knew the answer.

"Nothing solid. But Noah…" Amber hesitated. "Be careful. Both of you. These people… They don't play nice."

"Yeah, same advice to you, too. Watch your back," Noah said.

After they hung up, the silence felt heavier. Noah guided the truck through Stone River's quiet streets, past the diner where they'd had breakfast just days ago, past the tribal police station where he'd started his career. Everything looked different now, touched by shadow.

Jay Long was already hurrying toward them as they pulled into the station parking lot, his young face pinched with concern. "Noah, hey, got a minute?" Jay glanced uncertainly at Sophia before adding, "It's about Michael."

Noah's stomach dropped. Nothing good ever followed those words. "What happened?"

"He's in holding. Pretty messed up on something, possibly a hallucinogen. He was causing a scene at the mini-mart. We've got an ambulance coming to transport him to urgent care for evaluation." Jay shifted uncomfortably. "Thought you'd want to know before they take him."

Through the station's front windows, Noah could hear the muffled sound of someone shouting. Michael. His chest tightened with familiar guilt and worry.

"Go," Sophia said quietly. "I'll start the paperwork on the vandalism. Take whatever time you need."

Noah nodded gratefully and followed Jay inside.

The holding area was at the back of the station, a small space with two cells that smelled of disinfectant and the faint sour tinge of human despair. Michael's voice echoed off the walls, a stream of paranoid ranting that made Noah's heart ache.

But nothing prepared him for actually seeing his cousin in this state. Michael's ragged shirt hung from his rail-thin frame, his skin waxy and yellow, dark circles like bruises under his eyes. When he spotted Noah, he lunged for the bars, gripping them so tight his knuckles went white.

"Noah! Noah, you gotta listen to me!" Michael's eyes were wild, pupils blown wide from whatever he'd put into his body. "You gotta get out of Stone River, man. I'm sorry about before, being a dick, but you gotta leave before—before—" He broke off, glancing frantically around the cell. "It's not safe. Not safe anywhere. Gotta run, man!"

"Michael, hey, calm down." Noah approached carefully, using the same tone he'd used when Michael was a kid having nightmares. "The paramedics are coming to help you—"

"No! You're not listening!" Michael slammed his palm against the bars. "They have eyes everywhere, ears everywhere. You don't know what you're messing with. The less you know the better, so please—" His voice cracked. "Please just go before they kill you, too."

Noah studied his cousin's face, trying to separate drug-induced paranoia from genuine fear. "Who's watching, Michael? Who are you afraid of?"

But Michael just shook his head violently, backing away from the bars. "Can't say. Can't say, or they'll know. They always know." He pressed into the corner of the cell, wrapping his arms around himself. "Should've listened to Travis. Should've helped him. My fault, all my fault."

"What about Travis?" Noah asked, but Michael was already retreating into himself, muttering too quietly to hear.

The ambulance sirens wailed in the distance, getting closer.

Jay appeared at Noah's elbow. "Paramedics are just about here."

Noah nodded, his throat tight. "Take care of him, yeah?"

"Course." Jay's expression was sympathetic. "You want me to call your aunt?"

"No, I'll do it." It was the least Noah could do, even though the conversation would tear him up inside.

Michael's voice cracked as Noah turned to leave. "Noah! We were just kids, man. How were we supposed to know how bad it could get? Not our fault, man. Not our fault."

Noah froze. "What do you mean, Michael? What wasn't your fault?"

But Michael was gone, sliding down the wall to crouch in the corner, muttering unintelligible gibberish.

"Paramedics are here," Jay said quietly.

Noah nodded, his throat tight. Even through the drug-induced paranoia, Michael's words hit too close to their investigation for comfort. Had Michael and Travis stumbled on something fifteen years ago? And if that was the case, why had someone let Michael live and not Travis?

Maybe because unlike Michael, Travis's silence couldn't be bought.

But whatever secret Michael was carrying had to be the darkness that fed his addiction. Noah had to catch Michael sober, get him someplace safe and get him to share that secret before it killed him.

Noah stepped out of the way so the paramedics could take him to urgent care.

Watching Michael deteriorate like that hit him in the solar plexus. It was like watching one of his little brothers slowly cut themselves apart with a knife and being unable to wrench the weapon from their hands.

When Noah returned to the front office, Sophia was filling out paperwork, her expression carefully neutral. But he could see the questions in her eyes.

"You okay?" she asked.

"No." He dropped into the chair beside her desk. "But that's not exactly new when it comes to Michael."

"How bad?"

"Pretty bad. He's paranoid and not making much sense, but I can't shake this feeling that Michael might be hiding something that we need to know. The problem is it's buried beneath the drug addiction."

Sophia set down her pen. "I know the drugs are a factor, but sometimes paranoid people are paranoid because they really do have something to be afraid of."

Noah rubbed his face, suddenly exhausted. The adrenaline from finding the brick was wearing off, leaving him drained. "Yeah. That's what worries me."

They worked in companionable silence for a while, making quick work of filing the report and entering the brick into evidence. But Noah couldn't shake the feeling that his cousin was drowning in plain sight.

By the time they were finished and Noah was driving back to his mother's place to gather his things, he was certain whatever was happening in Stone River had roots that went far deeper than he ever imagined.

Chapter 22

Sophia sat cross-legged on the hotel bed, case files spread around her like tarot cards waiting to reveal their secrets. The scratching of her pen against paper felt loud in the quiet room as she tried to organize her thoughts.

Her phone buzzed, startling her from her concentration. A knock at the door followed immediately after. Her hand moved automatically to her weapon as she approached.

Another buzz: Don't shoot, it's just me. Brought sustenance.

Sophia smiled despite herself, checking through the peephole to confirm it was Noah before opening the door.

He stood there with a pizza box balanced on one hand and a six-pack of beer in the other, looking more relaxed in jeans and a faded Blackfeet Nation T-shirt than she'd seen him all week.

"I come bearing gifts," he said, lifting the pizza slightly. "Figured we could both use some comfort food right now."

Something warm unfurled in her chest at his quiet compassion. She stepped back to let him in, ignoring the flutter in her stomach that had nothing to do with physical hunger. The lines weren't so clear anymore. She felt as if she were falling down a rabbit hole, uncertain where she was about to land. "As long as there isn't any pineapple on that pizza."

"Please. I have better taste than that." He set everything

down on the small table by the window. "Though I can't vouch for the quality. Options are limited at 9:00 p.m. in Stone River."

"Beats protein bars and cold coffee." Sophia cleared her notes off the bed, hyperaware of Noah's presence in the small room. It felt different than sharing space during the investigation, more intimate somehow.

Noah cracked open two beers, handing her one before settling into the room's single chair. "So, what were you working on? Besides wearing a hole in that legal pad with your pen."

"Just trying to organize my thoughts, similar to our whiteboard back at the station." She sat on the edge of the bed, taking a long drink of beer. "Sometimes writing everything out helps me see connections I missed before." She gestured to the notepad. "I'm a little old-school when I need to think. There's something about the process of writing in longhand that helps pull my thoughts into some semblance of order."

"Share with the class?" He grabbed a slice of pizza, somehow making the casual gesture look masculine and attractive.

"Sure," Sophia said, handing him her legal pad. "I've been trying to organize everything we know for certain versus what we're speculating."

Noah took a bite of pizza as he studied her notes. "Travis's posed body bothers me," he said, tapping that line with his finger. "That's not something we focused on originally, but killers don't typically take time to pose victims unless there's a message or a personal connection."

"Exactly. And now we have another posed victim with a seemingly out-of-place message written on her." Sophia tucked one leg under her. "What are the odds of two unrelated killers taking time to position their victims in Stone River fifteen years apart?"

"Not great." Noah frowned at her notes. "Another thing that feels weirdly deliberate is Logan's original statement. He included all these specific details about what everyone was wearing, exact times, even the weather. Most witnesses can barely remember what they had for breakfast, let alone that kind of detail from days earlier."

"Especially if they were supposedly high at the time." Sophia leaned forward, warming to the discussion. "You interrogate enough people, you start to recognize when someone's testimony feels rehearsed."

"Like they were coached on exactly what to say." Noah met her eyes, and she could see he'd been thinking the same thing. "Question is, who was doing the coaching?"

"And why complicate it with a lie about drug-induced memory loss now?" Sophia grabbed a slice of pizza. "Unless whatever he's hiding is worse than admitting to lying in a police statement."

"What gets me is Michael's reaction today." Noah's voice softened with concern. "I've seen him strung out before, but this was different. He was terrified."

Sophia hesitated before asking, "Was Michael ever a resident at Clear Skies?"

Noah paused to remember, narrowing his gaze as he sifted through his memory. "Maybe? Briefly? I know my aunt was having issues with Michael around that time, but I thought it was typical teenager stuff, you know, back-talking and being a know-it-all shithead. Honestly, I wasn't really paying much attention to what my little cousin was doing. I was wrapped up in my own stuff at the time."

"Is it possible Logan and Michael were both at Clear Skies at the time when Travis was killed?"

"It's possible. I could probably ask my aunt if she remembers," Noah said. "But what I do know is that something bad enough happened that Michael turned to drugs to cope."

"What was Michael like before the drugs?"

Noah chuckled, shaking his head. "Like a bratty little brother that was always underfoot, trying to hang out with the big kids. Probably had ADHD, but I don't know if he was ever diagnosed. I remember him not liking school all that much, but he was always quick to laugh. I think that's what stands out the most in my memories of him. The man he is now? I don't think he's had much to laugh about in a long time."

"Drugs ruin people," Sophia agreed sadly. "Has Michael ever wanted to get sober?"

"Well, my aunt pinned her hope on this expensive rehab awhile ago, emptied out her savings to send him there, but it didn't stick. Michael was back to his old ways within a month. After that, my aunt stopped trying to help him kick the habit and just accepted that Michael was never going to quit."

"Empathy burn-out," Sophia said. "Addiction will gut everyone in its path, from the addict to the support system."

Noah nodded, exhaling. "Still, you hope for the best when it's someone you love."

"It's all you can do." She paused a minute before asking, "Do you think it might've been Michael who threw the brick, trying to get you to leave town?"

"I want to say no, but I can't assume anything at this point."

The easy rhythm of their back-and-forth felt as natural as breathing, which was a new experience for her.

"We're getting close to something." Sophia tucked a strand of hair behind her ear. "If it wasn't Michael trying to protect you in his own weird way, it means we're close enough to a hidden truth that someone's willing to escalate from hiding in shadows to direct threats."

"Good thing I don't scare easy." Noah's smile was warm enough to chase away the chill of the threat. "How about you, Agent Bennett? Ready to cut and run?"

"Not a chance." She returned his smile, savoring how comfortable this felt, sharing pizza and theories in her hotel room. "Though, I definitely need a fresh beer."

Noah reached for the six-pack without hesitation. "I think that can be arranged."

Sophia took a moment to crack her beer open. "Let me tell you what really bothers me about Clear Skies," she said finally. "It's how perfectly crafted everything seems. Like a mask that's too carefully maintained. I know I mentioned it before, but it's the thing that keeps coming back to me. Nothing is perfect, not when you're dealing with broken kids. They find trouble, they *make* trouble, and that can be as simple as graffiti and as dangerous as violence. There was nothing of the sort happening at Clear Skies, so far as I could tell. It was quiet, contained and, honestly, kinda creepy."

"So you're saying the absence of those things doesn't speak to Claire's management style but rather something darker?"

She took another drink, weighing how much to share. "When I was thirteen, I landed in a group home in Houston. The kind of place that looked great on paper. Director was this friendly guy, always talking about helping troubled kids find their path." Her voice turned bitter. "What the paperwork didn't show was how he liked to check on the girls at night when his wife was sleeping. How he'd sit too close, let his hands linger too long."

Noah's expression darkened. "Did he…"

"No. I learned early how to keep my distance, stay out of reach. But some of the other girls weren't so lucky." She shrugged, aiming for casual despite the old anger burning in her chest. "That's the thing about predators. They're good at hiding in plain sight, wrapping themselves in respectability."

"And you think Claire Redstone might be doing the same thing?"

"I don't know. Maybe I'm letting old trauma cloud my judgment. But something about that place feels wrong, Noah. The way those kids watch her, how tightly she controls everything. Logan's devotion goes beyond gratitude into something almost religious, and that freaks me out."

Noah was quiet for a moment, considering. "Then we dig deeper," he said finally. "Pull every record, interview every kid who's passed through those doors in the last fifteen years. If Clear Skies is clean, the evidence will show that. And if it's not..." He met her eyes steadily. "We take them down. Together."

The simple acceptance in his voice, the lack of dismissal or doubt, made something tight in Sophia's chest loosen slightly. She wasn't used to people taking her concerns seriously without demanding ironclad proof first. "Thank you," she said quietly.

"For what? Mediocre pizza and warm beer?"

"For listening. For not telling me I'm being paranoid or letting my past affect my judgment."

"Hey." Noah leaned forward, his expression serious. "Your past is what makes you good at this job. Those instincts you developed? They've kept you alive. Kept other people alive, too."

Sophia studied his face in the dim hotel lighting, noting the quiet strength there, the genuine kindness that somehow hadn't been worn away by years of seeing humanity at its worst. He was nothing like the men she usually encountered in law enforcement, with their hard edges and stunted emotional intelligence.

The pizza box lay empty between them, a comfortable silence settling in the room. Sophia was acutely aware of how Noah's presence filled the small space, not just physically but in a way that made her both unsettled and strangely at peace. She couldn't remember the last time she'd let someone see the real her, trusted someone enough to share confidences with them.

When Noah reached out to brush a strand of hair from her face, her breath caught. His touch was gentle, almost reverent, rough fingers surprisingly tender against her skin. A question lived in that touch, one that made her heart thunder against her ribs.

"We should probably get some rest," she said softly, but her body betrayed her words, leaning almost imperceptibly into his hand. "Long day tomorrow."

"Probably," Noah agreed, but his eyes held hers, dark and intent. Something electric crackled in the space between them, a current she'd been fighting since that first day.

The kiss, when it finally came, was the continuation of a conversation they'd started on their hike. They fell into a rhythm like two lovers who'd spent a lifetime mapping each other's bodies and knew every hill and valley.

Noah's lips met hers with the same careful consideration he brought to everything, as if he understood the magnitude of her letting him this close. No demands, no expectations, just the quiet exploration of two people who had been orbiting each other, drawing closer despite every professional boundary and personal wall.

Sophia felt something deep inside her shift, like tumblers in a lock finally aligning. A door she kept triple-bolted began to open, revealing possibilities she usually refused to acknowledge. Her hands found his shoulders, solid and real beneath her fingers. He tasted of beer and promise, of safety and danger all at once.

For the first time in her life, the warning voices in her head—the ones that whispered about keeping her distance, protecting herself, never letting anyone close enough to matter—fell quiet. The warmth of Noah's kiss drowned out everything except the thundering of her heart and the realization that she was tired of being alone.

For once, she didn't try to slam the door shut again. Instead, she let herself sink into the kiss, into the possibility that sometimes walls were meant to come down, that not every open door led to pain.

Even if tomorrow brought regret, tonight she would let herself have this moment of connection, this taste of what it meant to trust someone enough to be vulnerable.

For tonight, that was enough.

Chapter 23

Noah's hotel room felt smaller in the predawn hours, the walls pressing in with memories of last night's kiss. He stood at the window, watching frost creep across the glass while Stone River slept below, peaceful in its ignorance of the darkness they were uncovering. His coffee had gone cold, forgotten on the desk beside stacks of case files he couldn't focus on.

He had a feeling in his gut he couldn't shake—a looming sense of dread that seemed to shadow his every thought and kept him from catching a decent night of sleep. Worry over Michael, the overwhelming reach of this case, and the inability to trust the town he'd known his entire life were all weighing on him.

His phone buzzed—Amber—and he was almost relieved to have the distraction.

"Do you sleep?" he asked by way of greeting. "It's zero-dark-thirty."

"Need I point out, you're awake, too?" she returned without missing a beat. "Why are you awake so early?"

"Couldn't sleep, got tired of staring at the ceiling. You got something?"

"I've got something so good it's going to win me a Pulitzer. I've got a paper trail that's going to make your head spin." Amber's voice crackled with the energy he recognized from their dating days—the sound of someone who'd just broken a major story. "Remember that trucking company I mentioned? River Rock Transport?"

"Yeah, the one with routes through Montana, Idaho and Wyoming."

"It's owned by Mountain West Holdings, which then branches into three development companies—Mountain West Youth Services, Big Sky Educational Trust, and Frontier Development Group. All three have been making substantial donations to tribal youth programs across the tri-state area."

In an instant, the fatigue was gone, and his mind was sharp. Noah grabbed his notebook and a worn-down pencil. "How much are we talking?"

"Combined annual donations of around $750,000 per service region. Clear Skies is listed as one of several recipients under the Stone River allocation, but here's where it gets weird—when I tried to trace exactly how much money went where, the records get murky. It's like someone deliberately obscured the paper trail."

Noah tapped the pencil against the pad, speculating, "Could just be sloppy bookkeeping."

"Maybe. But one of your tribal council members, Vincent Marshall, sits on Mountain West Holdings's board of directors. He's also been pushing for increased tribal funding to youth programs through official channels. Why run money through private companies when there's already a legitimate funding stream?"

He knew Vincent through his mom's work at the tribal center. As far as he knew, Vincent was a solid guy. Noah wrote rapidly, documenting every detail in shorthand notes for himself. "Send me everything you've got—corporate filings, the whole trail."

"Even the stuff I obtained without a proper paper trail?" Amber asked.

"Yeah, send it all. We'll deal with the legality, later."

"Good, because I already did. Check your email." Amber paused. "Oh and there's something else. The timing of these private donation programs? They started the same month Travis died."

A knock at his door made Noah turn. He checked his watch. Damn, did none of the women in his life need sleep? He rose and quickly opened the door, motioning for Sophia to come in.

Her expression remained professional without showing even the smallest indication that last night's kiss weighed on her mind. Luckily, he didn't have time to marinate on that detail, either.

"You're on speaker. Sophia's here," he told Amber. "Put everything in a secure file and—"

"Way ahead of you. Already encrypted, password is the name of that bar in Billings where you proposed. You remember?"

"Yeah." He ignored Sophia's raised eyebrow. "Thanks, Amber. Be careful out there."

"You, too. And Noah? Dig deep into those financial records. The money always leads somewhere."

After hanging up, Noah quickly filled Sophia in on Amber's findings.

She listened intently, making notes, her investigator's mind already working the angles. "Financial records can be telling," she said finally. "But they can also be misleading. We need to verify where that money actually went. How'd she get this information?"

"You know she won't say, but if we can verify her numbers through legal channels, we might have the paper trail that'll lead us exactly to where these assholes are hiding."

"I like the thought of that," Sophia said, grinning.

Powered by the hotel's brown sludge masquerading as coffee, they spent the morning digging through Amber's files. But just as Amber warned, the more they looked, the less clear things became. The initial transfers seemed innocuous, allowing them to follow the money through a maze of legitimate-looking disbursements—facility improvements, staff training programs and educational initiatives—but the amounts themselves were highly irregular.

"Look at this," Noah said, frowning at his laptop screen. "The donations Amber flagged? They're part of a larger tribal development initiative. Clear Skies is just one of a dozen programs receiving funds. Look what other facility is listed." He tapped at a name on the screen. "Bright Horizons in Missoula."

"The same facility where Laramie Baker was last seen," Sophia murmured. "The most convenient way to hide illegal payments is to bury them in legitimate ones. On the surface, it wouldn't be unusual to receive disbursements for similar programs, but something tells me we need to dig deeper on this angle." She paused with a subtle frown. "Unless we're seeing conspiracy where there's just bureaucracy."

Noah rubbed his eyes, frustration building. Without concrete proof of wrongdoing, they had nothing but suspicion and coincidence, which wasn't enough.

"We need to talk to Claire," Sophia said finally. "Get her explanation for these transactions before we go too far down this rabbit hole."

"Yeah." Noah stared at the financial records, wondering if they were chasing shadows while the real threat operated elsewhere. "Michael's paranoia might be leading us astray."

"Speaking of Michael—any update?"

"Haven't heard anything since they took him to the hospital. Might be a good sign." But even as Noah said it, something cold settled in his gut. A premonition he couldn't shake.

They worked through the afternoon, ordering takeout from

the Red Feather as they tried to untangle the web of financial connections. But every promising lead seemed to dis-
solve under scrutiny, leaving them with more questions than
answers.

Before calling it a night, Sophia ducked out around five
with things to do, but Noah didn't want to stop. Before he
realized it, the dinner hour had come and gone, and he was
forced to munch on a package of stale peanuts he had found
in his travel bag to stop his stomach from growling.

Around nine o'clock, he decided to call it quits, but his cell
rang as he was gathering his papers together. Expecting to see
Sophia's number, he was surprised to see his aunt Twylla's
number instead.

"Noah?" His aunt's voice was raw, broken in a way he'd
never heard. "Michael... Oh god, Noah, he's gone. Michael's
g-gone."

Noah's lungs seized as he processed what his aunt was
saying. "What happened?" he asked, his voice strangled. "I
thought he was still in the hospital."

"He was," Twylla confirmed with a watery wail. "They're
saying his heart just stopped. But he was fine, he was getting
better... I was planning to see him tomorrow. I don't understand how this happened. Why didn't the doctors help him?"

The words washed over him like ice water as Twylla dis-
solved into sobs. Noah gripped the phone so tight he heard
the plastic casing protest, forcing himself to breathe through
the crushing weight in his chest.

"I don't know, Auntie, but I'll find out," he promised her.
A sudden cardiac arrest. Clean, simple and impossible to dis-
prove. Was it just like Michael had warned? They always
knew. They were always watching. Or maybe it truly was the
drugs. The human body could only take so much abuse before it collapsed. Lord only knew what kind of pharmaceuti-

cal horror show Michael had put his body through over the years. "Did you call Mom already?"

"I called her first," Twylla answered with a sniffed apology. "She told me I ought to call you right away because you might be able to get answers faster than any of us. I hope it's okay for me to ask."

"Of course, Auntie. I have my own questions, too. I know it's hard, but try to get some rest. Can Lynette come home to help with the arrangements?"

"Yes, she'll come. She's a good girl," Twylla said. If heartbreak had a sound, it was the grief in his aunt's voice. "Thank you, Noah. You were always so good to my boy. I wish he'd followed in your footsteps instead of getting mixed up with that group of his. Maybe things would've been different."

Noah swallowed the lump in his throat that tasted a lot like guilt for not being more attentive, more invested in making sure that Michael flew straight. Tears stung his eyes. "I'll check in with you tomorrow, okay? Get some rest. You'll need your strength."

Twylla clicked off, and Noah just stared at the phone in his hands for a long moment. Michael was dead. That poor, misguided, broken kid was finally at peace, but what about the people he left behind? Would his aunt be okay? She was such a sweet old lady; she deserved better than what life had put on her plate.

Thank God his cousin Lynette was a solid person.

Snow began to fall outside his window, each flake drifting to the ground with the cool indifference only Mother Nature could perfect. His dad used to remind him that they were nothing but ants in relation to Great Spirit, scurrying around thinking whatever they were doing was important to the world around them.

Michael's last words echoed in his mind: *You don't know*

what you're messing with... Please just go before they kill you, too.

Now, Michael would never be able to tell them what had him so spooked. Never explain what secrets someone felt were worth killing to protect.

The snow fell harder, burying Stone River beneath a blanket of pristine white, while somewhere in the darkness, monsters counted their money and planned their next move. Noah watched the snow, his reflection ghostlike in the window, and made a silent vow to his cousin. This time, he wouldn't fail. This time, the truth wouldn't stay buried.

He spun on his heel and went next door, his hand shaking slightly as he knocked.

The hallway felt too bright, too sterile, the fluorescent lights harsh against his raw nerves. Even in plain, comfortable clothes, he felt like something was banding his rib cage, squeezing the air from his lungs.

When Sophia opened the door, her expression shifted immediately from professional courtesy to concern as soon as she caught sight of his face. "What's wrong?"

"Can I come in?"

Sophia simply moved aside, and he brushed past her into the room, needing to move, to do something with the energy crackling under his skin. Best to rip the bandage. "Michael's dead." The words came out flat, hollow. "They're saying his heart stopped. Just like that. Cardiac arrest."

Sophia closed the door quietly, giving him space while staying close. "Noah, I'm so sorry."

"And maybe the cause of death is legit, but it feels awfully damn convenient that the minute Michael starts acting like a loose end, he gets snipped." He ran a hand through his hair, pacing the small space between bed and window. "In his own way, he was trying to warn us. He was scared of someone he thought could reach him, and he might've been right to be afraid. Damn it! I should've paid better attention instead of just writing him off as a paranoid drug addict."

"We need to be careful about jumping to conclusions," Sophia said, her voice gentle but decisive. "Drug use, especially meth, puts tremendous strain on the heart. Given his condition when they brought him in—"

"No." Noah turned to face her. "I can't ignore my gut on this. You didn't know him before—before the drugs, before Travis died. He was just a kid who got caught up in something too big for him to handle. And now…" His voice cracked slightly. "I should have protected him. Should have seen what was happening fifteen years ago."

Sophia stepped closer, close enough to touch him but maintaining that crucial professional distance. "This isn't your fault."

Logic told him Sophia was right, but logic wasn't in charge just then. He couldn't shake the guilt that he'd failed his young cousin, ignoring his cries for help because it was inconvenient to deal with an addict. "Goddamn it. I was so focused on Lionel Redhorse's crew, so sure I knew what happened to Travis that I completely ignored Michael's connection to all of it."

"We've all had cases where we missed a detail. You're only human, Noah," Sophia said with a concerned frown, but she followed with practical advice. "Don't beat yourself up over the past. It's counterproductive, and we still have a case to solve. I need you fully present, okay?"

Noah drew a deep breath. Of course, Sophia was spot-on. He didn't have the luxury of falling apart and drowning in guilt, but throttling that locomotive down? Damn near impossible. He pressed his forehead against the cold window glass, watching snow gather outside the ledge. "He tried to tell me yesterday, tried to warn me, and I couldn't understand through the paranoia. Now he's gone, and I'll never know what he was trying to say."

"Noah." Sophia's voice held a quiet authority that made him turn. "Listen to me. If Michael was murdered—and that's still an if until we have evidence—then the people responsible will have made mistakes. They had to move quickly, which means they left traces. We'll find them."

Sophia's quiet assurance calmed the storm raging inside him long enough for him to pull himself back together. Even though the rage still simmered, it wasn't sloshing over the sides anymore. "I can't shake the feeling that whoever's responsible is laughing at us, watching us fumble and chase dead ends. It makes me want to punch something."

"Everyone makes mistakes—we'll find who's responsible, and when we do, we'll build a case they can't wiggle out of. They might be feeling smug right now, but the clock is ticking on their ass. I can promise you that." She stepped closer, and this time she did touch him, her hand warm on his arm. "But you have to stay focused. Channel that anger into the investigation. Don't let it make you sloppy. I know it's asking a lot, but I need the agent I met on day one. The guy with a solid head on his shoulders and a dedication to the job, no matter what—even if it meant working with another agent that he didn't want to."

Noah looked down at her hand on his arm, that percolating anger starting to cool beneath her touch. Charging in half-cocked would only get more people killed. But God, it hurt to be rational when all he wanted was to burn the whole corrupt system to the ground. "That guy didn't realize how lucky he was to have Sophia Bennett working with him," he said, meeting her gaze.

Suddenly, the intimacy of last night's kiss returned, wrapping them in a warm cocoon of safety and appreciation. He pulled her gently to him, needing to feel her lips on his. She went willingly.

He didn't care about the rules right now. He needed to feel something good, something to blot out the pain and guilt cocktail mucking up his head.

Maybe he was making a huge mistake, but when Sophia wrapped her arms around his neck and hopped into his arms, he knew there was no stopping what they both wanted.

They'd deal with the consequences later.

Chapter 24

The room held that peculiar silence that comes with falling snow, a hushed intimacy that made the world beyond their door feel distant and unreal. Sophia was acutely aware of every sensation—the scratch of hotel sheets against her bare skin, the play of shadows across Noah's face, the thundering of her heart against her ribs. His hands moved over her body with careful reverence, each touch igniting nerve endings she'd forgotten she possessed.

The familiar scent of his skin—pine and brisk air, coffee and something uniquely Noah—filled her lungs as she breathed him in. How often had she caught that scent across a desk or in his truck and had to force herself not to lean closer? Now she could press her face into the curve of his neck, tasting salt and desire on her tongue.

Noah's weight settled over her, a delicious pressure that made her feel protected and desperately wanted. His hands smoothed down her sides, learning her body's language while his mouth traced a burning path down her throat. Each touch felt deliberate and purposeful like he was memorizing her responses for future reference.

Sophia had always kept tight control during intimate moments, maintaining that last crucial boundary between pleasure and true vulnerability. But something about Noah made her want to surrender that control, to let herself fall, knowing he would catch her. Maybe it was how well they worked together, that innate understanding that had developed between them. Or maybe it was simply that he saw her—really saw her—and wasn't afraid of what he found.

When his fingers found a sensitive spot that made her gasp, his smile held a flash of male satisfaction. "Want me to stop?"

The last man who'd seen her naked was an FBI tactical instructor two years ago, a brief fling that had fizzled precisely because he couldn't understand why she checked her phone during intimate moments or canceled dates for case developments. But Noah… Noah would understand the weight of responsibility she carried. He lived with those same demands, that same driving need for justice.

Instead of answering, she pulled him down for a kiss that held nothing back.

His response was immediate and hungry, deepening the kiss until she felt it in her bones. This wasn't the careful exploration of their first kiss; this was need and heat, and it was the release of tensions they'd both been carrying.

When his mouth found her breast, she arched into the contact with a gasp that surprised them both. His answering groan vibrated against her skin, sending shivers of pleasure racing along her nerves. She let her hands explore him in turn, tracing old scars and learning the map of his body. Each mark told a story—bullet grazes, knife wounds, the physical cost of their chosen profession written in silver lines across bronze skin.

"You're beautiful," he murmured against her collarbone, and for once, the words didn't make her want to retreat. In the dim light, with snow falling silent beyond their window, she could believe them.

Noah's first gentle slide into her body took her breath away, not just from the physical pleasure, but from the emotional impact of letting someone this close. Noah held still above her, his control evident in the way his muscles trembled while he waited for her to adjust. When she shifted her hips in silent permission, his slow withdrawal and deeper thrust made her dig her nails into his shoulders.

They found their rhythm naturally, the same intuitive synchronization they'd developed working together, translating to this most intimate dance. Each roll of his hips built the pressure higher, pleasure coiling tight in her core. She couldn't stop the small sounds escaping her throat, couldn't maintain her usual silent control.

"Let go," Noah whispered, his voice rough with exertion and need. "I've got you, Sophia. Let go."

The use of her first name, so intimate in this context, broke something loose inside her. She felt herself spiraling higher, pleasure building to almost unbearable levels. Noah's movements grew more urgent, his breathing harsh against her neck as he drove them both toward release.

When it finally crashed over her, the intensity took her by surprise. She cried out, her body arching as waves of pleasure washed through her, taking her careful control with them. Noah followed moments later, her name a broken prayer on his lips as he shuddered above her.

As their breathing slowly steadied in the quiet aftermath, Sophia waited for the usual urge to make any plausible excuse to escape. But it didn't come. Instead, she traced patterns on Noah's chest as he held her, neither quite ready to break this fragile peace.

The snow continued falling outside, coating Stone River in pristine white that would hide all manner of sins. But here, in this room, there was only truth between them, raw and real and terrifying in its intensity.

"I don't usually…" she started, then stopped, unsure how to explain.

"I know," Noah said simply, kissing her forehead. "Me, neither."

That simple acknowledgment, the understanding in his voice, made something in her chest ache. She knew this couldn't last; tomorrow would bring complications, consequences and the return of the weight of their professional responsibilities.

But for now, she let herself sink into his warmth, into the safety of being truly known and accepted.

Rain began tapping against the window, mixing with the snow in that peculiar way Montana weather had of keeping you guessing. The sound created a cocoon of privacy around them, making this generic hotel room feel like the only real place in the world.

"This job doesn't leave much room for relationships," she said, surprising herself with the admission. "My last attempt was with another agent, a tactical instructor. It seemed perfect on paper. He understood the demands of the job and the crazy hours. Until he didn't."

Noah's fingers continued their gentle exploration of her spine, encouraging without pushing. "What happened?"

"We were supposed to have dinner at this fancy Italian place he'd been talking about for weeks. I got a call about a trafficking victim willing to testify. Fourteen-year-old girl, terrified her pimp would find her before morning." Sophia closed her eyes, remembering. "I called to cancel, and Mark just…lost it. Said I was using work to avoid real intimacy. Maybe he was right."

Noah's hand stilled on her back. "What happened with the girl?"

"She testified. Three traffickers went to prison. More than worth missing pasta primavera."

His quiet chuckle rumbled against her cheek. "Before Mark?"

"A few attempts at relationships. Nothing stuck." Sophia drew a breath, voicing something she'd never admitted aloud. "I think I scared them. Not the job exactly, but...the intensity. The way I can't let go of cases, can't stop until justice is served. They wanted me to be softer somehow. More...normal."

"Normal's overrated." Noah's voice held no judgment, only understanding. "My marriage to the job killed things with Amber before they really started. She wanted stories. I wanted to protect my cases. Neither of us were wrong, we just...wanted different things."

"Who ended it? You or Amber?"

"It was mutual. We just kinda knew it was over. The breakup was pretty civil and boring by today's standards. Every now and again, she'd call me for help on something she was writing about, but until this case, I hadn't talked to her in years."

"Do you...miss her?"

Noah thought for a minute as if weighing his answer, finally saying decisively, "No." Then he clarified, "Amber is an amazing woman—smart, talented, tenacious and driven—but we didn't mesh well as romantic partners. Before we tried getting involved, we were great friends. We should've just kept our relationship at that level. My younger sister, Lila, still adores her. I think they're still on a group chat together, sending each other memes and shit like that."

Sophia chuckled, feeling a lot less *something* about his connection with Amber, which was good because she was really starting to like the woman. "With Mark, I kept waiting for that moment when he'd ask me to choose between the job and him. Figured it was probably best to cut my losses before things reached that point."

"Did you miss him after you cut him loose?"

Sophia's answer was quick, and a shudder of distaste followed. "Not even a little. I think my attraction to him was solely based on needing an itch scratched, and he was convenient. To be honest, he was kind of a jerk, and his personality sucked."

"Should I even ask what I am?" Noah asked with a tinge of self-deprecating humor.

She knew he was making light of the fact they'd ignored the rules and ended up in bed together, but she didn't want him to ever think that he was just a convenient lay.

Sitting up, she leaned forward to brush her lips across his. "You are so much more than anything I ever could've anticipated, Noah Thunderhawk. You are the opposite of a convenience—you are a complication that I smugly thought I'd never have to experience. But I regret nothing. Do you hear me? Nothing."

Noah responded by deepening the kiss and rolling her beneath him. The solid strength of his body pressing against her made her feel soft and feminine, protected and cherished.

"Me, either," he murmured as he nuzzled her neck, his lips pressing a trail of kisses to her collarbone, creating shivers of delight cascading down her body. "The question is…how am I going to pretend I haven't tasted your skin and memorized the sound of your moans when we leave this room?"

"That's a problem for a different day," Sophia answered, reaching between them to grasp his quickly hardening shaft. "For now, this is just about us. Are you okay with that?"

"Copy that, Agent Bennett," he said as he thickened against her palm with a guttural moan that immediately chased away any thought beyond the present moment.

The second time was slow and deliberate, with generous pauses filled with sensual kisses that left little room for thought or second-guessing.

Sophia had never in her life believed in the fairy tale of soulmates, but being with Noah challenged what she'd thought she knew, causing her to question what it meant to truly belong with someone.

The quiet intimacy of sharing his breath, of feeling his heart thundering against hers, created a cocoon of safety she'd never experienced before. Each touch felt like a revelation, each kiss a confession neither could voice aloud. This wasn't just sex— this was something far more dangerous.

Noah's hands traced paths across her skin that felt like promises, and for once, she didn't fear what those promises might mean. In the darkness of a Montana winter night, with snow falling silent beyond their window, she could admit— if only to herself—that she'd been waiting her whole life to feel this complete.

When pleasure finally overtook them again, it wasn't just physical release that washed through her body. It was acceptance, understanding, the recognition that some walls were meant to come down. Noah held her through the aftershocks, his breathing ragged against her neck, and she knew with bone-deep certainty that nothing would ever be the same between them.

Later, as the night deepened, and the storm gentled outside, Sophia lay awake listening to Noah's steady breathing. Tomorrow would bring reality crashing back—a dead cousin, a trafficking ring, professional boundaries they'd gleefully ignored. But for now, she let herself sink into this moment, memorizing the weight of his arm around her waist, the warmth of his body curved protectively around hers.

She'd spent her life building barriers to protect herself, learning the hard way that vulnerability was just another word for target. But here, in the quiet dark with Noah's heartbeat strong against her back, she realized some risks were worth taking. Some people were worth trusting. Some connections transcended all the careful rules she'd made for herself.

And that terrified her.

Because Sophia knew herself too well—she knew how she'd start pulling away the moment her demons whispered their familiar warnings. How she'd find reasons to establish distance, to rebuild those protective walls brick by careful brick. The better something felt, the harder she worked to destroy it before it could destroy her. It was a pattern written into her DNA by years of foster care and failed relationships.

Noah deserved better than her inevitable retreat. He deserved someone whole, someone who didn't view emotional intimacy as a threat to be neutralized.

Sleep hovered out of reach while her mind spun with possibilities and fears. The warmth of connection warred with the cold certainty that she'd find a way to ruin this. She always did.

Noah shifted in his sleep, his arm instinctively pulling her closer. The gesture was so natural and unguarded that it made her chest ache. This man had already slipped past defenses she'd spent years perfecting, and she didn't know what to do about it.

For now, she focused on his steady breathing, on the solid warmth of his body curled around hers, trying not to think about all the ways she could, no, would, screw this up.

Maybe that was the real terror. Not that she'd sabotage this connection, but that she desperately didn't want to for the first time in her life.

Chapter 25

Dawn crept over Stone River, painting the streets in shades of pink and gold. The rain had washed away most of the snow, leaving the town a sloppy mess of mud and wet gravel, but the air held a bitter bite as a reminder that winter was coming.

Noah stood at his hotel room window, coffee growing cold in his hands, his thoughts no longer sheltered by the solid feeling of Sophia nestled against him.

His phone buzzed: His mom. "The elders are planning to gather at the tribal center at nine," she said without preamble. "Vincent Marshall will be there to discuss arrangements. You should come."

The weight of obligation pressed against his chest. He needed to be there, to honor Michael and support his aunt Twylla. Time to return to the present.

"I'll be there," he promised.

A soft knock at his door made his heart stutter. He knew who it would be—they'd have to face each other eventually. When he opened the door, Sophia stood there looking as professional and put-together as ever in her FBI suit, red hair pulled back severely, no trace of last night's intimacy visible except perhaps in the slight softening of her gaze when their eyes met.

"Hey," she said quietly. "Any word on funeral arrangements yet?"

"Yeah." He struggled to find the right words, to bridge the gap between last night's vulnerability and today's return to cold reality. "My mom just called. The elders are planning to gather at the tribal center at nine. Vincent Marshall will be there. Would you like to come?"

"No, this is about your family right now. There'll be plenty of time to talk to Vincent later. I'll start interviewing the hospital staff about Michael's last hours while you're at the tribal center."

The courteous distance in her voice felt like a physical pain, but he understood it. They had a job to do, a killer to catch. Whatever was happening between them had to wait.

"Thank you," he said simply.

She nodded once, professional mask firmly in place. "I'll text if I find anything significant."

The drive to the tribal center gave him time to shift mental gears, to let the familiar rhythms of tribal custom settle over him. Wet pavement crunched under his boots as he made his way up the walk, the sound eerily loud in the morning stillness.

Inside, the center smelled of sage and coffee, voices murmuring in the community room where the elders always gathered.

Grace met him at the door, her silver hair freshly braided, wearing her best dress. "There you are," she said, pulling him into a quick hug. "Vincent's been asking for you."

The room was crowded with familiar faces—tribal elders he'd known since childhood, women who had watched him grow up, men who had served on the council when his father was a tribal cop. Vincent Marshall sat at the head of the table, his thin, wiry frame showcasing a strong body despite his age.

"Noah," Vincent said, rising to shake his hand. "I was sorry to hear about Michael. He was too young to leave us so soon."

Noah studied the older man, trying to reconcile the tribal leader he'd known all his life with Amber's financial discoveries. Nothing in Vincent's bearing suggested anything but genuine sympathy. "Thank you for coming," Noah said. "Aunt Twylla will appreciate the council's support."

As if summoned by the sound of her name, his aunt walked in, supported by his cousin Lynette who must've dropped everything to return home to help her mom prepare for the funeral. His mother hurried over to hug her sister-in-law, and Noah returned his attention to Vincent.

Vincent's expression was appropriately somber. "We take care of our own. Michael was a warrior fighting demons we could never know." His dark eyes were sharp despite his gentle tone. "Sadly, I understand you're investigating some sensitive matters lately that may have triggered Michael in some way?"

And there it was—the subtle probe beneath the sympathy. Noah kept his expression neutral. "Yes, I was questioning Michael about Travis's case. Trying to see if he remembered anything that might open up a new lead. It seemed to have upset him."

Vincent placed a comforting hand on Noah's shoulder. "You're just doing your job. Michael's burdens were not for you to carry. He is at peace now with our Creator, and for that we will rejoice."

Noah didn't know about rejoicing, but he accepted the condolences with a nod. "Thank you," he murmured.

Vincent turned back to the gathered elders. "The community will want to pay their respects. We should discuss arrangements that will honor both tradition and the family's wishes."

Noah watched the interplay of politics and tradition play out across the room, remembering how the community had gathered when his father died. The same rhythms would unfold—aunties bringing food, elders offering guidance, the tribal council ensuring all needs were met. Some things remained constant, even as the world changed around them.

But when the discussion turned to Michael's burial, Noah interjected, his tone carefully neutral, "Given the circumstances of Michael's passing, there may need to be some adjustments to accommodate the medical examiner's requirements."

Vincent's attention sharpened. "The medical examiner? I thought it was ruled natural causes. As I heard it, he suffered a cardiac arrest."

"Potentially, but there's concern that Michael's death may not have been completely natural. Standard procedure with any death involving substance abuse," Noah said smoothly.

There was a moment of confusion among the elders, but they didn't push back, not even Vincent.

"Of course, whatever is required," Vincent said, adding with conviction, "May the Creator guide you in your investigation so that you may do what's right for your people."

Noah paused at Vincent's comment before choosing to let it go. He and Sophia would have time to question Vincent later. For now, it was about Michael.

The morning passed in a blur of details—which families would bring food, who would prepare the ceremonial items, where the wake would be held. Noah participated mechanically, one part of his mind cataloging Vincent's subtle deflections whenever the conversation strayed toward Michael's death.

His phone buzzed just before eleven. Sophia.

Hospital security cameras were down last night. Maintenance issue. Convenient timing.

Noah looked up at Vincent, still holding court at the long table. He remembered Amber's discoveries about Mountain West Holdings. How deep did the connections run? How many coincidences were too many?

"So, it's settled," Vincent was saying. "We can begin the wake tomorrow evening."

Grace touched Noah's arm. "You'll help Twylla with the arrangements?"

"Of course." The words came automatically, loyalty to family ingrained in his DNA. "Whatever she needs."

Outside, fresh snow began to fall, making everything look clean and pure again after the rain had muddied everything. Noah watched the flakes swirl past the window, thinking about Michael's warnings, about surveillance cameras that failed at convenient times, about business connections that led in circles.

His phone buzzed again. Another text from Sophia.

ME's preliminary report shows unusual levels of potassium in blood work. Could indicate cardiac intervention. Nothing conclusive yet.

Noah slipped the phone back into his pocket, ice forming in his gut.

Across the table, Vincent caught his eye and smiled benevolently, every inch the concerned tribal elder. "Everything all right?" Vincent asked. "You seem troubled."

"Just grief," Noah lied smoothly. "It's never easy, losing family."

Vincent nodded sagely. "No, it never is. But we endure. The People endure." He rose, gathering his coat. "We'll have the wake, then burial at sunset. The council will cover all expenses, of course."

"That's very generous," Twylla said, tears of gratitude filling her eyes.

"We take care of our own," Vincent repeated, but this time the words carried a weight Noah couldn't ignore.

After the elders left, Noah helped his mother clean up and put away chairs, the familiar routine giving him time to think. Michael's paranoid ramblings about people watching, about consequences. The financial web Amber had uncovered. The too-convenient timing of everything. Ordinary events suddenly felt suspicious.

Once everything was put in its place and the center ready for the next gathering, his mother joined him, appreciative for his help but also concerned. She rubbed his shoulder with maternal affection, asking, "How are you doing? I know you're probably taking this harder than you should. Michael was a troubled boy and was since his father died. It's not your fault what happened. He made his choices."

He couldn't burden his mother with his suspicions, nor could he talk about an open case. He'd told her a story about needing to stay in a hotel because the case was keeping him up at odd hours, and he didn't want to disturb the house with his comings and goings. He wasn't sure if she bought his story, but she hadn't pushed back, either. Sometimes mothers just knew when the truth was something they'd rather not hear.

"Thanks, Mom, I appreciate that," he said, honoring the sentiment with a brief smile. "I just wish things would've ended differently."

"As do I, my son," Grace murmured, shaking her head. "As do I. The only silver lining is the hope for healing. Michael isn't hurting anymore. He's with Great Spirit, no more addiction, no more pain. He was an unhappy man in this life. His soul was very sad."

Noah respected his culture, appreciated his heritage, but

he'd seen too much death and misery to understand why Great Spirit was okay with any of it as part of some cosmic design. Or maybe he was just bitter and jaded right now.

"You know your father used to say that some choices echo through generations," she shared. "And now therapists are talking a lot about something called 'generational trauma,' which sounds like the same thing to me."

"Dad's wisdom was ahead of his time," Noah teased, coaxing a smile from his mother.

"He was a good man, your father. Smart in ways that mattered." Grace wound her multicolored shawl, probably crocheted by one of her friends, around her shoulders as she prepared to brave the weather. "I remember one time, back when you were maybe eight, this young man got arrested for drunk driving. John recognized him—the boy's father had been one of the worst drunks on the reservation, mean as a snake when he was deep in the bottle. Instead of processing him right away, your father sat with that boy all night in the holding cell, just talking."

She shook her head at the memory. "I was so mad—it was our anniversary, we had plans. But John said something I never forgot. He said, 'Grace, that boy is standing at a crossroad. He can turn left and follow his father's path or turn right and forge his own. Sometimes all it takes is one person showing them there's another way.'"

Grace's gaze met Noah's. "That boy ended up going to college, became a substance abuse counselor. Still works with troubled youth over in Browning. Your father understood that breaking cycles takes more than just arresting people—it takes someone willing to see past the surface to the pain underneath."

Noah felt the weight of her words, thinking about Michael, about all the crossroads where things might have gone differently. "Did he ever regret it? Getting so invested in other people's problems?"

"Never," Grace said softly. "But that's who he was. He couldn't see someone hurting and not try to help." She straightened, pushing the memories away. "Much like his son."

Noah choked up unexpectedly, looking away to hide the sudden tears in his eyes. All it took was talking about his dad to reveal the wound that never seemed to heal, no matter how much time had passed. He cleared his throat and grabbed his coat, following his mom to the door so she could lock up.

Was now the right time to ask about her new boyfriend? Was there such a thing as a right time to ask his mother about her love life? No. There was not. Instead, he pivoted in the opposite direction. "Do you know anything about Vincent's connection to Mountain West Holdings?"

She thought for a minute, recalling with an unsure expression, "It sounds familiar, is it that development company? If it's the one I'm thinking of, they've done a lot of good for the tribe. Why?"

Before Noah could answer, his phone buzzed again. Sophia had sent a photo—security footage from a gas station near the hospital, time-stamped the night Michael died. The image showed a black SUV with tinted windows. No visible plates.

"No reason," he told his mother. "Just curious."

Outside, the snow continued to fall, nature's own conspiracy of silence, while Noah's mind sifted through possibilities, each one darker than the last. He thought of Sophia's warmth last night, of Michael's broken warnings, of Vincent's benevolent smile.

Some choices did echo through generations. And some secrets were worth killing to protect.

The question was, how many more would die before they uncovered the truth?

Chapter 26

Two days later, Michael had been laid to rest, but Sophia and Noah were back at Michael's apartment, looking for clues as to what Michael had been running from. Noah had offered to search the apartment alone, but she wouldn't hear of it.

"We're partners," she'd said, and that was the end of that discussion.

The hallway of River Bend Apartments smelled of stale cigarettes, mildew and something darker that decades of poverty had embedded into the walls. Sophia watched Noah fumble with the key from the property manager, his hands steady but his jaw tight. She recognized the tension in his shoulders, the same rigid control he'd shown at Michael's funeral, only now layered with the intimacy of their night together.

The lock clicked, and he pushed the door open, revealing Michael's final days in harsh morning light.

The smell wafted out of the dank apartment, similar to what was likely baked into the very wood and steel of the building. Sophia couldn't help but feel bad for anyone who had to call this place home. If despair had an odor, this was it.

"Sorry," Noah said about the state of the apartment, grimacing as he opened up his forensic kit and pulled out two sets of gloves. "Let's get started."

The apartment was a single room with a kitchenette, every surface covered in the consequence of addiction. Fast food containers grew mold in towering stacks. It was a haz mat situation everywhere she looked.

But it was the walls that caught Sophia's attention. They were covered in what looked like random scribblings at first glance—dates, names, arrows connecting seemingly unrelated events. The work of a paranoid mind...or someone trying to piece together a larger pattern?

"Jesus, Michael," Noah breathed, taking in the chaos. His face held that careful blankness that spoke of emotions too deep to process.

She pointed to the scribblings on the walls. "Was all of that here the last time you saw him?"

"No, he must've done this sometime after I left. I would've noticed this," he said.

Sophia moved past him, automatically scanning the room with her investigator's eye. "Let's be systematic about this. You take the kitchen area, I'll start with the bathroom."

The bathroom was a biohazard, but Sophia had seen worse. She cataloged the prescription bottles—mostly empty, some with other people's names. Common occurrence with addicts. A bloody syringe in the trash made her glad she'd worn gloves. But behind the toilet tank, wrapped in plastic, she found something interesting—a composition notebook, its pages water-warped but legible.

"Noah," she called. "Got something."

He appeared in the doorway, holding a stack of past-due notices. The careful distance in his eyes cracked slightly when he saw the needle in the trash. Sophia quickly moved the bin aside.

"Look at this," she said, carefully unwrapping the notebook. The pages were a window into Michael's fractured mind, full of paranoid ramblings about government surveillance mixed with detailed observations of comings and goings at Clear

Skies. One page contained nothing but THEY'RE WATCH-
ING written over and over. The next held what looked like a
coherent log of dates and times, recording someone's car in
different locations. Then more spiral thoughts about chips
being implanted in his brain and how owls weren't real animals, but alien-made illusions created to monitor humans. Sophia glanced at Noah, admitting, "Wow, that's a lot to take in."

Noah agreed, his expression perplexed. "Some of this…"
He trailed off, shaking his head. "Some of this might be valid,
but how do we separate what's real and what's a figment of
his damaged brain?"

Sophia turned another page to find a crude drawing of
eyes watching from windows, but in the margin was something interesting:

Saw him again behind Red Feather. Says he's one of the
good guys but I know what they did. Says I don't understand what's really happening. Travis knew. Travis
tried to tell me.

"Any idea who he might be talking about?" Sophia asked.
"It has to be Logan Crowe. Michael references Clear Skies
here." Noah gestured to the section of the notebook with the
reference. "And he was probably tailing Logan. We can run
a plate search to verify if it was Logan's car. The question is
why? What was Michael trying to do?"

Between the pages, she found a crumpled receipt from the
Red Feather, dated just three days before Michael died. Two
meals, two coffees. "Look at this," she said. "Why do you
think Michael would've kept a receipt with his notes unless it
was connected to what he was documenting? Maybe he was
meeting with Logan?"

"If that's the case, Logan lied when he said he hadn't been

in contact with Michael in years," Noah said. He moved to study the wall of Michael's scribblings, random words and arrows connecting seemingly unrelated events. But now they could see fragments of truth buried in the chaos. Clear Skies. Logan. Travis. Mountain West Holdings. Like pieces of a puzzle scattered by Michael's broken mind.

"Most of this is probably drug-induced paranoia," Sophia said. "But mixed in with the delusions…"

"He was trying to say something." Noah touched one of the clearer passages:

He knows the truth about Travis. Said I better keep quiet or end up the same. They make people disappear. Clean up loose ends.

A flash of color caught her eye beneath the mattress. She pulled out a manila envelope, its contents spilling onto the floor. Mostly prints of blurry phone photos, clearly taken by shaking hands, useless except for one. Logan climbing into the same car photographed in the other pictures, behind the Red Feather, dated the same day as the receipt.

"No need to run those plates now," she said, holding up the photo. "Michael was tracking Logan's movements. Why?"

"Michael, you crazy sonofabitch, why didn't you talk to me?" Noah murmured, rubbing his forehead. "If he'd have come to me about all of this, maybe he'd still be alive."

"Maybe he was trying to protect you in his own way," Sophia suggested with a wave of empathy for tragically doomed Michael Thunderhawk. "I think he truly did care for you. He was trying to help in the only way his addiction would let him."

"Yeah, well, it got him killed," Noah said, his hands gentle as he gathered the photos and slipped them into an evidence bag. "Whoever killed him thought it would be easy to make Michael's death appear natural because of his drug abuse, but this right here proves that Michael was a threat."

Sophia touched his arm, feeling the tension thrumming through him. "We'll get them. All of them."

He met her stare, and the rawness there made her breath catch. The steel in that gaze wouldn't bend. She tried to smother a shiver of raw attraction at the strength she saw within Noah. But it was too late.

He clearly felt it, too. That undercurrent of primal need honed by extreme circumstances and sharpened by an emotional whetstone pulled them to each other. Noah claimed Sophia's mouth with a hunger that mirrored her own. Amid the ruin of another man's life, wedged between the devastation of grief and guilt, the tendril of want unfurled between them like a tenacious root pushing through the cracks of cement.

His tongue explored hers, blotting out their surroundings until there was nothing but each other in the space of a heartbeat.

Too soon, Noah pulled away, holding her gaze, wordlessly communicating the pain in his heart and conveying how much he appreciated her presence as its witness. "I can't stop feeling his death is my fault. I was a shitty cousin but possibly a worse cop. I should've put aside my personal feelings and looked at everything with an objective eye."

"Stop." Sophia cupped his jaw, still close enough to feel the heat radiating from his body. "You couldn't have known. But we can make it right. We can finish what Michael started. Honor his sacrifice. Make it mean something."

For a moment, she thought he might kiss her again. The air between them crackled with unspoken things. But then his phone buzzed with a text message—Amber.

"We need to finish up here. Amber's got something she wants to show us."

They were just finishing their search when a soft knock at the door made them both freeze. Noah's hand moved instinctively toward his weapon, but the voice that called out was thin and wavering.

"Michael? Is that you, dear?"

Noah opened the door to find a tiny woman in her eighties, her silver hair braided loosely in a single fraying plait that looked as though she had slept on it for days.

She blinked at him in confusion through thick glasses. "Oh! You're not… I heard movement and thought maybe…" Her voice trailed off as she took in both Noah and Sophia's presence. She blinked with owllike concern to ask, "Is Michael in trouble again?"

"Mrs…?" Noah prompted gently.

"Cutter. Marie Cutter. I live next door." Her eyes filled suddenly. "Something's happened to him, hasn't it? That's why you're here."

Sophia watched Noah's face soften as he broke the news.

The old woman's grief seemed genuine, her small hands fluttering to her throat. "Oh, that poor boy. I was afraid something like this might happen, especially after that awful argument last week."

Noah's attention sharpened. "Argument?"

"Some man came to see him. I couldn't hear everything through the walls, but their voices got very loud. Michael kept saying he wasn't scared anymore, that he knew what needed to be done." She shook her head. "He was different that day, clearer somehow. Not like when he was on those terrible drugs."

"Did you see who it was?" Sophia asked.

"No, but I heard a car afterward. One of those fancy ones.

Not the usual kinds we get around here." Mrs. Cutter twisted her hands in her housedress. "I should have checked on him, but…"

"It's not your fault," Noah assured her.

"He was such a sweet boy, when he was himself," she said suddenly. "Would bring my groceries up the stairs—my arthritis is real bad. Wouldn't take a penny for it, either, though Lord knows he needed it. Just last month he fixed my leaky faucet." Her eyes welled up again. "I know people thought he was just another junkie, but there was more to him than that."

Sophia saw the muscle jump in Noah's jaw, could sense the pain he was fighting to control. She stepped closer, letting her shoulder brush his in silent support. "Thank you for telling us, Mrs. Cutter," she said. "Is there anything else you remember about that day? The argument or the car?"

"Just that Michael seemed different after. More nervous. Kept watching out his window." Mrs. Cutter peered up at Noah. "Are you his cousin? The law man? He talked about you sometimes. Said you were one of the good ones."

Noah made a sound that might have been a laugh or a sob, uncomfortable with the praise. "I'm not sure he was right about that."

"Oh, he was." Mrs. Cutter reached up to pat his arm. "He said you were the only one who might understand, if he could just figure out how to explain it right." She sighed. "I should have done more…"

"You were kind to him," Sophia said. "That mattered."

They said their goodbyes, but as they turned to leave, Mrs. Cutter called after them. "Find out who hurt him. He deserved better than this."

"We will," Noah promised, his voice rough with emotion. "We will."

They worked quickly, gathering everything that might be

relevant. But as they left, Sophia caught Noah taking one last look at the apartment—at the ruins of his cousin's life, at the evidence of his final, coherent act of rebellion against the corruption that had helped destroy him.

Outside, fresh snow was falling, covering their tracks as they carried Michael's final testimony away.

But Sophia knew some tracks couldn't be erased, like the path that had led them here, to each other, to this moment of truth that would change everything.

Chapter 27

Noah pulled into the Lewis & Clark Motor Lodge parking lot, fat snowflakes catching in the beam of his headlights, turning Amber's silhouette into a dark smudge behind the neon vacancy sign. She paced as she waited, her investigative restlessness visible even through the curtain of snow.

Beside him, Sophia sat reviewing her notes from Michael's apartment, her presence both a comfort and a complication. Every time he glanced her way, he remembered the heat of her skin under his hands, the way she'd touched his face when Mrs. Cutter's words had cut too deep. But there wasn't time for those thoughts now. Michael's paranoid scribblings and carefully documented surveillance of Logan demanded their full attention.

"Ready?" Sophia asked, catching his gaze. The quiet understanding in her eyes made something in his chest warm.

"Yeah." He grabbed the evidence bags containing Michael's notebook and photos. "Let's see what Amber's got."

Amber was already moving toward them as they exited the truck, her dark hair collecting snow. "About time. You're not going to believe what I found." She gestured toward her room. "And we should probably take this inside. Stone River has too many eyes lately."

The motel room smelled of coffee and printer ink. Papers covered every surface—financial records, corporate filings, and property deeds, all organized by Amber's meticulous sticky-note system. A corkboard propped against the wall held what looked like a time line, with Clear Skies at its center.

"Before you start," Noah said, holding up the evidence bags, "we found something you need to see."

Amber's eyes widened at the photos of Logan's car. "Well, damn. Looks like Michael and I were working the same angle." She turned to her laptop, typing rapidly. "Because I just traced a series of payments from Mountain West Holdings to Clear Skies, routed through three different tribal programs. On paper, they're listed as consulting fees, but the amounts don't match any services actually rendered."

"How much are we talking about?" Sophia asked, moving closer to study the screen.

"Nearly two million over the past five years." Amber pulled up a spreadsheet. "All authorized by Vincent Marshall himself."

Noah felt the weight of that revelation settle in his gut. Vincent, who'd just arranged Michael's funeral. Vincent, who'd served on the tribal council with Noah's father. Vincent, whose signature appeared at the bottom of those suspicious payments.

"Show me," he said quietly, trying to reconcile the man he'd known all his life with the evidence mounting against him.

Outside, the storm picked up force, rattling the thin motel windows. But inside, surrounded by paper trails and Michael's final testimony, Noah felt the pieces starting to align. All those years ago, Travis had stumbled onto something at Clear Skies. Now, Michael had died trying to expose the same corruption.

Noah caught Sophia watching him, her expression both professional and intimate, the look of someone who knew exactly what it cost him to investigate his own community. At that moment, he wanted nothing more than to pull her close and find shelter in her strength. Instead, he forced himself to focus on Amber's evidence, on the conspiracy that had already claimed too many lives.

The storm howled against the windows, but Noah barely heard it. He was already thinking about his next move—confronting Logan, protecting his family and finding justice for Michael. And somehow, in the midst of it all, figuring out how to hold onto this unexpected connection with Sophia without letting it compromise either of them.

"Look at this," Amber said, spreading printouts across the bed. "Every time Mountain West Holdings made a payment to Clear Skies, there was a corresponding wire transfer to an account in Idaho." Her finger traced the pattern. "The amounts are always exactly forty percent of the original payment. My guess is that the payments are for supplying fresh victims for the trafficking organization. You need a secure supply chain, and that costs money."

"So the payments are kickbacks," Sophia said, leaning closer to study the numbers. "But why Idaho?"

"Because that's where the trucking company is registered." Amber pulled up another document. "River Rock Transport. They run routes through Montana, Idaho and Wyoming, focusing on rural areas and reservations. And guess who sits on their board of directors?"

"Vincent Marshall," Noah said, the name tasting bitter on his tongue.

A sharp knock at the door made them all freeze. Noah's hand moved instinctively toward his weapon as Amber checked the peephole. Her sharp intake of breath had him moving forward.

"Logan Crowe," she whispered.

Noah and Sophia exchanged quick glances, an entire conversation passing between them in seconds. She moved to cover the documents while he positioned himself beside the door, weapon ready but hidden. He nodded, giving her the okay to open the door.

"Logan, what are you doing here?" Sophia asked, deceptively calm and cordial. "Are you okay?"

"I came to talk to Noah Thunderhawk," Logan rasped, falling forward like a cut tree in the forest.

Noah caught Logan before he could hit the floor, lowering the man gently to the carpet. "Jesus, he's bleeding," he said as blood seeped between Noah's fingers from Logan's side. "Get me a towel, quick!"

"Call 911," Sophia ordered Amber, already moving to check Logan's wound with a towel in hand. "A deep stab wound, still bleeding freely. Looks like the liver's been nicked. Not good. He needs a hospital now."

"Logan, what happened? Tell me," Noah said, knowing they were racing against the clock as Logan's blood gushed against the white towel Sophia was pressing against the wound. "C'mon, hold on, stay with me."

"Vincent," Logan gasped, his grip tight on Noah's arm. "Vincent did this. But you need to know…about Travis. It was me. I killed Travis."

Noah went very still. "What?" Was Logan confessing to him right now? Or was it just the blood loss causing Logan to hallucinate? "Be still, buddy, try to conserve your strength."

But Logan was driven to keep going. Even as his bloodshot eyes struggled to focus, he wouldn't quit before he'd said his piece. "Accident," Logan's voice was choked up and gurgling. "We were arguing. He knew…knew something wasn't right at Clear Skies. I pushed him. His head…the rock… Claire said she'd fix everything. Said she knew how to make it go away… but I had to trust her."

Sophia pressed harder on the wound, trying to slow the bleeding while Logan confessed fifteen years of secrets.

"Why, Logan? Wasn't he your friend?" Noah asked, confused and angry but trying to keep Logan talking to keep him present. "Why did you push him?"

"I… I got mad. He was saying bad things about Claire, but Claire couldn't be doing the bad things he was saying. I didn't believe him. She was the best thing that ever h-happened to me. I didn't mean to hurt him, I didn't…"

"Ambulance is ten minutes out," Amber warned in a murmur, knowing just as he did that it didn't look good for Logan.

"But after Travis…everything changed. Secret meetings with Vincent. Kids showing up in the middle of the night, no paperwork. Always had good reasons… I believed her. She was doing good things…just bending the rules a little sometimes."

Noah was starting to understand. Logan had always been a kid just wanting to be loved and accepted. For the first time in his life, he thought he'd found that with Claire, and he'd acted like any kid desperate to protect what he thought was the only good person in his life—lashing out with violence at any perceived threat to it. But he was likely telling the truth about not meaning to hurt Travis. That part had been an accident.

"Why didn't you just tell me that back when it happened, man?" Noah asked, swearing beneath his breath. "I could've helped you."

"I didn't trust no one but her," Logan admitted, his eyes watering. "I would've done anything for her." He sputtered, coughing up blood. Damn it, Logan was going to die in Noah's arms if that ambulance didn't get here real quick. Logan's breath hitched with pain. "But after Laramie…heard Claire and Vincent fighting. Blaming each other. Vincent said Claire's fight with Delgado was what got Laramie dumped here. Wasn't supposed to happen…"

Rafael Delgado! The smooth, too-well-dressed director at

Bright Horizons who'd rubbed them both wrong. Noah shared a look with Sophia. Their instincts had been right about that prick, but if Logan died, they'd lose their most important witness. "Stay with us, Logan," Noah urged as Logan's eyes started to drift. "The ambulance is coming."

"Tried to confront Vincent. Protect Claire. But she...she just looked annoyed. Like I was..." Logan coughed with a bubble of blood landing on his chapped lips. "Then Vincent stabbed me. They left me for dead. Claire left me." His grip on Noah's arm was weak. "I'm sorry. About Travis. About everything. I didn't hurt that girl, and I didn't hurt Michael. Had to tell someone...before..."

Noah fought to keep his breathing steady despite the turmoil raging inside him. Claire, who'd helped so many kids. Vincent, who'd served alongside his father. The betrayal cut deep, but he couldn't afford to let it show. Not with Logan bleeding out under his hands.

"The evidence," Logan whispered, his voice growing weaker. "Claire's office... False bottom in the filing cabinet. She doesn't know I found it." His breathing became more labored. "The ledger...shows everything. Every kid. Every payment passed through the whole operation."

The sound of sirens grew closer. Logan's grip on Noah's arm tightened suddenly, a burst of desperate strength. "Watch the prison laundry. That's how...how they move them. Through River Rock's trucks. Warden Hayes...he's in Vincent's pocket..."

The EMTs burst through the door, equipment in hand. As they worked to stabilize Logan, Noah stood back, letting them take over. His hands were stained with Logan's blood, trembling slightly as the weight of revelation pressed down on him.

Sophia touched his arm, grounding him. "You okay?"

"No," he admitted quietly. "But that doesn't matter right now."

Logan thrashed weakly as the EMTs lifted him onto the gurney. "Noah..." His voice was barely audible over the chaos. "Claire's computer...password is Travis's birthday."

The realization that Claire Redstone had played everyone, had pretended to grieve alongside their community for the boy she'd known all along had been murdered by Logan Crowe, and then had the sick audacity to use Travis's birthday as her computer password burned a hole in his gut.

Then they were rushing Logan out, leaving Noah, Sophia and Amber in a room that suddenly felt too small, too full of ugly truths about people Noah had trusted his whole life.

But Sophia was quick to mobilize. "We need to move fast," she said, her tactical mind already working. "Before Claire realizes Logan survived long enough to talk to us."

"Right." Noah nodded, pushing down the personal betrayal to focus on the job.

Right now, they had evidence to secure and a trafficking ring to dismantle.

If Logan survived.

Chapter 28

Snow fell in thick curtains as Sophia coordinated with Stone River police and tribal law enforcement outside Clear Skies. Red and blue lights painted the pristine white landscape in alternating colors, creating an oddly festive atmosphere for such a grim operation. The warrant in her pocket felt heavy with purpose, but the weight was satisfying.

"Teams of two," she instructed the assembled officers. "Clear each room. Remember, this is still an active youth facility. Keep movements controlled, voices calm. These kids have been through enough trauma."

Noah stood beside her, face set in hard lines. She knew what this cost him—dismantling an institution many in Stone River had trusted. But Claire's mask had finally slipped, and the monster beneath needed to be exposed.

To watch Noah in action, you'd never know that he was struggling with a mental battle. He moved with stoic efficiency, directing the scene with confidence and sticking to protocol—which only deepened her respect and admiration for the man.

"Computers and phones are priority one," Noah added. "And watch for any attempts to destroy evidence. Claire's not here, but she's got loyal staff."

They moved in precise formation, badges visible, weapons ready but not drawn. The night staff surrendered access without resistance—they were mostly part-timers who'd had no idea what happened behind Claire's carefully maintained facade. Their expressions of fear and confusion were a good sign that Claire had conducted her dirty work behind closed doors. And while that might seem like an odd thing to be grateful for, it helped soften Sophia's jaded belief that all of the people drawn to damaged kids had some kind of sick agenda. Some people were actually in the business to help.

Claire's office felt different in the harsh glare of tactical flashlights. The framed photos of "success stories" on the walls now held a sinister undertone. How many of those smiling teens had disappeared into River Rock Transport trucks, never to be seen again? They might never truly know. Tears pricked her eyes but Sophia hid it well, sniffing back the moisture and refocusing on the win.

"Logan said false bottom in the filing cabinet," Sophia murmured, already pulling on evidence gloves. The metal drawer slid open with a soft scrape. "Help me empty this."

Together, they removed files, setting them aside for processing. When the drawer was empty, Sophia ran her fingers along the edges, searching. There—a slight catch in the metal. She pressed, and the false bottom popped up with a soft click.

"Got it." She lifted out a leather-bound ledger, its pages dog-eared with use. Opening it revealed columns of names, dates and dollar amounts. "These aren't just local kids. They were pulling them from reservations and institutions across three states. Bright Horizons being one of them."

Noah leaned closer, his breath warm against her neck. "Look at these amounts. Twenty thousand per kid, minimum." His voice held carefully controlled rage. "They were selling them like inventory." He traced a name across a line item, a code beside the name. He flipped to the back, finding the ledger key. His mouth tightened with disgust. "Goddamn it, just as I feared. Forced prostitution," he murmured. Until the appetite for young flesh ended, kids would always be in danger somewhere—and someone would always be willing to pay. He snapped the book closed and slid it carefully into an evidence bag before sealing it shut.

At Claire's computer, Sophia typed in Travis's birthday—04021991. The screen unlocked immediately. "Logan was right about the password. Claire was a piece of work. Seems sick to use Travis's birthday like it was some kind of trophy."

"Or a reminder," Noah said quietly. "Of what she had to lose if she slipped up."

Files populated the screen, spreadsheets tracking "shipments," emails coordinating with River Rock Transport, documentation of payments through Mountain West Holdings. Everything they needed to unravel the entire operation.

"Download everything," Sophia ordered the tech team. "I want triple backups."

Her phone buzzed—tribal police. "We've got movement at Vincent Marshall's house. Two vehicles just left, heading west."

"That's their escape route," Noah said. "Through Idaho."

"Not tonight." Sophia was already moving. "We've got local sheriff and FBI working to set up roadblocks. State police are covering the highways. They're not getting far."

Noah jerked a short nod and returned to his business. She caught him, standing in a quiet corner, updating his boss about the arrest.

A win was supposed to feel better than this, but she could only imagine how this moment was coated with emotional conflict for Noah, and that broke her heart for him. When had she fallen for Noah Thunderhawk? And what was she going to do with these feelings? She didn't know where to put them.

Noah returned, sharing, "My team's been updated on the situation. Any support needed is available, but I told them we've got this under control."

Sophia nodded, wishing she could wrap him in a tight hug. But that wouldn't be appropriate, and it would likely make Noah uncomfortable with so many people watching.

What they had—whatever it was—was private. And now wasn't the time to figure it out.

Vincent and Claire were caught thirty miles outside town, their vehicles stopped by tribal police just before the road blockade. Sophia and Noah left Clear Skies to go straight to the station where Claire and Vincent were in holding for transport in the morning into federal custody.

Sophia looked to Noah. "Do you want me to handle this?" she asked quietly, respecting how difficult this would be for him.

But Noah's stoic shake of his head told her he needed to do this himself.

Housed in separate cells, Claire clung to the bars and cried out when she saw Noah. "Oh, thank God you're here! There's been a terrible misunderstanding—"

"It's over Claire," Noah cut in, his gaze hard. Sophia suppressed a shudder at the frost in his stare. "We have the evidence to put you and your network down."

Claire's bottom lip trembled for a minute as if she might break down and beg for mercy, but suddenly, her eyes cleared, and she surprised them with a snarl. "I gave those kids purpose. Structure. What did their families ever do for them? I gave them a reason to get up in the morning. Because of me they weren't a drain on society. I should receive a goddamn medal for what I've done for this community."

"You sold them," Sophia said quietly. "Like cattle."

"I made them useful." Claire's smile was cruel. "And everyone got paid. The families never even looked for most of them. Know why? Because no one cares what happens to troubled Native kids. No one except me."

"Why'd you turn on Logan? He was loyal to you," Sophia asked, curious.

Claire's dead-eyed stare gave Sophia chills. This was the stare of a true sociopath. When she answered, "He'd outlived his usefulness and had become dead weight," Sophia knew she was seeing the real Claire Redstone, the one she'd sensed from the start.

Sophia felt Noah stiffen beside her, but his voice stayed professional. "Claire Redstone, you've been arrested for human trafficking, conspiracy to commit kidnapping and accessory to murder. I'm going to make sure you never see the light of day ever again."

"We'll see," Claire returned with a smug smile that immediately made Sophia want to slap her, but Noah appeared untouched. He looked hard as granite and just as unbreakable.

He swiveled his attention to Vincent down the hallway in his own cell. Unlike Claire who vibrated with venomous energy, Vincent was strangely quiet, almost reflective. Sophia watched as Noah left Claire to walk to Vincent's cell.

Sophia held her breath as Noah asked, "Did you kill Michael?"

Vincent looked up, his eyes dull. He didn't answer but spread his hands as if what happened couldn't be helped. Then, he said, "He was a troubled soul. He's at peace now."

Sophia's gaze flew to Noah, her feet rooted to the cold cement floor. The air in the room seemed to disappear as Noah processed what Vincent didn't say but Sophia and Noah both heard.

It would've been criminally easy for Vincent to walk into Michael's hospital room, shoot him up with potassium and walk out, with no one the wiser because he was trusted in this town. Nothing would've been more welcome than an elder coming to visit a troubled member of the tribe. No one would've thought twice. The fact that Vincent had played the part to perfection of an elder who cared was enough to make Sophia want to puke.

But Noah showed nothing of what he was feeling on the inside. All Sophia could do was watch and wait. The tension in the room felt like a blanket of ice settling on her shoulders, but Noah still didn't react.

Civilians didn't understand the strength of will it took not to react when faced with the temptation to exact personal vengeance. Not everyone who wore the badge could resist that urge to play judge, jury and executioner. But Noah wasn't like most people.

He turned to walk away, and Sophia released the breath she was holding, but then he stopped and pivoted, causing her breath to hitch again. He returned to Vincent with one final question. "What was the beef between Delgado and Claire?"

Excellent question, but would Vincent answer?

Vincent surprised her with one word. "Money."

"What does that mean?" The sharp demand in Noah's tone left no trace of the respect afforded an elder.

Vincent's sigh ended on a derisive chuckle. "I told her, don't shit where you eat. She didn't listen. And then, a dead girl shows up with the name of the boy she knew was murdered on this very land. In the end, it's always sex and money that gets us all."

"Claire and Delgado were sleeping together?"

Sophia didn't want to think about Claire and Delgado bumping uglies. Frankly, she never wanted to think of them ever again, and that went for Vincent, too, but she knew it was a different kind of pain for Noah.

But pride ballooned in her chest when Noah muttered, "I hope you rot in prison," as he walked away, leaving both of their sorry asses behind.

Dawn was breaking by the time they finished processing the paperwork. Evidence teams had found more hidden documents at Vincent's house, along with burner phones and offshore account numbers. The pieces were all there—they just had to assemble them properly.

Between the FBI and BIA teams working in tandem, the perps in this case had nowhere to run.

"Three River Rock Transport trucks were intercepted," Sophia reported, reading updates from her phone. "Twelve kids total were found inside, being moved under the guise of the prison laundry system. Apparently, Hayes likes to host exclusive 'parties' inside the prison. One of the trucks has a false wall. Hayes is in custody. His entire operation is rolling over on him, trying to cut deals." She swore beneath her breath. "It's Epstein Island all over again. It'd make you sick to know how much these assholes will pay to defile a child. I think they got a sick thrill out of operating right beneath our noses. Who would've suspected a prison as a pedophile playground?"

Noah nodded. "What's happening to the kids?"

"Social services is already working on placement with legitimate facilities." Sophia touched his arm lightly. "You okay?"

"No." He scrubbed a hand over his face. "I knew these people my whole life, Sophia. Trusted them. My dad worked with Vincent. And all this time..."

"You couldn't have known."

"Maybe I should have." He turned to face her, snowflakes catching in his dark hair. "All those missing kids over the years. The trafficking patterns. We just couldn't see it because it was hidden behind people we respected."

"That's how predators work," Sophia said. "They build

trust, create systems, make themselves invaluable to the community. Makes it harder for anyone to question them."

"And the tattoos?" Noah asked.

"Similar to the Mexican drug cartels, it's how they mark property. They don't see these kids are people…more like cattle, and it also helps keep rival operations from trying to steal their property. It's disgusting," Sopha said, her lip curling. "I'd risk a broken foot if it meant I could round up every single trafficker and kick them in the nuts."

They stood in silence for a moment, watching the sun rise over Stone River. The town would never be the same after this.

"Logan's out of surgery," Noah said finally. "They think he'll make it."

"Good. We'll need his testimony." Sophia hesitated, then added, "And he deserves a chance to make this right."

"Like Travis deserved?" Noah's voice was rough with emotion. "Fifteen years, Sophia. Fifteen years of wondering what really happened that night. And it all started because he saw something wrong and tried to stop it."

"Then we make sure it counts," Sophia said firmly. "We build a case so solid they never see daylight again. For Travis. For Laramie. For all of them."

Noah's hand found hers, warm despite the cold. For a moment, they just stood there, connected by more than just the job now. Whatever was growing between them would have to wait—there were statements to take, evidence to process, justice to secure. But after all of that, this thing between them would still be there, real and patient.

Outside, the snow fell steadily, covering Stone River in bright white, reminding humans that Mother Nature had her own way of cleaning. But some stains, Sophia knew, ran too deep for nature to wash away.

They had their arrests, their evidence, their confessions.

Now came the harder part—helping a community heal from betrayal while ensuring the truth was finally told.

Dawn painted the sky in shades of promise as Sophia and Noah walked back to their vehicles, professional masks firmly in place. There would be time later for everything else. For now, they had work to finish.

For all the lost children. For Travis. For Michael. For a town that deserved to know the monsters hiding behind trusted faces.

Justice was coming. And this time, it wouldn't look away.

Chapter 29

The scent of frying bread filled Grace's kitchen, carrying memories of countless homecomings and departures. Noah zipped his duffel bag, the familiar weight of his mother's gaze following his movements as she dropped another round of dough into the hot oil. Early morning light filtered through frost-edged windows, catching the silver threads in Grace's hair as she worked the dough with practiced hands.

His laptop and case files were already packed, evidence sealed and logged, paperwork as complete as it could be until he got back to Billings, and his broken truck window repaired. But something kept him lingering in his mother's kitchen. Maybe it was the warmth or the way the familiar scents of sage and fry bread seemed to soften the sharp edges of the past few weeks.

"Your father always said an empty stomach made for poor thinking," Grace said, her tone casual but her eyes tender as she watched him. "And you've got plenty to think about."

In his career, even when he worked as a tribal officer, he made it a point to keep work separate from his personal life, but he couldn't seem to shake the weight from his shoulders and the words just tumbled out.

"I keep wondering how I missed it," he admitted, the words bitter on his tongue. "All those years, they were right there, doing unspeakable things to kids who needed help. Kids like

Michael—and when Michael tried to tell me, I ignored him because I thought it was the drugs talking. I can't stop thinking about how alone he must've felt, how scared."

Grace was quiet for a moment, focusing on the bread as it turned golden in the oil. The kitchen filled with the soft sounds of cooking—the pop and sizzle of oil, the gentle tap of the wooden spoon against the pot's edge. When she spoke, her voice held the patience of someone who'd seen many storms pass through Stone River.

"Evil doesn't announce itself with bells and whistles," she said, lifting the bread carefully. "It comes wearing a kind smile and speaking gentle words. That's how it gets past our defenses."

"Doesn't that make you doubt everything? Everyone?" The question that had been haunting Noah since Claire's arrest finally escaped. "You defended Claire, trusted Vincent... How are you dealing with this level of betrayal, Mom?"

He was pleading with her to help him make sense of this upside-down situation. He felt like a boy again, needing a parent to soothe his fears after a nightmare—and that didn't sit well with him. He was a grown man, not a kid afraid of the dark. And yet...he desperately needed someone wiser than him to help quiet the noise in his head.

"People are imperfect, son." Grace sprinkled sugar over the hot bread with the same precise movements she used for her beadwork. "Am I disappointed? Yes, of course. Am I hurt? Yes. But am I going to let the actions of two imperfect humans affect the way I live my life? No. However, it will make me pay closer attention to what people do, not just what they say." She glanced at his phone, which had buzzed twice in the last hour—both times Sophia, updating him on Logan's condition. "Like that partner of yours."

Noah's hands stilled on his bag. "Sophia?"

"Mmm-hmm." Grace tested the oil's temperature with a small piece of dough. "She's got a good heart. I can tell by how she watches out for you."

Heat crept up Noah's neck. "Mom, it's not—"

"Oh hush, I was young once, too," Grace's gentle tone schooled him, reminding him that his mother was a powerful woman and could make a point without raising her voice. "It's been a long time since you let anyone close enough to see your true heart. Now, don't get me wrong, I have a soft spot for Amber and always will, but I knew from the start she wasn't right for you. But we have to let our children make their own mistakes to learn. The key, Noah, is to actually learn when the Universe teaches. You need someone smart like you, but also someone who shares a common philosophy. Amber could go toe-to-toe with you in the smarts, but you shared wildly different philosophies about life and priorities. That was a ticking time bomb waiting to explode. I don't see that issue with Sophia."

"Mom, to be fair, you've only met Sophia once—"

"First impressions are everything. I know what I know."

Noah thought of Sophia's steady presence through the interrogations, her quiet support when his world had tilted on its axis. "She's good at her job," he said carefully.

"Is that all it is?" Grace's knowing look made him feel like a teenager again, trying to hide his first crush.

"It's complicated." He busied himself checking his go-bag, though he knew everything was already properly packed. "The job comes first. Has to."

"Funny," Grace said, her smile soft with memory. "That's exactly what your father said when he first started courting me. Said being a tribal officer meant he couldn't offer any promises."

This was new information—he hadn't heard this story before. Noah looked up, curiosity overtaking his desire to avoid the conversation. "What changed his mind?"

"Nothing changed his mind. He was right—the job did come first, many times." Grace wrapped the cooling bread in foil, her movements deliberate. "But that didn't mean there wasn't room for love, too. Your father learned that the heart is bigger than we think. Has room for duty and devotion both."

"Dad was different." Noah's voice roughened. "He knew how to balance things."

"No, he didn't." Grace's laugh was gentle. "He was terrible at it, actually. Missed more dinners than he made. Worked too hard, slept too little. But he tried. That's what mattered." She handed him the wrapped bread, her eyes kind. "And he had someone who understood that life, who didn't expect him to be perfect, just present when it counted."

Noah's phone buzzed again. Sophia, with another update about Logan's condition. His fingers hovered over the keys, remembering how it felt to wake up with her in his arms, to feel completely known and accepted.

"I can't offer any promises, either," he said quietly.

"Then don't." Grace touched his cheek, her fingers rough from years of beadwork. "Just offer truth. That's all anyone can really ask."

Outside, snow began to fall again but softer now, like a benediction. Noah thought about Sophia's fierce dedication to justice, her way of protecting herself by keeping people at bay, the way she'd let him see past those defenses, just for a moment.

"What if I mess it up?" The question escaped before he could catch it.

"Then you mess it up." Grace's practicality was oddly comforting. "But at least you'll know you tried. You know what the ancestors say—a heart that never opens can never be filled."

"How do you know what the ancestors say?" Noah teased behind a smile.

"I know because it's in here." She tapped her chest lightly. Then she smiled and pressed more wrapped bread into his hands. "Take this. Share it. Sometimes the simplest offerings mean the most. And stop being a stranger. I hope it doesn't take another dead body to bring you home for a bit."

Noah hugged his mother, breathing in the familiar scent of fry bread and sage that meant home. "Thanks, Mom."

"For the bread?"

"For everything."

Grace patted his chest, right over his heart. "You're a good man, Noah Thunderhawk. Don't let what Vincent and Claire did make you forget that. Some people choose darkness, but that only makes it more important for the rest of us to choose light."

Noah gathered his bags, feeling the weight of his mother's words settle into his bones. She was right about evil's deceptive face, about watching actions over words. About paying attention to the small moments that revealed the truth of people's hearts.

And maybe she was right about other things, too. Like her new guy, Roy. Would Noah ever get used to the idea of his mother dating? Probably not. But it was happening. He supposed he could be grateful she hadn't started dating someone like Vincent.

He leaned forward and pressed a kiss to her soft forehead. "Roy had better treat you right, or he's going to have to answer to me," he murmured, pulling away with a knowing smile. "But I want you to be happy. It's your turn to do something for you."

Grace's gaze warmed with a subtle glaze, and her bottom lip trembled ever so slightly, but she simply nodded and followed him to the door with motherly instructions. "Call when you get to Billings. And, Noah? Don't let fear make your choices for you. Life's too short for that kind of regret."

He climbed into the truck and his phone buzzed again. This time, it was a text from Amber.

Thanks for the wild ride and the excellent story. Vice is already interested. I'm back, baby!
    But in all seriousness, don't screw up a chance with that amazing chick. She's awesome and I love her. Honestly, if you don't date her, maybe I will.

Noah guffawed at that, even though a part of him wouldn't even be surprised if Amber made good on her threat.

She ended with:

You did good work. Proud to call you my friend. Oh, and fair warning, I will tell Sophia about your weird obsession with the Star Wars franchise. Dude, grown men should not wear Chewbacca pajamas. Peace out.

Noah chuckled, realizing his mother was right. He and Amber were never destined to take things to the next level, but he was grateful for her friendship.

But what did that mean for him and Sophia?

He felt things for her that were deeper than anything he'd ever experienced. There was a hunger inside him that craved everything about Sophia. Was that love? Was it possible he'd fallen head over heels for the one woman he shouldn't? Even as he fought the truth staring him in the face, he knew the answer. Yeah, he'd gone and fallen in love with Sophia Bennett, and he didn't have an answer for how it'd happened so quickly.

It didn't make much sense to be this into a person he barely knew. And yet, he felt as if he'd known her for a lifetime. Like two old souls, fingers entwined, spending their lives walking beside one another.

But the practicality of trying a relationship with Sophia seemed daunting and out of reach. What was he supposed to do? Move to Washington, DC, so they could date?

Sophia was scheduled to meet up with his team back at headquarters before returning to DC for her debrief on her end. It would be his last chance to talk to her before their professional relationship came to an end.

The drive to Billings stretched ahead, five hours of Montana highway and whatever waited at the end. Noah typed a quick message to Sophia before starting the engine:

Hitting the road. See you back at BIA headquarters for debrief. Drive safe.

Sophia's response came quickly: Safe travels.

Professional, proper. But he remembered how she'd touched his face in the darkness, how she'd understood his silences. Maybe his mother was right about hearts being bigger than people thought.

Or maybe he was just tired of building walls closing off the parts of himself that felt the most vulnerable.

The snow fell steadily as Noah drove away from Stone River, his mother's fry bread filling the truck with the scent of home. Some doors, once opened, couldn't be easily closed again. He wasn't sure if he was ready to walk through this one, but at least now he could admit it existed.

For today, that would have to be enough.

Chapter 30

Sophia folded her suits with military precision, each crease sharp and deliberate as she packed her suitcase. The Whispering Pines room felt hollow now, stripped of case files and evidence that had covered every surface. Outside, weak morning sunlight painted Stone River in watercolors, the mountains a smudged outline against pearl-gray sky.

Amber had already packed up her stuff and left, no note or anything, but Sophia hadn't expected anything more. Still, it felt kind of weird to be sitting in the room alone after the energy it had housed during the final moments of the investigation. Was it crazy to admit that she'd miss Amber's organized chaos?

Her phone sat silent on the nightstand. No messages from Noah since his brief text about hitting the road. Professional. Proper.

A knock at her door made her pause. Through the peephole, she saw Amber's familiar silhouette. An unexpected spark of joy took her off guard as she opened the door.

"Thought I'd catch you before you left," Amber said when Sophia opened the door. She carried two coffee cups, offering one. "Peace offering?"

"For what?" Sophia accepted the coffee, the warmth seeping into her cold fingers.

"For being a pain in the ass during the investigation." Amber's smile held a hint of self-deprecation. "I know I pushed boundaries."

"You got results," Sophia corrected with a warm smile that she genuinely felt. "That's what matters."

"Can we talk? Woman to woman?"

Something in Amber's tone made Sophia pause with concern. The usual sharp humor was gone, replaced by an unexpected vulnerability. "Of course," Sophia said.

"I loved Noah once," Amber said quietly. "Or thought I did. But we would've destroyed each other if we'd stayed together. You know why?" She didn't wait for Sophia's response. "Because we were too alike in all the wrong ways. Both ambitious, both driven, both willing to sacrifice everything for our careers. There was no balance."

"Why are you telling me this?"

"Because you and Noah? You balance each other." Amber's dark eyes held no trace of jealousy, only certainty. "Don't let fear of complications keep you from something real."

Sophia's hands stilled on her suitcase. "It's not that simple. We live in different states, work different jurisdictions—"

"Please," Amber cut in with a snort. "Long distance is practically a dating requirement these days. You really going to let a few plane rides stand in the way?"

"I don't do relationships." The words sounded flat and rehearsed, even to her own ears.

"No, you don't do vulnerability. There's a difference." Amber's smile turned knowing. "Trust me, I get it. It's safer to be alone. No one can hurt you if you never let them close enough to try."

Sophia turned away, throat tight. When had she become so transparent?

"But here's the thing about walls," Amber continued softly. "They don't just keep pain out. They keep joy out, too. And from where I'm standing? You deserve some joy, Sophia Bennett."

The truth of those words settled into Sophia's bones like winter frost. How long had she been using work as a shield, keeping everyone at arm's length under the guise of professionalism? "I don't know how to do this," she admitted finally.

"None of us do." Amber's laugh held genuine warmth. "We're all just making it up as we go along. The trick is finding someone worth figuring it out with."

Sophia thought of Noah's quiet strength, how he'd held her through the night without demanding promises she wasn't ready to make. How he understood the weight she carried because he carried his own. "When did you get so wise?" she asked, managing a small smile.

"Oh honey, I'm still a disaster." Amber grinned. "Just one who's learned a few things about not letting the good ones get away." She headed for the door, pausing with her hand on the knob. "Watch for my byline. This story is going to make waves."

With a wink, she was gone, leaving Sophia alone with thoughts she couldn't ignore anymore.

Sophia touched her phone, Noah's last message glowing on the screen. Professional. Proper. Safe.

But maybe safe wasn't enough for her anymore.

After Amber left, Sophia stood at the window, watching snow gather on the ledge. The coffee's warmth seeped through the paper cup into her palms, grounding her in this moment of unexpected clarity.

She'd spent so many years becoming the perfect federal agent who never let emotion cloud her judgment. But Noah had managed to find a way past those defenses without even trying.

She moved to the bathroom, catching her reflection in the

mirror. The woman staring back looked different somehow—softer around the edges, less rigid. Was this what letting someone in did to you? Made you vulnerable? Or just more human?

Her phone buzzed, a text from her supervisor back in DC about the upcoming debriefing. The familiar rush of duty tried to reassert itself, but for once, it felt hollow. She'd caught the bad guys, saved lives, dismantled a trafficking ring. By any measure, this case was a success.

So why did the thought of returning to her empty DC apartment feel like returning to someone else's life?

Sophia did a final check to ensure she wasn't leaving anything behind, each motion precise and controlled, but her mind kept drifting. To Noah's hands on her skin. To late-night case discussions that felt like dancing. To the way he'd looked at her across crime scenes, like he saw her soul in ways that no one ever had.

The sound of a door slamming down the hall made her jump. Just another guest checking out, but it reminded her of all the times she'd walked away. From relationships. From connections. From anything that threatened the careful order of her life.

You deserve joy.

Amber's words echoed as Sophia zipped her suitcase. Did she? And whether she deserved it or not, after everything she'd seen, all the darkness she'd witnessed, was she still even capable of reaching for light?

The storm outside intensified, wind rattling the window in its frame. Montana weather, always pushing, always testing boundaries. Like Noah himself—steady but relentless, wearing down her resistance with quiet persistence.

Sophia checked her watch. Her flight wasn't for three hours. Plenty of time to grab coffee, maybe breakfast at the Red

Feather one last time. But the thought of sitting alone in their booth felt wrong somehow.

Her fingers hovered over her phone. One text could change everything. Or nothing. That was the terrifying part—not knowing. She'd always been good at calculating risks, weighing evidence, making informed decisions. But this? This was pure free fall.

We're all just making it up as we go along.

Maybe that was the real lesson here. That sometimes the bravest thing wasn't charging into danger or facing down criminals. Sometimes it was simply opening your heart and letting someone in.

The question was—was she brave enough to try?

Chapter 31

The fluorescent lights of BIA headquarters cast harsh shadows across the conference room as Noah walked through his presentation slides. The stale coffee and recycled air reminded him of countless other briefings, but this one felt different. Every crime scene photo, financial record and surveillance image that clicked by seemed to pulse with the weight of personal connection as he detailed the trafficking network's collapse. His attention kept drifting to Sophia, seated at the far end of the table.

She looked exactly as she had that first day in Stone River—composed, professional, red hair pulled back severely. No trace of the woman who'd curled into him on a cold Montana night, whose quiet strength had anchored him through the storm of betrayal and loss. The memory of her skin against his made his voice catch slightly as he outlined Clear Skies's involvement.

The days since returning from Stone River had given him time to settle back into his routine, but something felt fundamentally wrong. Like a bone that had healed crooked, everything was functional but slightly off. It wasn't until he saw Sophia sitting in the conference room, pen poised over her notepad with that familiar focus, that he understood. The missing piece was her.

"Excellent work," Isaac said when Noah finished, his deep

voice carrying the weight of genuine pride. "Both of you. The attorney general's office is particularly pleased with how cleanly this wrapped up."

"We got lucky," Sophia murmured, characteristically deflecting praise. "There was a point when we were chasing our tails. Logan Crowe made this case come together."

"And he came through surgery okay? He'll be able to testify?" Nizhoni Gray, a task force member hired alongside Noah, leaned forward with concern. Her silver threaded hair caught the fluorescent glare as she added, "His injuries were pretty severe from what you shared."

"The man has nine lives," Noah said, remembering Logan's pale face in the ambulance. "He came through surgery despite a five percent chance of survival. Maybe this is the Universe's way of clearing the path so Logan can truly make amends. He seems like a man determined to make things right. He even apologized for busting my window. I think it's a good sign that Logan is redeemable."

He caught Sophia's private smile at his mention of the Universe—she knew his complicated relationship with faith and destiny. His heart skipped a beat at that shared understanding. Clearing his throat, he forced himself back to the presentation.

"It wasn't until we had Delgado in custody that we learned what happened to Laramie and who had written Travis's name on her body," Noah shared.

The team quieted with appropriate sobriety as Sophia took point on this part. "As we feared, Laramie was one of the trafficked victims sent to one of the warden's secret parties. Except, this particular party was the worst kind possible. We uncovered a particularly heinous type of abuse. Not only was Laramie used for prostitution but also as a punching bag. The poor teen was beaten to death."

"Good God, how awful," Nizhoni murmured, sharing a look with Dakota Foster. "That poor kid."

This was the worst part of the debrief, reliving the horror of their findings.

Noah continued, "One of Delgado's disgruntled employees in on the scheme, Wes Quiller, was in charge of the body disposal after the party, but Delgado and Quiller got into it over money, and Quiller decided to screw him over for it. Quiller knew about Claire's dirty secret, and he also knew that if he took down Delgado, the whole deck of cards would come tumbling down. Except, he never expected to get caught in the cross fire. The problem with doing business with terrible people—at some point, they will turn on you. We caught Quiller trying to leave the country under an assumed name. Thankfully for us, they're all willing to cannibalize the other to save their own ass."

"Well, we can all thank God for the weak character of bad people working in our favor," Isaac said, satisfied with the closure. "Excellent work."

The task force team broke into congratulatory murmurs and good-natured ribbing. The lightheartedness might seem inappropriate to most people, but it was how they coped with the terrible things they saw on the job.

Agent Kira Redfeather, fresh off her own major case victory, leaned back in her chair with a grin that lit up her entire face. "Look who went full warrior on his first cold case. Thunderhawk bringing home the win and taking down a corrupt prison warden while he's at it. The list of charges being thrown at Warden Hayes for his involvement is impressive—and horrifying at the same time. Damn, an inmate murder cover-up, sex crimes—he had his own little den of inequity going on. Like I said, freakin' impressive."

"Just needed a white hat and a sunset to ride into," Agent

Dakota Foster added, scrolling through the financial records with an impressed whistle that echoed off the conference room walls. "Seven point two million in seized assets. That's going to look damn good on the quarterly report."

"Don't forget the truck fleet," Nizhoni chimed in, her turquoise jewelry catching the light as she gestured. "Fourteen semis, each worth about a hundred fifty K. Plus the warehouses in Idaho."

"Not bad for a reservation cop," Foster quipped with a wink, but her smile was warm, respectful. They'd all started somewhere and worked their way up. Noah had earned his place on the task force twice over with this case.

The friendly banter washed over Noah, familiar as breathing despite being one of the newest with the team. But his attention kept drifting to Sophia, watching how she quietly observed with that laser focus he'd come to admire. To crave.

He wanted to draw attention to how important Sophia's presence had been on this case. It felt important to acknowledge that he couldn't have done it without her help. Maybe he needed her to know he felt that way.

"Agent Bennett's assistance was invaluable," Noah said, keeping his tone neutral. "The FBI's assistance helped us crack this case wide open. Without her... I don't think we could've closed this case."

"Just doing my job," Sophia replied smoothly. But her fingers tightened almost imperceptibly around her pen. "It helps to have a capable and professional partner to work with. Agent Thunderhawk is a credit to your team."

"We love a fruitful collaboration with our federal family," Isaac said, closing his folder with a satisfied snap. Rising, he signaled the meeting finished. "Take some time off, Noah. Two weeks minimum. You've earned it." He clapped Noah's shoulder as he left, the rest of the team trailing after him with final congratulations.

Then it was just the two of them, the air suddenly thick with everything unsaid.

Sophia stood, gathering her files with precise movements. The conference room felt too small, too charged with memory and possibility. "You didn't have to give me a shout-out in front of your team," she said. "But I appreciate the gesture."

"No, I did need to... I was serious. I couldn't have done this without you," he said, resolute.

"Debatable but thank you." She lifted her briefcase and straightened her shoulders, preparing to leave, but she lingered. "Feel good to sleep in your own bed?"

Not really. Without Sophia beside him, it felt as foreign as another hotel bed, but could he say that? "I... Actually, it was weird. It'll probably take a few more days to adjust to being home."

"Sounds about right. I live out of suitcases so often, sometimes my own apartment feels like someone else's, until I see my name on all of the bills," she admitted with a short chuckle. She glanced around, as if seeking another reason to stay. "Your team seems awesome. Close-knit group. It's not like that in my office. We're all lone wolves in my department. You should see our company potlucks. Very awkward."

He smiled at her dry humor. "Yeah, they're great. Nizhoni and I were hired together. I think Isaac is going to hand her the next big case. She's a solid investigator, though. No worries there."

Were they going to dance around how they truly felt and make small talk until one of them gave up and walked away? *Take the chance, Noah! Don't be a coward. Just put yourself out there!* But his mouth refused to form the words.

A long, pregnant pause stretched between them until it was

obviously painfully awkward for the both of them. A flash of disappointment flared behind Sophia's eyes, but she didn't act on it. When it became apparent he wasn't going to stop her from leaving, she graced him with a short smile and a final goodbye before heading for the door.

If you let her walk away, you'll regret it for the rest of your life.

Something clawed its way free and pushed its way out of his mouth.

"So," Noah said, almost desperately. "What's your opinion on Star Wars?"

Sophia's hands stilled on the door handle. When she looked up, her professional mask had cracked just enough to reveal a hint of mischief and a tentative hope that bordered on vulnerability. "I might own a Princess Leia slave costume."

The tension shattered. Noah crossed the room in three strides, pulling her into his arms. Her briefcase dropped to the floor with a dull thud as he claimed her mouth, tasting coffee and promise on her lips.

In that moment, he realized feelings as real and true as what he felt for Sophia didn't follow rules of engagement, didn't politely adhere to social norms and laughed in the face of common sense. The heart wants what the heart wants, and it didn't matter if they'd known each other a lifetime or a few weeks.

This woman was his other half—and it was finally time to stop fighting that fact. When you realize the truth of your connection, you don't want to waste another moment questioning the how and why it worked.

"I have two weeks off," he murmured against her skin. "My place or yours?"

She smiled against his mouth. "DC is beautiful this time of year. Not too cold, not too warm, just right."

"I've always wanted to see the cherry blossoms."

"That's not until spring."

"Guess I'll have more than one reason to come back."

Her fingers curled into his shirt. "Guess you will."

Outside, winter sun painted the mountains gold. But Noah barely noticed, too lost in Sophia's eyes, in the feel of her pressed against him, in the knowledge that some leaps were worth taking blind.

They had two weeks to figure out the rest.

Time to book a flight.

* * * * *

Get up to 4 Free Books!

We'll send you 2 free books from each series you try
PLUS a free Mystery Gift.

FREE Value Over **$25**

Both the **Harlequin Intrigue®** and **Harlequin® Romantic Suspense** series feature compelling novels filled with heart-racing action-packed romance that will keep you on the edge of your seat.

YES! Please send me 2 FREE novels from the Harlequin Intrigue or Harlequin Romantic Suspense series and my FREE gift (gift is worth about $10 retail). I may cancel anytime by emailing ReaderServiceInfo@Harlequin.com or by calling 1-800-873-8635. If I don't cancel, I will receive 6 brand-new Harlequin Intrigue Larger-Print books every month and be billed just $7.19 each in the U.S. or $7.99 each in Canada, or 4 brand-new Harlequin Romantic Suspense books every month and be billed just $6.39 each in the U.S. or $7.19 each in Canada, a savings of 20% off the cover price. It's quite a bargain! Shipping and handling is just 75¢ per book in the U.S. and $1.75 per book in Canada.* I understand that accepting the free books and gift places me under no obligation to buy anything—they are mine to keep for free no matter what I decide.

Choose one:
☐ **Harlequin Intrigue Larger-Print** (199/399 BPA G3CD)
☐ **Harlequin Romantic Suspense** (240/340 BPA G3CD)
☐ **Or Try Both!** (199/399 & 240/340 BPA G3CE)

Name (please print)

Address   Apt. #

City   State/Province   Zip/Postal Code

Email: Please check this box ☐ if you would like to receive newsletters and promotional emails from Harlequin Enterprises ULC and its affiliates. You can unsubscribe anytime.

Mail to the **Harlequin Reader Service:**
IN U.S.A.: P.O. Box 1341, Buffalo, NY 14240-8531
IN CANADA: P.O. Box 603, Fort Erie, Ontario L2A 5X3

Want to explore our other series or interested in ebooks? Visit www.ReaderService.com or call 1-800-873-8635.

*Terms and prices subject to change without notice. Prices do not include sales taxes, which will be charged (if applicable) based on your state or country of residence. Canadian residents will be charged applicable taxes. Offer not valid in Quebec. This offer is limited to one order per household. Books received may not be as shown. Not valid for current subscribers to the Harlequin Intrigue or Harlequin Romantic Suspense series. All orders subject to approval. Credit or debit balances in a customer's account(s) may be offset by any other outstanding balance owed by or to the customer. Please allow 4 to 6 weeks for delivery. Offer available while quantities last.

Your Privacy — Your information is being collected by Harlequin Enterprises ULC, operating as Harlequin Reader Service. For a complete summary of the information we collect, how we use this information and to whom it is disclosed, please visit our privacy notice located at https://corporate.harlequin.com/privacy-notice. Notice to California Residents—Under California law, you have specific rights to control and access your data. For more information on these rights and how to exercise them, visit https://corporate.harlequin.com/california-privacy. For additional information for residents of other U.S. states that provide their residents with certain rights with respect to personal data, visit https://corporate.harlequin.com/other-state-residents-privacy-rights.

HIHRS2603